McDermott's
Sky

McDermott's Sky

Robert Serling

LG

The Laurel Group, Inc.

New York

Published By:
  The Laurel Group, Inc.
  150 East 58th Street
  New York, New York 10022

This Edition Distributed By:
  Stein & Day
  Scarborough House
  Briarcliff Manor, New York 10510

Library of Congress Cataloging in Publication Data

Serling, Robert J
  McDermott's sky.

  I. Title.
PZ4.S4854Mac   [PS3569.E7]   813'.5'4   77–14000
ISBN 0–930392–00–0

McDermott's
Sky

Prologue

They still talk about a stewardess named Rebel Martin—in crew lounges, on layovers, in cockpits, and in the homes and apartments of airline people who knew her.

They talk about those who loved her and those who hated her, the latter being considerably more numerous.

They talk about her with fond memories, unvarnished contempt, wistful regrets and the venom of righteous morality—a divergence of views inevitable inasmuch as Rebel Martin was nectar to some and poison to others.

They talk with bitterness about the lives she ruined, yet with a semi-sweet tinge of pity, for among them was her own.

They all remember Rebel. For many reasons and for many things. Her incredible beauty, admired by the pilots and envied (or resented) by the stewardesses. Her chameleon personality, assuming the viciousness of a barracuda one minute and the insecure unhappiness of a frightened child the next. Her insensitivity, a mask of cruelty occasionally and very briefly raised to reveal a capacity for deep love.

And sometimes, particularly by her fellow stewardesses, she is remembered with a chill of fear. They drive by the house where she once lived and point it out in nervous whispers. Not one girl can stand by the stewardess mailboxes in Flight Operations without her glance being drawn irresistibly to Number 101—empty and unused since the

1

day of her last flight. Nor was any explanation ever offered for its abandonment, no sane person in the stewardess office being willing to admit that the dusty little cavern was considered jinxed.

Most of all, the stewardesses think of Rebel on dark, lonely nights, when strange creaks seem like the lurking steps of an unseen invader and when imagination distorts every shadow and sound into terror.

The uniform fitted him badly. There was a small burn from pipe ashes in the jacket coat and his somewhat scuffed shoes would never have passed a martinet's inspection, but that was not what the pilots and stewardesses noticed when Max McDermott first walked into Operations that day.

"There," a stewardess whispered to a flight engineer, "is the ugliest man I ever saw."

Ugly *was* the word for Captain McDermott. At 5'8" and one hundred and ninety-two pounds, his burly frame gave him the appearance of a beer barrel with arms and legs. A Prussian crew-cut roofed his pock-marked face, and a thin pink scar ran a jagged path from the top of one cheekbone down to the corner of his mouth. His nose was a mere caricature of that olfactory organ, smashed almost flat as if someone had held him down and tried to hammer it into his skull. A massive jaw hinged to McDermott's broad, craggy features completed the picture above the bull-neck, a picture so unattractive that few noticed two redeeming qualities—the massive shoulders that moved like oscillating waves under the jacket, and his deep-set, icy blue eyes.

Coastal Airlines already had announced officially, via company teletype, that Captain McDermott was being reassigned from Chicago to Washington as a check pilot on the Boeing 727. Unofficially, the airline grapevine—considerably faster and more efficient than any teletype system—also had spread the word that Captain Mc-

Dermott was slightly harder than chrome steel.

"That must be him," a copilot was telling several stewardesses gathered around the battered coffee urn in the crew lounge. "I hear he chews senior captains up and spits out the pieces."

The object of the *sotto voce* comments nodded brusquely in the direction of the Crew Scheduler on duty, aimed a tight, humorless smile at the dispatchers directly across from Crew Schedule, and marched into an ante room just outside the office of Chief Pilot Roger Blake.

"Mornin'," McDermott growled to Blake's secretary, an attractive woman in her early thirties. "Captain Blake in?"

"Bright-eyed and bushy-tailed, Captain McDermott," she smiled. "He's expecting you." She ushered him into Blake's office, murmuring a polite "Captain McDermott" to Blake and then closing the door behind her.

Blake rose from behind his cluttered desk and greeted the newcomer warmly. "Max, how the hell are you? Sorry I wasn't here when you reported in last week. Went down to Dallas for the ALPA Safety Forum. Have a seat."

McDermott sat down heavily in the chair Blake offered. "Your secretary took good care of me," he said. "What's her name—Mrs. Boatdeck or something?"

"Boadwine," Blake laughed. "You fly here or drive?"

"Drove. Figured I'd need my car. I'm only about ten minutes from National Airport but I hear bus service is lousy."

"You're all settled, then? Where'd you get located?"

"Thanks to Mrs. Boadwine, yeah, I'm all unpacked, more or less permanently. A high-rise—River House. Got me a little furnished efficiency. Hell of a view. I can see the whole damned city of Washington, not to mention National. Which reminds me, Rog, I also got a good view of a Coastal three-holer coming in on final yesterday afternoon. I wish I had been check-riding the sonofabitch. He went over the fence at about four hundred feet and damned near pan-

4

caked that bird in. Don't you run stabilized approaches at this base?"

The chief pilot chuckled, albeit wryly. "Same old Max. On a nice Sunday afternoon, you've got nothing better to do than look out your window and see who's making lousy landings. About what time was it, Max?"

"None of your goddamned business," McDermott said. "I don't turn guys in unless I'm in that cockpit seeing personally what they're doing wrong."

Blake dropped the subject. "How do you feel about the transfer, Max? This base is quite a bit smaller than Chicago."

McDermott reached in a pocket and brought out a heavily-caked pipe with a well-chewed stem. He filled it from an equally disreputable tobacco pouch and lit it before answering.

"Frankly, I was glad. Chicago's an ice box in the winter, a bloody oven in the summer, and our base there is too damned big. Hell, I never got to know half the guys there. Always liked Washington, Rog. I think I can do you a pretty good job here."

Blake nodded. He was well aware of McDermott's reputation as a check captain. Rough but fair. Extremely thorough. And a deep sense of dedication to the first rule of a supervisory pilot: an airline owes its passengers the safest, most responsible flight deck crew possible, and not even the strongest personal friendship warrants priority over a stiff check ride. McDermott, Blake knew, was one of those check pilots who would wash out his own father if he felt proficiency were unsatisfactory. Max was not Coastal's most popular check captain, to put it charitably. Blake remembered the case of Roy Stephenson, who had flown with McDermott in Korea and was his closest friend. Stephenson had a liquor problem and it steadily deteriorated his flying to the point where he drew Max for a six-months' check ride and butchered it. McDermott promptly gave him an Unsatisfactory rating and recommended his demotion to first

5

officer. Stephenson never spoke to him after that, and neither did a few other pilots.

Blake looked at McDermott with something akin to ungrudging respect. Max was a pro, no doubt about it. A kind of lone wolf, apparently living only for his job, never married and, if he had any kind of a social or sex life, he had managed to keep it totally private. Which on an airline was no mean accomplishment.

"Like to have you out to dinner, Max," Blake ventured. "My wife's heard a lot about you. You've got a certain claim to fame. An airline captain who used to be a homicide detective."

McDermott grimaced. "That's not fame, Rog. It's notoriety. I'd like to forget that little chunk of my life."

"Where was it, Max—Dayton, Ohio, wasn't it?"

"Yeah. Look, chum, let's cut out the small talk. When do I go to work?"

"Today, if you feel like it."

"I feel like it. Who's my pigeon?"

"Jim Lindsay. Only he's more of an eagle than a pigeon. One of our best captains—solid, dependable kind of guy. I think he must have been born in a 727. Only one thing . . ."

Blake hesitated, frowning.

"I'm always interested in that one thing," McDermott rasped.

"Well, Jim's a happily married man with a damned cute wife and two great kids. Now it seems one of our stews got her hooks into him but good. The word around the airline is that he's. . . ."

"Skip the gossip crap," McDermott interrupted. "The only time I get interested in shacking is when it affects a guy's flying. What's this Lindsay drawing today—a six-month check?"

Blake sighed, childishly disappointed that the check captain wasn't panting for additional sordid details. "Negative.

6

Route qualification, Chicago-Salt Lake City. Washington crews have just started flying Salt Lake and Jim's never pulled a trip there. You lay over in Chicago tonight and go to Salt Lake City tomorrow. Lindsay doesn't need any checking between here and O'Hare but you'll probably like to see how he operates. That reminds me—got an overnight bag or do you wanna go home and grab one?"

"Already brought it. I didn't know what you'd be handing me today so I didn't take any chances."

Blake rose. "Fine, Max. That trip number is Flight 208. Leaves at 0900 so Lindsay should be checking in any minute. I'll introduce you."

"If I see him first, I'll introduce myself," McDermott rasped. His voice, Blake noted, went with the man—low, rather harsh and gravelly as if the words were being sifted through pebbles in the throat.

"He's a tall guy, on the slender side, with sandy hair," the chief pilot said. "Good looking cuss; you can't miss him. Buy you a coffee, Max?"

McDermott shook his head. "Kinda like to wander around Operations, Rog, until Lindsay signs in. Get the feel of the joint. It's sure smaller than O'Hare."

"A small, happy family," Blake grinned. "That's the advantage of DCA. Have a good trip, Max. Don't be too hard on our boy. Like I said, he's one hell of a good pilot. Matter of fact, he won the ALPA Safety Award couple of years back; he's something of an expert on turbulence."

McDermott merely emitted a noncommittal grunt and left, unbending just enough to mumble "Thanks" to Mrs. Boadwine as he walked by her desk enroute to Operations. He peered at two pilots studying weather advisories at the Dispatch desk but decided neither of them could be Lindsay and strode into the Crew Lounge adjoining Operations. Except for its size, he could have been back in Chicago, for all airline crew lounges look about the same and the DCA one was no exception. About as tidy as an unmade bed, a

7

profusion of stub-filled ashtrays, a floor that badly needed both cleaning and waxing, and a general atmosphere of cheerful, informal sloppiness in stark, incongruous contrast to the well-groomed inhabitants of the lounge.

Said inhabitants, at the moment McDermott entered, consisted of five stewardesses, a captain and two copilots, all of whom looked at the stocky check captain with frank curiosity. He nodded in their general direction, a gesture that was more of a grudging acknowledgement of their presence than a salutation. Conscious of their continuing stares, McDermott occupied himself by perusing the various pilot and stewardess bulletin boards, which also could have been hanging in Chicago, Los Angeles, New York and any other base as well as Washington. The pilot board contained an updated seniority list, a few three-by-five cards offering for sale such items as a 1967 Cougar and an outboard motor, and a reminder signed by Blake that five pages of Boeing 727 manual revisions were in pilot mailboxes. The stewardess board was filled largely with facsimiles of passenger commendation letters, and McDermott noted that of the six letters posted, four referred to a "Miss Martin"—all four signed by male passengers.

McDermott turned away just in time to collide with a stewardess who had come up behind him unnoticed to check the board.

"Sorry," McDermott muttered perfunctorily.

"Quite all right, Captain," the girl smiled. She was tiny, yet sturdily built, her hair light brown, a thin aquiline nose with pinched nostrils, small delicate mouth and deep-set blue eyes. McDermott liked those eyes; they had the disturbing quality of being simultaneously demure and wickedly sexy, and he also examined the rest of her with more than casual interest, because he preferred small women.

The stewardess in turn fluttered a cautiously quizzical salute with eyelashes so long they resembled miniature awnings. "Are you Captain McDermott?"

"Yeah." The single word from McDermott was a compliment. Ordinarily he would have merely nodded.

"Heard you were coming. Welcome to DCA."

McDermott uttered one of his noncommittal grunts, but it was not sufficiently tough to deter the girl from friendliness.

"I'm Betty Roberts," she introduced herself.

"Well," McDermott growled, "you already know my name."

Miss Roberts looked startled momentarily, then laughed. "Boy, they said you were tough and I can believe it."

McDermott began a frown, then looked at her pixie face and could not prevent the corners of his wide mouth from crinkling slightly in what for him was a wide grin. But before the stewardess could say anything further, he walked away with a rudeness that failed to register. Betty Roberts was too busy thinking, "Now there's a guy so ugly he's got sex appeal."

McDermott consulted his wristwatch, noted that Lindsay still had another ten minutes before his required hour-before-departure sign-in, and for want of anything better to do picked up a fat, looseleaf notebook labelled *Stewardess Briefing Book*. He was idly perusing its contents, mostly cabin service bulletins, informal chit-chat and admonitions signed by someone called "Mike," when the soft voice of Miss Roberts tinkled at his elbow.

"That's our briefing book," she informed him gravely.

McDermott glared. "Miss Roberts, I think I've been with Coastal long enough to know a stewardess briefing book when I see one." Before she had a chance to look hurt, he relented to the point of quickly asking, "Who's this Mike that signs all this crud?"

"Michelle Hunter, our chief stewardess supervisor. Everybody calls her Mike. Haven't you ever met her? She's quite a gal. I thought nobody could work for Coastal and not know Mike."

McDermott *had* heard of her, come to think of it. A rather fabulous Character—Max mentally capitalized the word—who was as much a Coastal institution as a mere employee. Any comment he was about to make to Stewardess Roberts, however, suddenly evaporated. A stewardess had just entered the Crew Lounge and even McDermott, inherently suspicious of and hostile to women of great beauty, did a double-take. The newcomer was tall, with honey-blonde hair, a magnificent figure and perfectly chiseled features. Only this female went beyond mere pulchritude, McDermott decided. She also breathed seduction, yet with that rare, dignified aloofness that suggests, rather than promises; that hints without openly exposing.

Even Max McDermott's facade of sour indifference cracked momentarily, his lips pursing in a soundless whistle that did not escape the alert eyes of Betty Roberts.

"That's Rebel Martin," she informed McDermott matter-of-factly. "She of the four passenger commendation letters I saw you reading."

The check pilot wrenched his eyes away from the blonde, impulsively patted Betty on the head in what may have been a kind of patronizing you're-a-good-kid-but-not-in-the-same-league-as-that-dish gesture, and strode out of the lounge. He had the uncomfortable feeling that he was retreating rather than leaving, but he temporarily forgot his first sight of Rebel Martin when he caught his first glimpse of Jim Lindsay.

McDermott thought the tall captain initialing the schedule sign-in sheet might be Lindsay—why, he could not say, except that the pilot fitted the mental picture he already had formulated from Blake's brief remarks. His guess was confirmed when he heard the crew scheduler's joking "Captain Lindsay, you've ruined my day on account of in twenty-seven more seconds I was gonna mark you A.W. O.L."

"Love suspense," Lindsay replied with a grin and McDer-

10

mott, who occasionally judged a man (1) by the way he smiled and (2) by the way he shook hands, was impressed on the first count. He was quickly impressed on the second count, too, after he introduced himself.

"Lindsay? I'm Max McDermott. I'm riding with you today. And tomorrow."

Linday's handshake was firm. "You're the new check captain, right? I figured Blake would be riding shotgun on that route qualification leg but glad you'll be on board. Want to meet the crew?"

McDermott nodded. Lindsay steered him over to Dispatch where the first officer, a pleasant-faced youngster named Bill Foley, was checking weather. Foley seemed a little nervous at the introduction. He, too, had heard tales of the redoubtable Captain McDermott, including a well-founded report that he monitored *all* crew performances on a flight, including those of the cabin attendants who could never be sure they wouldn't be quizzed on some aspect of cabin emergency procedures.

"Where's our flight engineer?" Lindsay was asking Foley.

"In the lounge—sir." Foley obviously was taking no chances that McDermott might even write him up for a protocol slip, and McDermott smiled wryly.

"Let's get something straight, both of you," the check pilot said softly but firmly. "I don't go for any phony military dialogue or sugar-covered salutations. If you two guys call each other Jim and Bill, keep it that way and can the sir crap. Read me?"

"Yes, sir," Foley gulped, and Lindsay laughed.

"Foley hasn't called me sir since our second trip," he chuckled. "But we might as well establish our ground rules. As far as I'm concerned, I'm Jim to you or any other check captain and if you don't want me to call you by your first name, say so now."

"Max will do fine, and that goes for you too, Foley. I might even get around to using Bill after I see how you operate."

11

Foley managed to look relieved and apprehensive simultaneously as Lindsay and McDermott walked away toward the lounge. "Seems like a nice kid," Max observed.

"A good boy and sharp," Lindsay said. "Ex-military like most of our newer pilots. So's our FE over there—Dean Mueller. Navy-trained, I think. I'll introduce you."

McDermott found himself talking to Mueller, a lanky, freckle-faced boy, when Lindsay tapped his elbow. The check captain turned to discover Rebel Martin standing by Lindsay's side, a wisp of a smile on her full, sensuous lips. Lindsay introduced her with what McDermott uncomfortably sensed was a feeling of both pride and possession. "Max, want you to meet one of our stewardesses, Rebel Martin. She'll be flying with us today. Rebel, this is Captain McDermott."

Max nodded, rather curtly, adding a gruff acknowledgement. "Miss Martin."

"It's my pleasure," Rebel said in a low and husky voice that managed to be about as routine as a trumpet sounding a cavalry charge. It was a voice that perfectly matched her face and figure and, McDermott thought, could have made a prosaic statement like "I hate prunes" sound like "Let's go to bed." Rebel's green eyes were fixed on the burly check captain's face, on a level slightly above his own, staring with a frankness that seemed to be measuring his virility.

McDermott decided suddenly there was something about the girl he didn't like, more from instinct and impression than conviction. She was almost too beautiful, and those green eyes bothered him. At close range, they were a little too narrow, with just a suggestion of cold calculation. And under her carefully-applied makeup, there was a hint of wear and tear that seemed out of character. Like a scratch on a new car, almost but not quite hidden by buffed polish.

Lindsay's quiet voice interrupted McDermott's uncom-

12

plimentary thoughts. "I'm going to make out our flight plan, Max," he was saying. "Meanwhile here's one of our other girls on 208. This is Betty Roberts."

The diminutive Miss Roberts had just joined their little group, and McDermott growled "I've already met Miss Roberts" as Lindsay, with a small, tight smile aimed at Rebel, turned and walked away. The tall stewardess looked at the departing figure, and her pink tongue slithered out to lick her lips. It was quick and almost imperceptible, and appeared to be purely instinctive, but McDermott's cold eyes, intercepting the gesture, narrowed suspiciously. Rebel turned back to him.

"I'm glad you're going with us, Captain McDermott," she said pleasantly enough. "You'll like Jim. He's an absolute darling."

"He's a good Joe," Betty Roberts said with a trace of tartness. "I'll let Rebel put him in the darling category."

McDermott was surprised by the venom in her voice and the frown on her tiny face that bordered on open dislike. But Rebel, either ignoring or oblivious to Betty's antagonism, merely asked, "Anything in the briefing book, Bets?"

"Notice from cabin service that next month we start serving complimentary liquor on all Washington-New York flights after 11 A.M., plus snacks up to four o'clock. That should worry the hell out of Eastern's shuttle. Remind me not to bid any New York trips, Rebel."

"I don't mind New York," the tall beauty said. "You meet an awful lot of influential men on that leg."

"Your stable's pretty full of influential men already, isn't it?" Betty snapped. "If Jim Lindsay knew. . . ."

"Jim's married," Rebel interrupted, her voice an octave lower and taking on the tone of a don't-push-me-too-far warning. "He's not holding any reins on me."

McDermott decided he had had enough. "You two broads can take this female cat fight out of Operations," he

13

rumbled. "Or would you like to discuss a few emergency procedures instead of your social life?"

Betty Roberts flushed. Rebel smiled, but McDermott could swear it was close to a sad smile. She said nothing and sauntered away, toward the full length mirror hanging on the wall of the Lounge. McDermott could not resist watching the rolling sway of her slim hips. Now she was primping in front of the mirror, turning sideways to check for any sign of a slip showing. Even in her rather restrictive powder-blue uniform jacket—Coastal was one of the few airlines that still insisted on stewardesses looking somewhat more military than feminine—her bust line was something to behold. Full without being grossly buxom and in symmetric proportion to the rest of her lithe body. If that's the babe Lindsay is banging, Max thought sourly, he is one lucky bastard. Betty Roberts intruded on what McDermott knew was nothing but a throb of envy, surprisingly close to jealousy.

"If you want to get interested in Rebel," she said in an exasperating demonstration of woman's intuition, "you'll have to get in line. She dates a different guy every night. Also you don't just date her. You have to fall in love with her. It's as natural as breathing."

Max whirled around, anger blending with embarrassment. He doused an urge to curse her, but she was only too aware that the cold eyes were impaling her on a spear of unspoken resentment.

"Miss Roberts," he said very slowly, "I am very strongly tempted to ask you the precise location of the walkaround oxygen bottle on the 727-200 series. Not only to test your knowledge of cabin attendant emergency procedures but to keep your goddamned mind off unofficial subjects. I'll refrain this time, and I'll add this bit of advice. If you ever stick your nose into my personal life, I'll kick that cute little butt of yours bloody."

He was out of the lounge and into Operations before

Betty could close her mouth. She was chastened, flustered, and—woman-like—she also was intrigued. She even had the impulse to apologize to Rebel, but the latter already had gone into Operations, preceding McDermott by a few seconds before he joined Lindsay at the Dispatch desk. As Max approached, Lindsay was telling her, "Looks like a smooth trip, Rebel. You can start serving as soon as we reach cruising altitude. For your cabin PA, we'll be at twenty-eight thousand, flying time an hour and thirty-nine minutes. Who are the girls?"

"Cathy Burkhart, Jim. The fourth girl's Chicago-based. I don't know her. Seems okay."

"Fine. Cathy's got almost as much seniority as you and Betty. I don't think a briefing's necessary."

"Or a quiz either," Rebel grinned. "I remember our first trip together. You made me show you how to hook up the rear lounge chute on the Electra. I could have killed you."

Lindsay patted her cheeck affectionately. It looked perfectly innocent and it was devoid of anything physical, yet McDermott, listening to their banter, sensed a kind of electricity between them, almost a deliberately suppressed emotional contact.

"I've got to get out to the plane, Jim," she said and departed with a wink at Max, who now found himself torn between liking her, distrusting her and wanting her.

"Quite a dish," he commented to Lindsay in a rare expression of non-aeronautical opinion.

"She's a fine girl," Lindsay replied. He hesitated, then added, "you'll hear a lot of rumors about Rebel, Max. Don't believe all of them."

"I never listen to rumors," McDermott said.

Lindsay ignored this mild reassurance, plowing ahead, as if an emotional dam had been pierced by the very presence of a man new to the Washington base and therefore totally objective on the subject of Rebel Martin. "She's supposed to collect men like a philatelist collects stamps, but Christ, that's par for anyone that beautiful. The other stews hate her because they envy her and they're jealous. You know airline people. They're the greatest bunch in the world, but they have over-sized mouths occupied by flapping tongues. Rebel's a good kid, no matter what lousy, goddamned gossip you hear."

McDermott took out his pipe, scooped the bowl into a tobacco pouch, and lit it, examining Lindsay shrewdly through the acrid smoke.

"You seem a bit touchy about her, chum," he observed. "By the way, what's her real name?"

"It's really Rebel. She once told me her father was an unreconstructed Southerner, sort of a Civil War buff. That's what he named her. Her parents died in a car accident when she was a kid and she was raised by some aunt in Pittsburgh. She's had a pretty tough life. Married some good-looking but worthless bum when she was eighteen. He beat her up about once a week and she finally divorced him. Worked as a secretary for a couple of years and then came with us."

Apparently, McDermott decided, Captain Lindsay was willing to talk about the girl forever. "Suppose we get out to our bird," Max said abruptly. "And, by the way, if you have no objections, let Foley make the takeoff and landing today, I'd like to see how he operates."

"Thought you were checking me," Lindsay smiled. Again, McDermott found himself drawn to the man. When Lindsay grinned, the crow's feet on the fringes of his eyes —that facial brand so typical of most pilots—furrowed into deeper ridges that somehow softened his rather stern features. Max could not even feel a tinge of annoyance at Lindsay's impressive physical appearance. The check captain had the normal aversion of short, homely men to tall, handsome men, and Lindsay was definitely of the Greek God variety—two inches over six feet, with wavy, brown hair graying maturely at the temples and a slim, yet wiry

16

physique. But there was nothing of the pretty boy about him and Max instinctively respected him.

The respect went from instinctive theory to accomplished fact once Flight 208 was underway. Lindsay, McDermott quickly observed, was not just a good captain but an excellent one. His handling of First Officer Foley, who was understandably jittery, and Flight Engineer Mueller was deft, with just the right blending of easy banter and crisp discipline. McDermott had the notion that check-riding Lindsay the next day would be a waste of time; the man obviously knew his job and his airplane.

They had been airborne about an hour, bouncing a bit through some choppy air, when Rebel unlocked the cockpit door and poked her head in to ask if anyone wanted to eat before they landed at O'Hare. Flight Engineer Mueller, who would not lose his appetite in the middle of a thunderstorm with one engine on fire, nodded happily. Foley, intent on flying and still acutely conscious of McDermott's presence, shook his head.

"How about you, Max?" Lindsay inquired. "We've got the whole day and evening to kill in Chicago and you probably know some good restaurants."

"Guess I'm not much of a gourmet," McDermott said, "but I do have a little spaghetti joint I kinda like if you guys dig Italian food. And a hamburger for lunch after we land will do me fine."

"Max passes and so will I, Rebel. Why don't you and the other girls plan on having dinner with us tonight?"

She gave him a smile that seemed to light up the whole flight deck. "Love to. I'll tell Betty. Cathy has a boy friend here and I know she won't come. Neither will the gal already based here." She closed the door, leaving behind an aroma of perfume that hung in the cockpit like a jet contrail frozen into a thin blue sky.

"That perfume," Mueller remarked, "would turn a monk into Jack the Ripper."

McDermott grunted, Lindsay laughed and Foley smiled faintly. Encouraged, Mueller went on. "Yes, sir, if I was married to that babe, I don't think I'd ever get out of bed. Boy, I'd . . ."

"Knock it off, Dean." Lindsay's voice was sharp. The flight engineer looked reproachful, like a little boy unexpectedly scolded by a favorite teacher. Evidently, McDermott thought, the youthful FE wasn't aware that something might be going on between Rebel and the captain. For that matter, neither was Max although he would have wagered a month's pay that Blake's gossip applied directly to Stewardess Martin. Lindsay's almost petulant reaction to Mueller's harmless remark was tangible evidence, added to Max's intuitive suspicions. There was an uneasy if momentary silence in the cockpit, reminding McDermott of the ominous calm before a violent storm.

The voice of Chicago Enroute Control broke the spell. "Coastal 208, you have unidentified high speed traffic at one mile, four o'clock and closing fast."

Four pairs of eyes swiveled instantly to the four o'clock position. Lindsay had just started to tell Enroute Control "We don't see him . . ." when McDermott yelled, "There he is! Climb!"

A small jet had appeared out of a thin, almost opaque overcast, streaking at the 727 from above at a slight descending angle and about to bisect a collision course. The shout of "climb" was barely out of McDermott's mouth when Lindsay grabbed the yoke, pulling it back almost to his lap and hard over to his left with one hand, simultaneously ramming the three throttles forward to full power with the other. The maneuver, precisely and perfectly timed, sent the 727 into a climbing turn so steep that Lindsay rolled the big jet nearly ninety degrees, virtually standing it on one wing. The smaller plane flashed by not more than a hundred feet away.

There was silence in 208's cockpit again as Lindsay leveled the 727, but this time it was a silence born of sheer relief and a chilling knowledge of what might have been.

"Jesus, that was close," Lindsay finally breathed. "Bill, I'm sorry I grabbed that yoke. Nothing personal. Just instinct."

"I'm damned glad you did," Foley assured him. "That was one hell of a job of flying."

"That it was," McDermott agreed and there was no trace of the usual grudging gruffness in his voice.

Lindsay ignored the praise, not from modesty but from a sense of unfinished duty which did not escape the check pilot in Max.

"Dean," the captain ordered, "would you go back and check for any injuries? That seatbelt sign was on but God knows who might have been walking up the aisle when we rolled—probably the stews. See if Rebel's okay. And Cathy and Betty." He added the last two names hastily as if to hide his overriding concern for the one girl. Foley, still shaken, didn't notice and neither did Mueller, who already was out of his seat and donning his uniform jacket. But McDermott had, mentally chalking up another indication of Lindsay's involvement and for some strange reason regretting it—not from envy or jealousy this time, but because it represented a nagging imperfection, a slight blurring of the professional image Lindsay had given him.

"Coastal 208, have you spotted that traffic yet?" Enroute Control was asking.

"Take it, Bill," Lindsay told Foley. "I'll talk to them. Enroute Control, this is Coastal 208. Yeah, we spotted them. We had a near-miss. Looked like a military trainer, twin-jet. I'll file a report when we land."

"Coastal 208, can you estimate your separation from that traffic?"

"About three inches from our eyeballs," Lindsay answered grimly. "Coastal 208 out."

He clicked off his mike transmitter button abruptly, a rebuke delivered in sound rather than words, and glanced

19

at Foley, whose youthful face was drawn and tense. "We're all pretty shook up, Bill. Tell you what—suppose I make the landing at O'Hare. You've earned your pay on this trip."

"Okay with me," Foley said without resentment, and he seemed to visibly relax out of sheer gratitude.

Neatly done, McDermott thought. No bruised ego on the part of the young copilot and a subtle reminder to Max of Lindsay's command authority, check pilot or no check pilot. A more subservient, brown-nosing captain would have asked McDermott's permission to change his landing responsibility.

Mueller returned to report one minor injury. The passengers, miracle of miracles, all had their belts fastened but Cathy Burkhart had bruised her elbow.

"She fell against the galley," the flight engineer explained. "The stew from Chicago was already in a seat, Betty Roberts flipped into an empty seat and Rebel wound up parked in some guy's lap. He was very happy."

"I'll bet," Lindsay said. "Well, into the valley of public relations rides your undaunted captain." He picked up the cabin PA mike. "Ladies and gentlemen, this is Captain Lindsay. I'd like to apologize for and explain that sudden maneuver a few moments ago. It seems we had some, uh, conflicting traffic and we were unsure as to his intentions. We took precautionary evasive action to assure safe separation. I hope no one was too alarmed and I apologize for any discomfort. Now, I'm going to ask our stewardesses to check through the cabin and make sure everyone's okay. We'll be landing in Chicago on schedule and we'll try to make the rest of your flight a lot smoother. Thank you."

"Well," Foley sighed, "I just learned a new lesson. How to sugarcoat a PA."

"Thank God they were all strapped in," Lindsay said soberly. "We could have wound up with about seventy lawsuits."

"If there are any lawyers aboard, you'll still draw some,"

McDermott predicted sourly. He hesitated momentarily, reluctant to bestow further public praise on any captain, and the reluctance won out. Instead, he cleared his throat as if he were removing mental obstructions to what he was about to say.

"That dinner tonight is on me," McDermott growled, making it sound more like an order than a gracious gesture.

Order or gesture, it was a pleasant evening. McDermott's little restaurant was short on decor but long on culinary perfection, and even the dour check captain unbent, albeit a bit ponderously. He even was mildly polite to the saucy Miss Roberts, and halfway gallant to Rebel—out of respect for Lindsay, he admitted to himself. She paid most of her attention to the captain who was rather quiet but obviously enjoyed her teasing and cheerful chatter. Mueller and Foley also were quiet, the former because his mouth was full 98 percent of the time, and the latter because he still was in awe of McDermott, to the point of refusing a glass of wine with dinner. Max knew why, and put him straight in his blunt way.

"Look, Foley, if you like wine with dinner, go ahead and have it. Nobody's gonna turn you in, we're all out of uniform, and it won't hurt you. That no-drinking-24-hours-before-flight rule is a guideline, not an absolute rule. It applies to hard stuff and specifically too much hard stuff. Me, I've got my own drinking rule: I know how much it takes to give me a hangover and I always stop before I get even close to that point."

Lindsay nodded sagely, and a twinkle softened his deep-set brown eyes.

"I've heard a few stories about your off-duty drinking, Max," he said. "The word is that you could drink a thirsty camel under a table."

McDermott was lighting his pipe, the epitome of relaxation for pipe smokers with full stomachs.

"I never challenged a camel the night before I knew I had a trip," he said good-naturedly, but looking at Foley as if to remind him that rank hath its privileges along with mature judgment.

"I also hear," Lindsay went on, "that you used to be a detective before you started flying."

"A detective?" Rebel said excitedly. "A real detective? A private eye?"

"Just a plain cop," Max said. "Homicide, but don't start imagining I was Ellery Queen. I majored in criminology in college and got a job with the Dayton, Ohio, police force when I graduated back in 1940. I was lucky. Never even had to walk a patrolman's beat. Detective, second grade, right from the start."

"A real detective," Rebel repeated. "Did you solve any murders?"

McDermott snorted. "Hell, the only homicides I worked on were cut and dried. A jilted suitor shooting his ex-girl friend. A drunk husband clobbering the hell out of his wife with a baseball bat. You mention murder to the average person and he thinks of Agatha Christie stuff—all carefully premeditated with hidden clues, fifteen suspects and every damned one with a logical motive and a foolproof alibi. I wish to God real police work had been that interesting."

"I take it you didn't like the work or you wouldn't have changed professions," Lindsay remarked. His lean face was alive with interest, as if Max had opened a Pandora's box of stimulating talk.

McDermott puffed away meditatively. "Not exactly. You might say that I liked flying a helluva lot more, so much that I never wanted to go back to police work. I could have been an MP Officer in World War II but I joined the Air Corps instead. I learned a lot in the two years I spent in Homicide, and I've got a tremendous amount of respect for cops. They don't have a job anyone can really like, unless you're some kind of nut or sadist. You see too much of the seamy side of

22

life. Some guys put up with it because they enjoy the authority of a badge and a gun. Some actually like the work because there's a certain challenge, particularly in homicide. But I never knew a cop who didn't acquire a large coat of cynicism about people. And cynicism can be a kind of malignancy. It eats away your sense of values or judgment and even the ability to enjoy life, to like or love or trust someone."

Betty Roberts was staring at McDermott with an expression of startling discovery, as if Max had suddenly transformed himself from a Hyde to a Jekyll.

"I've never known a detective in my whole life," she breathed. "And a philosophical one at that. You've assumed romantic proportions, Captain McDermott."

"Romantic, my ass," McDermott said. "Police work is tiresome, dirty and boring. It's ninety-five percent legwork, hours of checking and rechecking, and knowing that you probably won't solve a tough case unless some stool pigeon spills. So even success makes you cynical. Tell you something, I'm supposed to be something of a tough guy, but I threw up at the first homicide I worked on. It was brutal, vicious and bloody—like a slaughterhouse."

"The taking of any human life is theoretically brutal and vicious," Lindsay philosophied thoughtfully.

"That's the Quaker in you, Jim," Rebel said.

"Didn't know you're a Quaker," Max remarked in mild surprise.

"Was. Or rather my parents were and they raised me in that faith. World War II came along, I was nineteen, very idealistic and completely sold on it being a justified war. So I went into the Navy and later went back in during the Korean War, as a reserve commander flying transports. I never returned to the Quaker faith, though. I had killed, and I found it hadn't bothered my conscience too much. I won't say I enjoyed killing another human being, but I supposed most of us rationalized we were killing Hitler or

23

Tojo when we were slaughtering some poor guy no different than ourselves."

"I suppose you also could rationalize murder," Foley suggested. "Often wondered why people do commit murder. I suppose there's a kind of pattern to it."

"Somewhat," McDermott said. "I think you'd find at least one of three elements in every homicide. Sex, money, or alcohol. Add drugs to alcohol, maybe. Anyway, it's one of these or a combination of them."

"You left out insanity," Lindsay objected.

Max shook his head. "Insanity is merely the culmination of the other factors. It isn't the basis for murder, it's just the final triggering act. A man needs dough so desperately, he may kill to get it—either in a moment of panic or going off his rocker. A woman can get jealous enough to shoot her husband or lover. Sure, some murders are committed by plain, pathological kooks. But most homicides involve people who are pretty normal to begin with, before their troubles start eating away at their sense of right-versus-wrong. I agree with Jim, here, that you'd have to be insane to commit murder. But it's usually not the kind of insanity you can wrap up in a nice neat little medical category with a fancy label, like schizophrenia."

"Insanity defined as self-destruction of reason and conscience," Lindsay said.

"Not bad," McDermott complimented him. "And that's what I learned in my two years as a cop. Anyone can go insane to a degree, if you accept Jim's definition. Likewise, anyone is capable of murder. Which is why I wasn't immune to cynicism, not even in a relatively short span. I saw enough in those two years to convince me there's potential evil in a saint."

Betty looked at him demurely. "And I suppose that's why you're also immune to marriage?"

Max started to glower but decided against it and managed a tolerant smile. "From that remark, I assume my marital status or rather lack of same has already been the subject of discussion around the base."

"It's been the subject of discussion among stewardesses," Rebel laughed. "Any newly-arrived captain is immediately categorized as to availability. You were no exception."

"Even with that prizefighter puss of yours," Betty added merrily. Foley's jaw dropped, Mueller whistled, Rebel swallowed and Lindsay frowned, but McDermott merely shook his head as if in disbelief at her impertinence.

"I'm not immune to marriage, Miss Roberts," he said in a tone so gentle its very softness was a verbal spanking. "I'm merely immune to premature marriages, marriages for purely physical reasons, or marriages just for the sake of marriage."

"Or marriages to stewardesses with large mouths and very little respect for senior check captains," Mueller muttered, and everyone laughed except McDermott, whose faint grin admittedly was for him the equivalent of a hilarious reaction.

Rebel turned suddenly to Jim. "Speaking of marriages, how's Norma and the kids?"

"All fine."

A perfectly routine question and conventional answer, but McDermott saw Lindsay's jawbone muscles tighten as if his teeth were a hidden vise. Nor could Max resist a sneaking look at Rebel, whose face for a split second was clouded with a mask of sympathy and affection.

"How many kids you got, skipper?" Mueller asked—he was junior enough and inexperienced enough not to realize that ninety-nine percent of airline captains hate to be called "skipper."

"Two. Boy and a girl. Kevin's eleven and Debbie's four."

"His wife's very attractive," Rebel said, and to anyone but McDermott her tone was a model of sincerity. Max sensed something else, a glimmer of taunting superiority. "She was a registered nurse, wasn't she, Jim?" Rebel was continuing.

Again, a perfectly prosaic question but one which bugged McDermott. There was just the hint of a jealous needle in her inflection.

"Yes." Lindsay's answer was so short it was almost rude.

"I thought most pilots married stewardesses," Mueller said, reaching for the last piece of garlic bread on the table.

"Not enough of them," Rebel remarked matter-of-factly.

"A lot of them marry stewardesses the second time around," Lindsay said in a flat voice, gazing squarely at Rebel as he spoke. Again, that momentary mask of affection dropped over her face and Max thought he detected a vestige of a flush. He found himself wondering about Mrs. James Lindsay, mother of two and ex-R.N. A shrew? A matrimonial iceberg, passions frozen by too many years of sameness and taken-for-granted intimacy?

The odds were very much against her coming within ten miles of Rebel's physical beauty. But Max could not rid himself of the image Lindsay had planted in his brain—so solid, dependable, straightforward that infidelity seemed out of character. Yet there was Rebel, and McDermott admitted to himself that even instinctively disliking the girl, he was attracted to her sensually.

"Where did you get that scar?" Betty Roberts was asking him, and for once Max welcomed her peskiness. He worried that the Lindsay-Rebel relationship might have finally percolated through the flying and gastronomical preoccupations of First Officer Foley and Flight Engineer Mueller respectively. McDermott was an aeronautical purist, to whom personal distractions were an anathema on any well-run flight deck. A captain with emotional involvements might well lose stature in the eyes of younger crew members—that was Max's theory, at any rate, and he was glad that Betty had diverted the conversation, so glad that his reply was actually cordial.

"Some young punk with a fifth of rotgut whiskey in his belly and a switchblade in his paw," he recounted in a rare mood for reminiscing. He was prevailed on to tell the whole story, and from there went into other experiences of his police days. One account of a particularly brutal murder renewed the earlier discussion.

"You told us," Lindsay was saying, "that most murders are committed by relatively normal persons pushed into a form of temporary insanity."

"That's right, I did."

"Okay, then by implication you're saying that anyone could murder, under the right circumstances."

"It's not an implication," McDermott declared, "It's a fact. Let me put it this way. Every person sitting at this table is a potential killer. And so are all your friends and acquaintences and relatives. Mind you, I'm not using homicide as a synonym for crime. I'll concede there are forms of justifiable homicide. If a mother caught some pervert molesting a five-year-old kid and bashed in the bastard's skull with a hammer, I suspect a jury wouldn't debate two minutes before acquittal. But it's still murder."

"You think, say, even someone like a priest or a devout Quaker, could commit murder?" Lindsay pressed.

"Suppose a Quaker came home and found a lunatic beating and trying to rape his wife. What the hell is he supposed to do—stand there and proclaim 'thou should take thy hands off my wife and I must ask thee to leave immediately?' Let me tell you something, Jim, I've argued this point with Quakers before, and every damned one of them finally came around to admitting that really strong motivation, such as protecting a loved one from physical harm, would override all the religious convictions in the world, no matter how deeply inbred."

"Motivation," Lindsay repeated thoughtfully. "I guess that's the magic word."

"The conversation's getting unpleasant," Rebel grimaced. "Let's get out of here."

McDermott rode with Betty, Rebel and Jim in one taxi

back to the O'Hare Inn, where Coastal crews stayed on layovers, while Foley and Mueller took another cab. Max sat with the driver, deliberately keeping his eyes on the road after a brief glimpse of Rebel and the captain holding hands. Suspicions confirmed, he thought, and then cursed himself for this adolescent curiosity about their relationship.

The pilots had separate rooms. Rebel, as the senior stewardess, also drew her own room. But McDermott's suspicions suffered a setback when they arrived at the motel. In Betty's box was a note from Cathy:

"Meet you in Ops tomorrow. Staying with a friend."

"Lucky Cathy," Rebel remarked. "Well, Betty, why don't I move my stuff down to your room? I don't feel like staying alone."

"Fine with me," Betty agreed. "Good night, you guys. Thanks for the dinner and the lecture, Captain McDermott."

Max bowed his head in gruff acknowledgement, conscious of both relief and puzzlement at the girls' sleeping arrangements. He had been positive that Rebel and Jim would be shacking up. He was so pleased, in fact, after the stewardesses left he indulged in the unusual amenity of inviting Lindsay to have some coffee.

"No thanks," Jim said glumly. "Guess I'll hit the hay, Max. Our crew pickup tomorrow morning is six-forty-five if you want to leave a call."

McDermott watched his tall frame stride down the corridor toward his room. Lindsay was walking slowly, his shoulders slumping. There was something bothering him, Max knew, and it didn't take an ex-detective to arrive at Rebel Martin as the source of Lindsay's inner conflicts. The stewardess had him hooked but good, that was for sure. McDermott mentally shrugged the other man's dilemma from his mind for the time being and went to his own room, where he fell asleep almost immediately.

He was sleeping so soundly that when the telephone jangled harshly and impatiently, he thought it was his wakeup call.

"McDermott," he answered, expecting to hear the voice of the switchboard operator. The voice was female, but it was no operator.

"Hi. Did I wake you up?"

"Who the hell is this?"

"Betty Roberts."

"Yes, you woke me up. And for a damned good reason, I hope."

"A very good reason, Captain McDermott."

McDermott looked at his wristwatch; he had been asleep for only a half-hour.

"Okay," he muttered. "Let me have the reason and then I'll decide whether to hang up."

"I'd like to talk to you."

"What about?"

"Anything you'd like to talk about."

"Horsecrap. That means you're horny."

"You put things so delicately. But you're right."

McDermott was interested but wary. "And I assume your roommate is listening with all eardrums at full throttle?"

"Oh, Rebel's not here," Betty said in a tone blending reassurance with surprise that Max had even asked.

He was silent for so long that she asked teasingly, "What's the matter, Captain—surprised?"

"Not exactly. But what was that little charade about staying with you?"

"For outward appearances, and probably because you're a check captain with the reported disposition of a constipated crocodile. She didn't want you lowering any boom on her beloved. And I mean beloved. They're nuts about each other or hadn't you guessed?"

McDermott was still chuckling inwardly at her reptilian analogy. He liked the spunky little vixen and, being a normal male with a strong sexual appetite, he was intrigued by her bluntness.

"Knock twice and the password is turbine," he told her.

"Oh, no, you come down here. I'd have to get dressed."

"So would I," Max growled. "And I don't like sneaking down motel corridors to a dame's room. If you're that horny, you can do the sneaking yourself."

He hung up before she had a chance to debate the matter.

And there were two discreet taps at his door fifteen minutes later, followed by a tiny voice whispering, "Turbine, you sonofabitch."

She was good in bed—affectionate, uninhibited and anxious to please even as she received pleasure. But as McDermott pounded at her slim, twisting little body and heard her moan the litany of satisfied desire, he would not prevent Rebel from straying uninvited into his mind.

He thought about it after Betty left—under duress because she was the post-sex snuggling type—and wondered anew at the extent of his involvement with another man's love affair. It was unlike Max, whose interest in gossip and concern with another man's troubles depended entirely on whether they affected a pilot's flying proficiency. McDermott wasn't even sure that Lindsay's conflict interested him less than Rebel did, and this nagged at his conscience.

Or was he getting involved because of his pilot instinct for spotting potential trouble, a kind of uneasy sixth sense that could see a boiling, angry, deadly thunderstorm lurking behind a bank of innocent clouds? Come to think of it, that could be a cop's instinct, too.

As Maximilian McDermott turned over and went back to sleep, it was just as well he could not know how deeply he was to become involved with a girl named Rebel Martin.

2

McDermott met the captain in the motel coffee shop at
six-fifteen. Lindsay looked tired, but Max thought wryly
that a night in bed with someone like Rebel could have
exhausted Errol Flynn. And he also noticed it was not so
much physical fatigue as an emotional exhaustion that
showed in Jim's usually clear eyes. The two captains sat
down with Foley and Mueller, McDermott ordering corned
beef hash and a poached egg and Lindsay just toast and
coffee. Jim said little except for a quiet "good morning" to
his copilot and flight engineer plus some desultory small
talk. He wore the air of a man desperate to confide in
somebody but at the same time unwilling to do the confid-
ing to someone like McDermott, whom he did not really
know, and certainly not to a couple of subordinates.

"Sleep well?" he asked Max.

"Yeah." McDermott wasn't volunteering anything more
than that. He was one of those relatively rare men who
never discussed sexual conquests with other males, and regarded such boasting as the ultimate in adolescent behavior.

"You're lucky," Lindsay murmured. "I'm having a hell of
a time falling asleep these days." Again, he seemed on the
verge of telling Max something, but his jaw muscles went
taut, as if they were closing a vise on his tongue. That jaw
muscle bit, McDermott thought, seemed to be an emotional
reflex; he had first noticed it when Lindsay had snapped at

31

Mueller, and he had seen it again last night at the restaurant.

Rebel and Betty poked their heads into the coffee shop to announce that the crew pickup limo was ready. McDermott, on the short ride to the airport, marveled as usual at the ability of some women—stewardesses were especially adept—to look absolutely virginal and untouched after a night of wholehearted sinning. Both girls were freshly-scrubbed and bright-eyed, their makeup applied perfectly and their outward attitude one of either forgetfulness or innocence. They chattered away while Lindsay, up front with the driver this time in what might have been an effort to maintain a captain's aloof decorum, listened idly and rather absent-mindedly.

Max had no fears about Miss Roberts dropping coy innuendos about the previous night. Despite the jaunty, almost insolent air she had affected toward him publicly, she was a little afraid of the burly check pilot. In fact, she had started to leave his room the night before with a light-hearted sally, "Can't wait to tell Rebel I scored," when McDermott grabbed her arm and with one swift, powerful motion, had plopped her back on the bed. She rubbed it ruefully, almost in tears, as he lit into her.

"I don't like stupid bastards who brag about their sex lives, and I dislike the habit even more in dames," he had snarled. "You open your damned mouth about tonight and you won't be able to sit down on foam rubber."

"I'm sorry, Max, I was just kidding," she had gulped.

His anger had softened, but his sternness was undiluted. "I'm a tough old rooster, Betty, but I've always regarded sex as something very personal, very intimate and nobody else's goddamned business. If you want to regard the last hour with all the simpering immaturity of a snot-nosed teenager, then from now on it's *Captain McDermott* to you and it's *Miss Roberts* to me."

She had half-sniffled a penitent, "Okay, Max," but at this

moment Miss Roberts was unconcernedly buffing her fingernails while Rebel inspected her makeup in a small hand mirror. Lindsay watched her even as he spoke to McDermott, giving Max the uneasy impression he was being addressed by a disembodied voice.

"I suppose you'd like to have the right seat today, Max," the captain ventured. "I know some check pilots prefer to ride copilot."

"If it's okay with Foley, it's fine with me," McDermott said. Foley nodded, whether out of necessary deference or alacrity at the prospect of a workless payday, Max could not tell. He knew he could have monitored Lindsay just as efficiently from the jump seat, but like most check captains he welcomed an occasional chance for some actual cockpit chores.

As McDermott had suspected, route-checking Lindsay was the equivalent of teaching Lindbergh how to fly. It took Max about thirty minutes to renew his previous conviction that Lindsay was a competent pro, and they were only an hour out of Chicago when McDermott gruffly announced he was going to the Blue Room (the time-honored airline nomenclature for toilet) and that Foley could have the right seat back for the rest of the trip.

They had a two-hour layover in Salt Lake City before their turnaround, Washington via O'Hare again. Takeoff was delayed while snow plows lumbered down their assigned runway, clearing one side first and then forming a huge circle at one end before peeling off to go down the other side.

"Looks like a bunch of covered wagons," Foley commented, watching the plows go into the circling maneuver.

"Maybe they're expecting an Indian attack," Mueller chuckled, but the little sally drew no response from Lindsay except a grouchy, "I wish to hell they'd hurry up." McDermott noticed that Lindsay had failed to brief the passengers on the reason for the delay; he would mention it to him later and in private, for Max never issued the mildest reprimand or reminder to a captain in front of other crew members. But just as he was writing a "remind L no cabin PA explng dly" in the margin of the route qualification check sheet, Lindsay picked up the PA mike and provided the cabin with a polite explanation. Max shook his head and crossed out the notation.

They landed in Washington at ten-forty, an hour at which Operations was almost deserted. Max went into Blake's empty office, dropped the check sheet on the chief pilot's desk, and emerged to see Lindsay standing alone by the pilots' mailboxes. Jim looked up as McDermott approached, a tired smile on his face.

"Any criticism, suggestions or advice, Max?"

"Nope. You run a good trip. See you again one of these days."

"Thanks. By the way, let's make 'one of these days' pretty soon. If you're not doing anything tomorrow night, how about coming out to the house for dinner? Like you to meet Norma and the kids."

Normally, McDermott tried to avoid social contacts with the men whose professional proficiency he had to judge. And he scrupulously rejected any socializing that involved going to a married pilot's home; Max was one of those bachelors to whom an invitation for a home-cooked meal was culinary hypocrisy. He claimed he had yet to meet any wife who could turn out a better meal than a good restaurant chef.

But this time he hesitated uncertainly. For the life of him, he could not suppress his curiosity. Maybe he just wanted to meet Rebel's competition. Maybe the check pilot in him subconsciously worried that a good captain was being endangered by personal troubles. And maybe the latter was pure rationalization; more likely, the ex-cop in him was having premonitions. Now why the hell was he thinking

34

like that? As if he smelled crime. As if he sensed tragedy.

"Think you can make it, Max?" Lindsay was saying.

"Uh, I think so. I don't know what Blake's got for me tomorrow. I'll give you a ring."

"Crew sked will have my number," Jim said. "Hi, Rebel. Want a ride home?"

"Love one." God, she was beautiful, Max mused. Two days of tough work and she still looked like a walking advertisement for stewardess recruitment. Betty Roberts, who had just joined them at the pilot mailboxes, looked bedraggled by comparison.

"Well, Foley's going to walk Cathy and me up to the parking lot," Betty said, giving McDermott a look that was one-third uncertain, one-third pleading and one-third defiant. McDermott offered absolutely nothing except a conventional "Good night, Betty." This time she positively glared at him and marched off.

"I'm ready anytime, Jim," Rebel said. Max noticed she was carrying an oblong, gift-wrapped box she hadn't bothered to open.

"Let me call home first. I'll tell Norma I'm playing bus driver."

He left to use a pay phone in the crew lounge, and Max went back into Blake's office, where he typed out a brief note to the chief pilot, informing him he would be in about eight A.M. to talk to him about getting some office space. When he returned to Operations, Lindsay had just hung up the phone and approached Rebel frowning.

"Sorry, honey, but Debbie's been sick all day and I'd better get right home."

Over Rebel's face dropped an almost imperceptible shadow of bitterness, erased immediately by apparently genuine concern.

"Nothing serious, is it, Jim?"

"No, just a little fever. Max, I forgot about you. How are you getting home?"

"I've got wheels," McDermott said. "Uh . . ." He paused, and Lindsay seemed to read his mind.

"Maybe you'd take Rebel home, then? Mueller and Foley already have left. It's pretty late to be catching a bus."

"Yeah, I'll take her." McDermott was thinking that Lindsay had no qualms about trusting his paramour with an ugly old bear. "If the lady doesn't object," he added gruffly.

Rebel smiled and it would have defrosted an iceberg. "That's sweet of you, Max. Jim, I hope Debbie will be all right."

For a moment, McDermott thought she was going to kiss Lindsay right in front of him, and Lindsay looked as if he would have welcomed it. But she turned away suddenly, with almost an effort, telling McDermott, "I'll wait for you guys outside."

"If that little girl of yours is sick, better forget about tomorrow," Max offered.

"Like I told Rebel, just a slight fever. Kids are that way. It'll probably be normal by morning or maybe even by the time I get home. Call me anyway, Max."

"Will do."

The three of them walked to the employees' parking lot, disdaining the usual shuttle bus which operated infrequently after ten o'clock. Lindsay carried Rebel's overnight bag along with his own. They reached Jim's car first, a 1970 Buick Riviera, and again McDermott got the feeling Lindsay and Rebel wished he was five miles away—or totally blind. They shook hands discreetly, but even in the darkness Max could have sworn the brief contact was more of a squeeze.

"Night, Jim."

"Good night, Rebel."

There was affection in her voice and sadness in his, Max thought.

"My car's up another row," McDermott said abruptly. "Let's go, young lady."

She followed him to a Mercedes four-door sedan, McDermott tossing her overnight bag in the back seat and then scolding himself for sneaking a look at her long, graceful legs as she slid in, her skirt hoisted almost to her thighs.

"I live on King Street in Alexandria," she told him, after he climbed in and had nursed the Mercedes' cold engine into a reluctant start. "Know where it is?"

"You navigate and I'll drive," Max said. "I'm not even sure where the hell our hangars are at this airport."

They proceeded toward Alexandria, starting with small talk.

"Nice car," Rebel observed. "Mercedes, isn't it?"

"Yeah, a brand-new '71 280SE."

"Hmm. About eight thousand, they run, don't they?"

"About." Trust Rebel to know the price tag.

"For another two thousand, you could have gotten an SL sports coupe, Max. A four-door's kind of square for a bachelor, isn't it?"

He glowered, "To you, it's square. To me, it's practical. I've got a cottage up in the Finger Lakes, near Ithaca, New York. An SL's too small for all the gear I take there every summer."

"Well," Rebel condescended, "it *is* a nice car. I love good cars." She stretched her long legs and leaned her head back against the deep, luxurious upholstery, fingering the little gift-wrapped package absent-mindedly.

"Why the hell don't you open it?" Max asked. "Or do you already know what's inside?"

"Probably a bracelet. The creep's liable to leave anything in my mailbox. Except an engagement ring, which is par for the male sex."

"You sound bitter. You also sound like you want to get married."

"Could be." Her voice dropped a couple of octaves.

"Picked out the guy?"

"Don't be a stuffy damned fool," she snapped and started

to cry, a development both unexpected and unwelcome for McDermott. He resented a woman's tears, regarding them more as a female weapon than a legitimate emotional outlet. But he was better than most men at divining when a lachrymose display was strategic rather than real, and something told him that Rebel's soft sobs were no act.

"I'm sorry, kid," he said, and Rebel sensed that in his own gruff way, he *was* sorry. She stopped crying and put her hand over his. Max squirmed mentally. Her touch was electrifying.

"I'd like to cry on your shoulder sometime," she murmured, and coming from anyone but Rebel it would have sounded like a phony come-on, a patent bid for sympathy. Rebel's low, deep voice coated it with sincerity and Max resisted an impulse to pat her clumsily.

"I make a punk Dear Abby," McDermott muttered. "What you could use is a nice, sensible, mature confidant of your own sex."

"Bull," Rebel said with open bitterness. "Women are too hypocritical to make good friends."

"That why you wouldn't exactly win a popularity contest among your colleagues?"

"When did you deduce I wasn't popular?"

"Male intuition. Plus that little scene in Ops yesterday. I gathered Miss Roberts wouldn't trust you farther than she could throw a 727 fuselage."

"She's a jealous little bitch. We used to date the same guy. She was nuts about him and he didn't mean anything to me, but he stopped seeing her. So she hates my guts for it."

"Justifiably," Max said laconically. "If he meant nothing to you and a hell of a lot to her, why'd you do it?"

"Don't ask so many questions," Rebel said mildly.

"I'll ask all the questions I want. You're the one who wanted a water-proof shoulder. I'd like to know what makes you tick so loudly—a kind of female time bomb. Why'd you

38

grab Betty's guy, with malice aforethought, as we cops say?"

"Female perverseness, I guess," she answered after a pause. "The instinctive desire to take somebody's man away from her even if you don't want him yourself. I suppose it's a challenge."

"Baloney," McDermott said with open anger. "It's cruel and mean and any dame that pulls that crap is a spoiled brat. You're a female dog in the manger."

"Turn left at the next corner," Rebel said without a trace of resentment. It was almost as if she hadn't even been listening. "Mine's the third house on the right after we turn. Number 6016."

She lived in one of those old Alexandria homes closely resembling the Colonial restorations in Georgetown, where even a coat of fresh paint fails to hide an air of antiquity. Max would not have been surprised if her door had been opened by a servant in a powdered wig. It wasn't a big house; two stories, he noted, but with narrow frontage, and he suspected the interior didn't have much more square footage than the average apartment.

"Live here alone?" He knew the answer but asked anyway. Rebel wan't the "Hi, roomie" type.

"Alone." Her reply carried just a suggestion of defiance, almost as if she were inviting further questions. Max had an obvious one which he refrained from asking: how she afforded a house on stewardess pay. She groped for the key in the depths of her handbag, which like all women's pocketbooks bulged with enough contents to outfit a pawn shop. Somehow, Max thought, that only too human touch made her seem a little less formidable and a little more vulnerable, like the discovery of a minor flaw in someone whose perfection was frightening.

Rebel handed him the key and he dutifully unlocked the door. "I'd like very much to mix you a drink," she said. "Not just for the ride home but—well, I feel like talking some more. And I like the way you say what you're thinking. Maybe you can talk some sense into me. About . . . some problems I've got."

"My advice may wind up as twenty ungentle slaps on your rear end," Max said bluntly.

She laughed, but it was a sound of derision, not humor.

"I'll give you odds you'll flip me over on my back before you get to ten," she said softly. "Come on in."

He did. He followed her inside, conscious that his very entrance was a form of surrender. One big hand tightened around the clasp of her valise, which he was carrying, and the other balled into a heavy fist.

Her house was a perfect example of the incongruity McDermott occasionally found in some women—those who would rather be caught naked than without proper makeup and smart clothes, yet never seemed to mind dwelling in an atmosphere of careless dishevelment. Rebel's living room wasn't exactly a pigpen, but McDermott's eyes roved disapprovingly over ashtrays crammed with stained cigarette butts, old newspapers strewn on the floor, and a layer of dust on a marred coffee table. He was willing to bet the kitchen sink was full of dirty dishes.

She read his mind. "The place is a mess, Max, but I don't seem to be home enough to keep it clean. I'm not that bad a housekeeper, honest."

McDermott politely refrained from saying aloud what he was thinking. It wasn't lack of time but lack of interest. It occurred to him that if he went to the Lindsay's home the following night, he'd probably find it a model of well-scrubbed suburbia. Damned if he could keep this tangled triangle out of his mind.

"Scotch all right?" Rebel asked.

"I'd rather have a straight shot of bourbon, if there's any on hand. On the rocks, no water."

"I think I've got some. I'll go see."

She went into the kitchen and McDermott had an im-

40

pulse to tidy up the living room mess. He rejected this in favor of inspecting the room. It was sparsely furnished with no attempt at interior decorating or color coordination. A large, rather faded gold couch, the dusty coffee table, a walnut telephone stand, a green easy chair with a jarringly modernistic floor lamp next to it, a small bookcase, and a nondescript rug that once might have been an attractive rust color under the coffee table, lapping up to the edge of the couch—this comprised her furniture. The living room itself was attractive in an antique sort of way, with a high ceiling and a fireplace opposite the couch, but the whole house smelled musty.

McDermott heard Rebel coaxing ice out of the refrigerator and grinned as he heard her curse, "These goddamned trays." He might have helped her but he didn't want to see that kitchen; it had to be like the living room, and this sloppy atmosphere, so sharply in contrast to the girl herself, bothered him. He remembered that when they had dinner in Chicago, Rebel was dressed in a simple but obviously expensive black sheath; and Max, while no expert on jewelry, could have sworn the lustrous pearls around her white neck were real.

He busied himself by browsing through what might charitably have been called her "library." It consisted of her stewardess manual, two gothic novels he had never heard of, a thick tome titled *Sex Education for the Mature Adult* and a half-dozen paperback mysteries. He picked up the sex instruction book, having noted the "Profusely Illustrated" under the title, but put it down hastily when he heard Rebel's footsteps.

She handed him his drink and sat down on the couch, sipping at the scotch and water she had mixed for herself, and surveying Max through eyes that suddenly seemed tired and spiritless.

"I won't bite," she said finally. "Sit here with me."

McDermott obliged, acutely conscious both of her per-

41

fume and her body. She had left her uniform jacket in the kitchen and without it, her v-neck, white blouse was about as impersonal as a transparent negligee. It accentuated her firm bust line as if it had been painted on instead of worn.

"It's your move, young lady," McDermott said. "Or if you don't feel like talking now, I'll finish up this drink and get the hell out of here."

Instead of replying, Rebel started crying again—retching, heaving sobs this time, that came from the depths of whatever was torturing her. Max waited uncomfortably, while her tears carved rivulets through her makeup. Awkwardly, he patted her slim hand with his own hairy paw, the effect being that of a bear trying to caress a baby without breaking it in two.

"Okay, unload," he said with a harshness he did not feel. "And I've got a sneaking hunch Captain Lindsay is the reason for this female flood."

Her sobs dwindled to a few half-hearted sniffles. "Loan me your handkerchief, Max. Funny, but a handkerchief is the one accessory we never have around when we decide to bawl seriously."

Wordlessly, he gave it to her, his expression stern and yet not forboding enough to intimidate her.

"Yes, it's Jim. I love him and he loves me. Only neither of us want to hurt his wife or his children. Typical triangle, isn't it? Like something out of a bad soap opera."

"There's a geometric inevitability to a triangle, Rebel," Max said. "One side of it has to get hurt."

"I know. And I suppose it has to be me. I'm the other woman. And it's my decision. Jim can't make it. He's too nice and too honorable. He's also the most wonderful man I've ever known. He's even a gentle lover. Gentle and strong at the same time. You could jump into a thousand beds and never find somebody like that."

Max swallowed half his drink with one gulp before responding. "What the hell do you want me to tell you, Rebel:

42

Go get him, tiger, and screw the wife and kids? That what you want to hear?"

"I don't know what I want to hear. I just wanted to talk to somebody. Maybe you think it's just a cheap pilot/stewardess affair. It isn't, dammit. I didn't even intend for it to develop into anything serious. We went to bed casually and all of a sudden we found out there was more than just sex between us. So much more that even when we have sex, it's frustrating because we know he eventually has to go home. To his family."

McDermott downed the rest of his drink in another gulp, as if he were taking on fuel to make his tongue move with the right words. "You said it was your decision, not Lindsay's. Only you used the words 'nice' and 'honorable.' Gutless would be more appropriate." She sucked in her breath at his attack, but he ignored her. "He's got it made, girl. He has you to satisfy his libido and a family to satisfy his urge for paternalism. Christ, he could drag that arrangement on until you'd be dyeing the gray out of your hair. So make up your mind, Rebel—it's a case of piss or get off the pot. Triangles that go on too long get kinda lopsided."

"Want another drink?" He shook his head. "Okay, so I make the move. But what move? Stop seeing him unless he agrees to divorce his wife? I couldn't do that to him. He's as torn up inside as I am. Anyway, I'm not quite ready to issue ultimatums. I suppose what I should do is forget him and marry the lovesick creep who sent me this." She gestured toward the little package, which she had tossed still unopened into the easy chair. "He's married too, but I wouldn't mind breaking up *his* marriage. It would serve him right. Besides at least he's wealthy."

"You seem to have a propensity for attracting married men," McDermott observed with more sarcasm than rancor.

"Married, single, what the hell, they're all men. They're all the same. Except Jim. He's a tender sensitive human being. Everytime I look at him, he sends me. Like the way he tightens his jaw when he's mad or upset; it actually makes me hot." She paused, as if testing his reaction to her bluntness. Max said nothing. "I go out almost every night, Max, and usually I sleep with my dates. You know why? Because I miss Jim so damned much. I drink too much and I screw too much because that's the only way I can stop thinking about him for at least a little while. A couple more drinks tonight and I'd go to bed with you. I'd even enjoy it, until after you left and I'd start thinking again about being Jim Lindsay's wife instead of the other woman."

He wasn't quite sure whether Rebel had invited him to bed or insulted him, but her intensity kept a lid on his annoyance. He was even clumsily sympathetic. "Maybe things will work out, kid. You aren't the first dame to get into this kind of mess and Lindsay isn't the first guy. Sometimes people reach a solution, nobody's entirely happy but at least minds are made up and there's no more uncertainty. Ride with the punches for a while longer and see what happens. Maybe Jim will make the move."

Her green eyes were bloodshot and still misty. "I've already let things ride for a long time. Like about six months. And every day without him is just a little bit worse than the time before. Right now I have a very strong urge to marry Daddy Warbucks and let fifty charge accounts sublimate how I feel about Jim."

"Daddy Warbucks? The guy who gave you that package."

She nodded, got up and walked to the easy chair. She picked up the box, tore off the wrapping with more impatience than eagerness, and opened it. She smiled but there was not an iota of surprise, gratitude or pleasure in the smile, for it never reached her eyes. A cynical, take-it-for-granted expression, McDermott thought, and he had a perverse wish that the sucker who had given her the gift could have been here to see her unguarded reaction.

Rebel gave him the box. Inside was a jade pendant which

44

Max figured must have cost several hundred dollars. There was a card underneath the shining jewelry, and McDermott handed the box back. "Here. Aren't you interested in the donor's name?"

"I already know. I told him I wanted a jade pendant. Go ahead and read it. Max. I don't have any secrets where you're concerned. I've already confessed more to you in the last ten minutes than I have to anyone in my whole life, except Jim."

She took the card from the box and Max read it.

"To Rebel. Just a small, insufficient token of how I feel about you. Love, Frank."

"Very touching," Max said. "Where'd he make his dough —writing greeting cards?"

"He's in the airline business."

McDermott's cold blue eyes narrowed. "By airlines, you wouldn't mean Coastal?"

"The name is Frank Gilcannon. Incidentally, he pays part of the rent on this place. Ever hear of him?"

Max whistled, an inadvertent outlet for surprise tinged with admiration for her audacity. "Yeah, I've heard of him. Our esteemed executive vice president. Supposed to be Belnap's hand-picked successor when the old man retires. I'll say this much for you, Rebel, when you play around, you don't fool with second-stringers."

She looked pleased, as if he had paid her the highest of compliments, but she shook her head. "There's at least one second-stringer, in a way."

"Now *that* remark intrigues me," McDermott said. "Just for the record, young lady, how many lovesick swains do you have in that stable?"

"Really want to know?"

"Yeah."

"Why?"

45

"Maybe I'd like to find out what a damned fine airline captain is letting himself in for."

She flushed, hurt and angry. "Go to hell. I told you why I sleep around. Jim's my guy. The rest are therapy for too many goddamned lonely nights without him."

"Okay, so don't tell me."

"Actually," she pouted, "there aren't as many as you might think. Frank you already know about. Then there's Lyle Tarkington. He owns a big chain of women's stores. And Bob Denham. I guess you might call him my second-stringer."

"Any reason for that lowly status? No, don't tell me. I can guess. Mr. Denham hasn't got any dough."

Rebel sat down next to him, disturbingly close. "Correct. He's a Coastal ramp agent. Very poor and very handsome. Even better-looking than Jim. Six-feet-two and wavy blonde hair—the Greek God type. He wants to marry me in the worst way. So does Lyle. And Frank would, too, if I gave him any encouragement."

"Marrying you," McDermott grunted, "*would* be the worst way." She was sitting so close to him their thighs touched and he moved just far enough to break the contact.

"You don't like me, do you, Max?" she asked without rancor.

"Not particularly."

"Why?"

"Without knowing what Jim Lindsay's home life is like, I'd say you stand a pretty good chance of lousing up one of our better pilots."

"That's Jim's business, not yours."

"It's my business if all this hanky-panky with you starts affecting the way he flies an airplane."

She ignored this and deliberately moved back toward him, leaning over so her full lips were close to his taut face. "You don't like me, but I'll bet you'd go to bed with me."

"That an invitation or an inquiry?"

46

She didn't answer, but mashed her mouth against his, her lips incredibly soft and then opening wide. For just a couple of seconds, McDermott responded but disgust overrode desire. He put one beefy hand against her face and shoved, so hard that she fell off the couch. Surprise and then anger distorted her features, but her ignominious posture—she was sprawled on her rump with one leg still on the couch —was all Max needed to completely douse the fire she had built in his loins.

He got to his feet and looked down at her flushed face.

"You dirty bastard," she said, but the epithet was a flabby defense against the fury in his icy eyes, and she started to cry again.

That was the way he left her, still on the floor, a tinge of guilt discoloring his contempt. He drove to his apartment, his mind a kaleidoscope of turmoil. Like any normal male, he was now regretting his impulsive rejection. He could still see her sitting, humiliated, on the floor but far sharper was the remembered image of her swollen breasts, her warm mouth, and her unspoken offer of satiating pleasure. Also, if the truth be known, McDermott felt sorry for her. He was cynical, but not to the extent of letting cynicism cloud his judgment of people, and he was convinced of one thing: Rebel had the moral stability of a nymphomaniac, but in her own twisted way she really loved Jim Lindsay.

And Lindsay must love her, too, Max reflected. Maybe he should take Jim up on that dinner invitation. For the first time in his life he was sticking his squashed nose into someone else's squalidly private business and he still couldn't explain exactly why. Unless—That damned nagging premonition again. That vague stir of uneasiness. The last hour with Rebel had fortified it. The girl was juggling dynamite —four panting suitors and at least three of them were going to get hurt. Maybe all four, Rebel being what she is. Four lovers with the potentiality of becoming enemies.

Lindsay. Gilcannon. Tarkington. Denham.

He shook his head, ruefully aware that he was listing those names like a cop running down a roster of suspects. He forced them from his thoughts and concentrated on his driving. Not only were the streets unfamiliar, but he was squinting through the windshield at the clammy, ghostly fingers of a gathering night fog.

Like all pilots, he hated and dreaded fog. An insidious, malevolent killer, its very silence the epitome of lurking death. This was the kind of night, he speculated gloomily, when evil is planned and plotted.

Which was what someone was doing.

3

Roger Blake the next morning managed to find McDermott what could have been euphemistically labeled as office space, a cubbyhole that had once been a storeroom.

"All I need now is a pay phone and folding doors," Max complained. "This isn't a room; it's a goddamned booth."

"I'm sorry, Max." Blake apologized. "Space is a bit tight around here. I'll try to get you bigger quarters if anything opens up, but meanwhile I've ordered you a phone which should be installed in about an hour. And a filing cabinet. How do you like the desk?"

"Where's the plaque?"

"Plaque?"

"The one that says the desk belonged to Orville Wright's father. Aw, skip it, Rog"—Blake looked hurt—"I'm just kidding. Any chance for a typewriter?"

"I'll dig one up. Make yourself at home. No check rides on tap today, so you can just get settled."

The phone was installed within an hour, and McDermott's first call was to Jim Lindsay, accepting the dinner invitation for that evening. Lindsay sounded pleased, adding "Norma's anxious to meet you" before proceeding to the laborious task of outlining directions, including those little directional clues understood only by the one supplying the directions.

"There's a Texaco station on the right side of route 236 just about four miles after you leave the Beltway, only that's not where you turn. You go another seven-tenths of a mile and there's what looks like a big school only it's a . . . ." Ten minutes of monologue like this and McDermott was convinced Admiral Byrd couldn't have found his way to Lindsay's house, but he dutifully wrote down all details of the verbal map.

"I'll call you if I get lost, which is highly possible," Max said wearily.

"It's not as complicated as it sounds, Max," Lindsay assured him with that irksome confidence of a driver so familiar with a route that he can't understand why anyone should have trouble. "By the way, dress informal. You show up with a tie and coat, I'll poison your drinks."

McDermott got lost four times enroute, finally solved his dilemma by asking at a gas station, and thanks to the foresight of leaving his apartment thirty minutes early, he arrived at the Lindsay's only ten minutes late.

The house was a contemporary rambler, large but not pretentious, the lawn well-manicured and the furnishings inside chosen with obvious good taste and decorative sense. He remembered his prediction of stark contrast to Rebel's home, but this line of reflection ended abruptly when Jim introduced him to his wife.

McDermott was pleasantly surprised, half expecting an unattractive shrew. Norma Lindsay was neither shrewish nor unattractive. She was a tiny woman, slender but with good legs, a trim figure and warm, gracious personality. McDermott guessed she was in her late thirties or early forties, a blonde who hadn't been afraid to let her close-cropped hair turn into a silvery shade. Except for that matronly steel in her hair, she could have passed for twenty-five. She had a cute pug nose and a sprinkling of freckles that gave her a marked resemblance to Doris Day. Central Casting's version of The Perfect Wife, Max ruminated. He liked her instantly, as he had warmed to Lindsay at first meeting, but he still could not resist comparing her to Rebel

50

and his favorable impression collided with an admission that Norma Lindsay was overmatched.

He realized something else. With all her easy, natural friendliness and poise, there was something about Norma that didn't ring true. She almost seemed to be reading Perfect Wife lines, carefully memorized and rehearsed for McDermott's benefit. Her laugh, for example, skirted the fringes of a girlish giggle, yet there was a brittleness there as if the merry tinkle could unexpectedly shatter into a crash of broken, jagged glass.

If well-behaved yet ingratiating children are barometers of successful matrimony, there wasn't much doubt in Max's mind that Rebel had invaded what had been a happy marriage. McDermott was slightly afraid of kids; he hid this fear under an air of aloof indifference, but the Lindsay offspring quickly punctured his facade. Kevin, the boy, was one of those mannered youngsters who called an adult "sir" and made it sound respectful rather than belligerantly forced. He was all-boy, too, a solidly-built kid with a crew-cut and a smile remarkably like his father's. Debbie, at four, was an accomplished flirt who climbed literally into McDermott's lap and figuratively into his heart.

Introduced conventionally by her mother—"this is Captain McDermott, Debbie"—she surveyed him solemnly and then blurted, "I like you, honey. What's your first name?"

"Max," he said with equal solemnity, as her parents laughed.

"I guess she picked up that 'honey' bit from me," Lindsay explained. "That's what I call Norma all the time. Debbie asked me why about a month ago and I told her it's a special name people use for someone they like a lot. You must be something special, Max. That's the first time she's pulled it on anybody. Better get off Captain McDermott's lap, Debbie. We're ready to serve drinks."

"I want to stay on his lap," she insisted. "He's got a nice face, like George."

"Who's George?" Max asked.

"Her stuffed gorilla," Jim chuckled. "Boy, now *that's* a compliment. Debbie, off!"

"Let her stay," Max said placidly. Her chubby little arms went around his neck, and for the first time in his life he felt the mysterious, unquestioning trust of a child.

"Only until we serve the drinks," her father warned.

"Hokay," Debbie said contentedly, and McDermott resisted an impulse to squeeze her, both from fear of crushing her and because he really didn't know how. Instead he engaged Kevin in conversation, as if he were trying to impress on a four-year old that a rock-tough airline captain never plays favorites.

"You going to be a pilot, like your dad?" Max was uncomfortably conscious that the boy probably had been asked this about fifty times.

"No, sir, I don't think so. I'd like to be a doctor."

Jim leaned forward and rubbed his hand over his son's bristly hair, a gesture so paternally affectionate that McDermott felt a new thrust of antipathy toward Rebel. "It's a little too early for career decisions, but I've told Kevin he can be what he wants to be, so long as he wants it hard enough to work for it."

"I may want to be an airline pilot later," Kevin said hastily, as if he were afraid of hurting his father's feelings. "I'm very proud of Dad. I know it takes a lot to be an airline captain. It's just that he's taken me flying a couple of times and, well, I liked it okay but, well, it wasn't as much fun as I thought it would be."

Jim smiled. "It wasn't as much fun as *I* thought it would be," he admitted. "I rented a Cessna one Sunday and took Kevin up, only it was pretty choppy and he got sick. Next time it was smoother, but he still didn't flip the way I expected."

"Or hoped," Norma called out from the kitchen.

"Hoped is closer," Lindsay conceded. "I guess every father wants a son to follow in his footsteps, so to speak. You try to mold a boy in your own image. Maybe in another year or two, Kevin, I'll take you flying again. Maybe the bug will hit you then like it did me a long time ago, and Max here."

"Did you always want to be a pilot, Captain McDermott?" the youngster asked.

"The bug, as your father put it," Max said dryly, "bit me a little late in life."

"The captain was a police detective before he got his wings, Kevin," Lindsay told the boy.

Max was adjusting Debbie's weight on his lap and picked that moment to observe the look on Norma Lindsay's face. She had come in from the kitchen in time to hear what her husband had divulged. It was hard for Max to describe it, for what crossed her features was more of a shifting canvas of moods than a single expression. Interest, puzzlement—maybe alarm?

"That's very interesting," she said quietly.

"It sure is," Kevin said, eyeing McDermott with fresh respect. "Dad lets me read a few murder mysteries, Captain McDermott. Did you solve any murder cases?"

Max felt obliged to repeat, in a digested form, what he had told his little dinner party of two nights before, while the Lindsays went into the kitchen to mix drinks. He found that talking to Kevin was like conversing with an adult, and he was fascinated by the boy's quick mind and excellent vocabulary. But Debbie squirmed considerably during the discussion and finally gave Max up as an unexpected bore, sliding off his lap and trotting toward her playroom with the admonition, "You have to see some of my dolls." Even at four, McDermott reflected, she was a woman, hating to surrender the center of attention.

The dolls arrived just before the drinks, and Max forced himself to show huge interest as he was properly introduced to "Snuggles," quickly followed by "Glenda," "Dorothy" and "Wendy." The fifth and final doll was an exquisite mannequin in miniature with long blonde hair.

"This is Rebel," Debbie announced just as Lindsay walked in carrying a tray of cocktails. "I named her after my friend. She works with Daddy."

McDermott winced inwardly at Jim's reaction. The captain's face turned the color of an open wound, but his voice was steady and, by obvious effort, very matter-of-fact. "Rebel came over here a few times for dinner when she was new to the base. She and Debbie had quite a mutual admiration society. She gave her that doll."

"She hasn't been here for a long time," the little girl informed Max. "I miss her. She's my very bestest girl friend. When is she coming again, Daddy?"

"She's pretty busy flying," Lindsay said softly, "but everytime I see her she wants to know how you are."

"I think she should come see me," Debbie persisted.

"I think you should put away your dolls and let Captain McDermott enjoy his drink." Norma had just reentered and Max knew she had heard. Her face was calm, but it was a pinched kind of calm, as if she had screwed bolts onto her facial muscles.

Max sipped his Manhattan gratefully. It was not his favorite drink—Jim had pressed it on him with the plea that "You just try one the way I mix them"—but at this point McDermott would have welcomed anything with alcohol in it, if only to induce a modicum of relaxation in the midst of the tension that hung in the air like the heavy, humid stillness preceeding a summer thunderstorm. It was made even more noticeable by the Lindsay's efforts to cover it under a blanket of apparent matrimonial bliss. Jim never called his wife anything but "honey" and Norma, in turn, alternated "Jim, dear," with "Jim, darling," and McDermott had the distinct feeling they'd rather be going at each other with knives.

Lindsay used an indoor gas barbecue to charcoal thick, succulent steaks and the strained atmosphere did ease somewhat between the delicious food and Kevin and Debbie competing for McDermott's embarrassed attention.

"I'll help with the dishes," Max volunteered after dinner, in a tone suggesting martyrdom combined with a silent prayer that the Lindsays possessed an automatic dishwasher.

Norma rescued him from a menial task he hated. "The dishwasher does all the work," she laughed, "but you can help me clear the table while Jim reads Debbie a bedtime story."

"I want my boy friend to read me a story," Debbie protested.

"Take your choice of free-meal penitence, Max," Lindsay said. "Clear the table or read."

Max weighed both prospects unhappily and chose the latter, mainly because if there was one thing he detested, it was dirty dishes. Debbie handed him a book titled *Bertram The Bear,* which she had heard read at least twenty times, and climbed into his lap. McDermott, cognizant that he couldn't have looked more ill-at-ease if he had been crocheting, tried bravely to put some feeling into his rendition of Bertram's adventures. Unfortunately, he read with all the dramatic impact of a man reciting stock quotations aloud, his rasping voice delivering the simple words in a deadly monotone. Debbie made things even worse by constantly anticipating what was due on the next page.

"Bertram was sad and lonely because the other animals wouldn't talk to him," McDermott mumbled. "They were . . ."

"They won't stay mad at him," Debbie confided, with the air of a person giving the plot away so Max could stand the suspense. He managed to stagger through both the rest of the story and Debbie's interruptions, looking helplessly at Lindsay when the little girl said, "Read me another," and felt eternal gratitude when Jim shook his head.

"Bedtime, Debbie. Captain McDermott will read to you the next time he's here, I think."

"When is he coming again?" she asked, with the magnificent if embarrassing directness of a child.

"Soon, I hope."

"Maybe he can bring Rebel with him. Can you, honey?"

Lindsay saved Max from committing perjury. "We don't call grown-ups 'honey.' I shouldn't have let you get away with that the first time. Off to bed, young lady, and no more questions."

"Hokay," She gave McDermott a quick hug, whispered, "I like you, honey," in direct defiance of parental orders, and flung herself into her father's arms to be carried out. The sight of father and daughter renewed McDermott's distaste for the triangle, and on impulse he walked into the kitchen, where Norma Lindsay was stacking dishes into the washer.

"I should have picked table clearing," Max grumbled. "I'd like to retitle that book, 'Bertram the Bore.'"

"Debbie's running commentary doesn't help," Norma admitted. "Like most children, she gets enamored with one or two books and seems to get most of her enjoyment out of their familiarity. Bertram, for example. By the way, what do you think of Rebel Martin? Jim said you took her home last night."

Her shift of subjects startled him.

"Seems to be a capable stew," the check captain in him replied. Then the man in him added, "Very pretty girl."

"A very beautiful girl," Norma corrected, looking at McDermott sideways as if she were waiting for him to make the next verbal move. She was poised to spring with open claws if he said the wrong thing. All McDermott could do was hedge.

"If you like the type," he allowed.

"Jim says you're a bachelor."

"Yeah. Perennial, confirmed and whatever other cliché adjective precedes that word."

"The way you got along with Debbie, you seemed to be a frustrated father."

"Frustrated grandfather would be more like it. I'm too old for the paternal bit, Mrs. Lindsay."

"If you're going to call my husband Jim, I wish you'd call me Norma." She smiled, and it removed ten years from her chronological age. "I asked you to earlier but I guess it went over your head."

"And out my ears," McDermott apologized. "Okay, it's Norma. And Max to you."

"You've never been married, Max?"

"Nope."

"Ever come close? Or am I prying?"

"Negative to both questions. I'm a great believer in that male adage, Norma—for a man, the only true aphrodasiac is variety." The words were out his mouth like spit watermelon seeds, impossible to recall, and he could have kicked himself. Norma Lindsay turned white and she slammed the dishwasher door shut with a force that was rebuke, pain and jealousy, all rolled into one angry sound.

"Let's go back into the living room," she said quietly. "Jim must have Debbie ready for bed."

Uncomfortable was the word for the rest of the evening. The two pilots engaged in desultory shop talk, most of it on Lindsay's theories concerning aircraft handling in turbulence while Norma Lindsay sewed, a brooding expression on her pretty face. McDermott finally announced that he had a seven A.M. checkride and that it was time to leave. He thanked Norma with elephantine politeness, miserably conscious of the hurt still in her eyes.

Lindsay walked McDermott to his car, putting his hand on the check pilot's shoulder just as Max started to open the Mercedes' door.

"Things seemed a little on the tense side tonight, Max. I'm sorry. I figured having company would help Norma but . . . uh, she hasn't been feeling well."

Max could have given him some prosaic and phony assurance of understanding, but the temptation never got by his memory of Norma Lindsay's unhappiness.

"Bullshit," he snapped. "Since when was justified jealousy diagnosed as a medical ailment?"

Lindsay's face sagged into a look of misery, visible even in the dark. "I take it you had a talk with Rebel last night."

"Yeah. Look, Jim, I wouldn't give you any advice even if you asked for it. But I saw those two youngsters of yours tonight. They're good kids, And I liked Norma. So let's try a simple observation on for size."

"Which is?" Lindsay's voice took on a tone of belligerance.

"You're a damned fool."

McDermott sensed the captain's fists clenching, without actually seeing them. But Jim's reply was calm, almost resigned.

"I probably am," he said, "but there doesn't seem to be much I can do about it."

They stared at each other, Max's eyes challenging and accusing, Lindsay's at first defiant and then dropping like flags dipped in surrender.

"Thanks for that dinner," McDermott said. "Tell me something, Jim. Why'd you invite me?"

"I wanted you to meet my family." Jim's voice was low but firm.

"A very incomplete answer."

"I know. Maybe it was a kind of last grasp at sanity. At decency. There was only one thing wrong."

"Yeah," McDermott said. "It didn't work. Good night, Jim."

The next time Max talked to Jim Lindsay was on a layover in Chicago, about four weeks later.

McDermott had been checkriding a younger captain, Ron Davilla, who had the positive conviction he could have taught Jimmy Doolittle how to fly. McDermott conceded his natural ability but he didn't like the way he cut an occasional corner—minor transgressions, but enough of them to build in McDermott's discipline-oriented mind a pattern of potential trouble.

Most pilots, including the corner-cutters, wore figurative halos around their heads when flying with Maximilian McDermott. Unfortunately for Davilla, self-confidence drifted unchecked into over-confidence and he operated the checkride exactly as he had been operating all his trips in the six months he had been flying in the left seat.

When they landed at O'Hare, Davilla breezily asked Max, "Any complaints?"

The flight engineer and copilot were still in the cockpit, so McDermott swallowed the fire and smoke about to emerge from his throat and merely said ominously, "I'll see you in Operations." Fifteen minutes later without raising his voice, he had dismembered Captain Davilla.

"The FAA inspector who gave you that fourth stripe must have been your father," was McDermott's opening line, and he went on from there to list Davilla's sins. No one heard the reaming—the debriefing was in a small office adjoining Coastal's Operations room at O'Hare—which in a way was too bad because when Max bawled out an erring airman, the mental scars never really healed.

"And one more thing, Davilla," Max concluded. "You're a swell-headed young punk. You can probably fly rings around most guys including me, but with that attitude of yours I wouldn't trust you on a bicycle. For your information, chum, you've just flunked your six-month check and for the next ninety days you can go back to the right seat and learn some manners."

"You can't talk to me like that," Davilla sputtered. I'm an airline captain, same as you."

McDermott rose, put out one huge hand, closed his fist around Davilla's tie and yanked the younger man out of his seat.

"Davilla, just because you put four stripes on a jackass doesn't mean you get a zebra. Go grab yourself a W-2 pass for a deadhead ride home on the next flight, and by that time I'll have phoned Rog Blake your sad story."

Max walked out of the room, leaving Davilla quivering in humiliation. He stopped by the chief pilot's office to request a reserve captain for what would have been Davilla's return flight to Washington, and as he emerged Jim Lindsay was waiting for him outside.

"Hi, Max. Saw you go in so I figured I'd catch you before I go to the motel. Time for a coffee?"

Max surveyed him with concern. Lindsay looked ten years older, his face drawn and his eyes a trifle bloodshot. "Sure. Nothing to do until our next flight home."

"How's the family?" Max asked, after they sat down in one of O'Hare's coffee shops.

"Fine. Debbie keeps asking about you."

"How's Rebel?"

That jaw muscle reflex again.

"You have a way of getting right to the point," Lindsay murmured.

"Just thought I'd ask. Not that I give a damn about your extra-curricular activities, but you look like an accident going someplace to happen. And *that* chum, bothers the hell out of me, for obvious reasons."

"Rebel's fine," the captain answered after a pause. "Look, Max, I'd really like to talk to somebody. You have to catch 205 home?"

McDermott hesitated, torn between not wanting to listen to Lindsay's sordid troubles and yet unable to shake his

60

fascination with them. "Well, 205's our next to last of the
night and I'd hate . . ." He stopped, impaled on Lindsay's
almost pleading expression. "Okay. Wanna have some dinner and we can talk?"

"Great, Max. But why don't you just lay over? We'd have
to rush dinner. I'm sure you could get a room at the Inn,
then take 215 home with me first thing in the morning.
Unless you've got to get back tonight."

"No," McDermott said slowly. "Nothing on tap tomorrow
except a pile of paperwork. I've got to call Blake anyway
about another matter. I'll check and make sure it's kosher
with him. Finish your coffee and I'll use the tieline."

He made the call to Blake, who put him in a good mood
by not arguing about the Davilla case. It was one of Roger's
virtues, McDermott realized, that he invariably backed up
his check pilots. Nor did the chief pilot object to his staying
in Chicago.

"It's fine with me if you can give me a written report on
Davilla by noon," Blake said. "I'll have to call the bastard
in for a little talk."

"I can still get back tonight," Max offered.

"The hell with it. Have some fun. You've been working
your butt off. See you in the morning."

McDermott had no difficulty getting a room at the
O'Hare Inn. He had brought an overnight bag and a civilian
suit along even though he had expected to return that same
day. Weather vagaries dictated this precaution for nearly all
pilots and stewardesses, who never knew when a turnaround might develop into an unscheduled layover.

He ate with Jim at the motel, tolerantly accepting Lindsay's attempt to delay mention of Rebel by discussing
Coastal's recent purchase of Boeing 737s. Max agreed that
the new plane was supposed to be a very efficient, sweet-
handling little bird, nodded sagely at Jim's views on the
forthcoming DC-10, and waited patiently for the captain to
get around to what he really wanted to talk about.

He finally did. He pushed aside a half-eaten steak and toyed with his fork, batting it aimlessly against a water glass. He wasn't frowning, but he was on the verge of looking sad without quite reaching a facial expression that conveyed sadness.

"Okay," Max rumbled. "Spill."

"I guess you might as well know about it. Norma and I are getting a divorce."

"I take it you're gonna marry Rebel."

Lindsay nodded. "As soon as the divorce is final. I've been in love with her from the day I met her. I never dreamed it would happen this way and, so help me God, I didn't want it to happen. Norma's a fine person, a wonderful wife and mother, and believe me I know what this is going to do to my kids. But I can't go on leading a double life. I live for the few times a month when Rebel bids my trips. I hate myself for what I've done to my family, but I hate myself just as much for what I've done to Rebel. We can't go on just having an affair, a few flings on layovers."

His voice was close to breaking. McDermott peered at him, the cold eyes narrowing to questioning slits.

"You want comment, my blessings, advice—or should I mind my own business?"

"Let's start with comment."

"You may want to slug me when I get through commenting."

"I'd appreciate your being as honest as you can. Not that you can talk me out of it."

"I won't even try, friend. A few weeks ago I called you a damned fool and I still put you in that category. Sure Rebel's beautiful. The most gorgeous dish I've ever seen. But for Christ's sake, Jim, you can't spend your life in bed. This could be pure physical attraction and while that's a fine basis for screwing, it doesn't guarantee a happy marriage. If it wears off, and most physical attractions do, you're gonna kick yourself from Washington to Hong Kong."

"I'll concede the strong sex attraction," Lindsay said. "But Rebel's more than that. She's got a sense of humor, she's fun, she's intelligent and she's . . . she's youth. My God, Max, I remember when I used to feel absolute disgust for guys who left their wives and kids for some young chick. But now I understand how it can happen even when you fight against it. As God is my witness, I fought. But you've seen Rebel. She makes me feel ten years younger and ten feet taller. I didn't have a chance."

"Your wife didn't have a chance," McDermott said.

"No," Jim agreed with a shade of reluctance at the admission. "Not from the first time I brought Rebel home to dinner and started comparing her with Norma. They were standing together in the kitchen and I knew I wanted to go to bed with her."

"Have you asked your wife for a divorce?"

"Yes."

"How'd she take it?"

"A few tears. She wants the kids taken care of. I told her not to have any worries on that score. She . . . well, I won't say she's happy about the whole thing but she seems resigned. I guess she halfway expected it."

"You said you wanted honesty. Still feel that way? Even if it hurts like hell?"

"Go ahead, although I think I know what you're going to say. About Rebel's alleged morals."

"Or alleged lack of same. She's got the reputation of being a swinger and I'm not quoting any cheap gossip. She told me a few things herself. Such as the fact that you're not the only married man in her entourage. If you'll pardon a lousy play on words, you're ditching a square-shooter for a pair of round heels."

Instinctively, McDermott tensed, expecting from Lindsay's crimson face that the captain might swing on him. But the blood suddenly fled, the momentary surge of fury replaced by an air of intenseness that bordered on pleading.

For understanding, Max decided, and for Rebel, not Jim.

"I know all about Rebel's affairs," Lindsay said, in a smothered voice. "What the hell kind of hypocrite am I supposed to be? I go home to Norma after a trip. Rebel's a healthy young woman, and loving a married man can be lonely and frustrating. She's only human, Max. She wasn't sure until now that I was willing to divorce my wife. She had every right to do anything she damned pleased and with anybody. Sure she cheated on me. She even told me so. But it was to forget me. Maybe it was a way of getting back at me for my indecision."

"Well," Max said grudgingly, "I suppose any decision's better than indecision."

"I like to think so," Jim agreed. His eyes widened and he looked beyond McDermott, across the room. "I'll be damned. I thought I saw Rebel sitting over there."

Max turned around. There was an attractive girl sitting at a faraway table with an older man, and from a distance there was a vague, superficial resemblance—mostly because she, too, had long, blonde hair. Max kept staring at her, hoping, he admitted to himself, if it were Rebel, she had trotted all the way to Chicago for a date with some clown and Lindsay might as well go back to his family.

He turned back to Jim, who smiled faintly. "Good thing it's not Rebel, or you'd be recommending a reassessment of the whole mess. No; Max, she's no tramp. I couldn't be in love with a tramp, not after all those years with Norma. I've got a better sense of values than that, no matter what you or anyone else thinks. Finish your coffee and let's get some sack time."

McDermott went right to bed, spurning Lindsay's suggestion that they have a beer in the cocktail lounge. His last thoughts before falling asleep were not of Jim or Norma, but of the two children, Debbie in particular. The innocent bystanders. The most tragic bystanders of a dying marriage. Damn that Lindsay. Damn Rebel . . .

The telephone jarred him awake. It was Jim.

"I guess I woke you. I'm sorry but I just can't sleep. Thought you might stagger down to the lounge for a beer. Bar's open until two."

"What time is it now?" McDermott mumbled groggily, trying to focus on the luminous dial of his wristwatch.

"Five after twelve. You sound like you've been asleep for a week. Look, I apologize again. I just felt like talking some more, what the hell—. But I'm too old to need hand-holding. Go on back to sleep, friend. Unless you . . ." He left the implied question hanging, as if he were too embarrassed to complete it.

"I'll pass," Max said, too sleepy to express the annoyance he felt. "See you in the morning."

He hung up before Lindsay had a chance to continue the conversation, and was snoring gently within seconds. At eight A.M. when he walked up to the front desk with his room key, Jim was already there, freshly shaved and smiling. Apparently, Max deduced, his getting that Gordian knot of a decision into the open last night had done him a world of good.

"You go down to get that beer anyway?" McDermott asked.

"Nope. Decided I needed sleep more than another dose of self-pity. Took a mild sedative and dropped off in five minutes. You look like a walking insomnia case. Couldn't you go back to sleep after that stupid call of mine?"

"Yeah. But I guess I must have dreamed all night. Damned if I know how that can tire you out."

"That's why I took the sedative," Lindsay said, his cheerful mood dissipating as if his conscience had suddenly remembered a reason for hurting. "I haven't slept well for a couple of months. By the way, thanks for letting me unload last night."

Max merely nodded, with the reluctant air of a man being thanked for something he didn't want to do in the first place. He was in a foul mood all the way to the airport, conversing with Lindsay and his copilot in grouchy monosyllables and not really knowing why the dyspeptic disposition. He should have felt relieved, he reasoned, for Lindsay's solution to his marital troubles—however ethically questionable—had at least ended any threats to Jim's cockpit professionalism.

If McDermott had been clairvoyant, his mood would have been worse.

Even as he waited in Operations for Lindsay to sign the dispatch release for their flight home, a man named Joe Dempsey was walking up the sidewalk to 6016 Bennett Avenue, Alexandria, Virginia.

6016 Bennett Avenue was the address of the house where Rebel Martin lived.

And at this very moment, the lived was past tense.

Joseph J. Dempsey had a mild crush on the occupant at 6016 Bennett Avenue.

The address was on his route as a driver for Dominion Dry Cleaners. The occupant was friendly (in a nice way), generous (she was one of his few customers who tipped him at Christmastime) and thoughtfully hospitable (she often gave him a cup of coffee on cold mornings).

Miss Martin also was beautiful, so much so that Joe Dempsey yearned for her in the abstract, fantasy fashion of an adolescent day-dreaming about a torrid affair with a movie star. Which pretty well described his chances. He was bald, five-feet-five, weighed two hundred and twenty pounds, perspired too freely and averaged only ninety-two dollars a week after deductions.

He knew the clothes he picked up and delivered at 6016 Bennett Avenue were expensive. Miss Martin had more wearing apparel than anyone else on his route except for the wealthy Mrs. Fenimore, who never offered him coffee and whose annual Christmas rememberance was a perfunctory verbal greeting.

The knowledge that one of her smartly-tailored suits must have cost more than he made in a week was only one reason he kept his desires in a reverie category. Their difference in height was another, for his occasional chimera of Miss Martin welcoming him some morning in a flimsy negligee and a look of uncontrollable passion in her green eyes, was invariably followed by a more logical image of her towering over him like a haughty Cadillac dwarfing a VW.

Miss Martin herself discouraged any fulfillment of his more erotic visions. She always greeted him with a more or less cheery "Hi, Joe," which was about as seductively suggestive as a belch. Usually she was dressed in an old flannel robe, one that would have looked more appropriate on Mrs. Fenimore, and if she had ever worn the negligee of his daydreams, Joe Dempsey probably would have turned around and fled.

Nevertheless, he looked forward to his twice-weekly visit to 6016, Tuesday for picking up cleaning and Friday for returning it. She wasn't always home, but if she were away on a trip, she would leave a note taped to her front door, an established arrangement for collecting or returning her clothes at a neighbor's. He always felt a throb of disappointment when he sighted the little slip of paper above the doorbell that signaled her absence.

This was Tuesday, and he hoped he wouldn't have to wake her up as he often did. She kept late hours and frequently her "Hi, Joe" was delivered in a voice coated with sleepiness or with the definite hint of a painful hangover. It was on such occasions that his guilt for getting her out of bed mingled with envy for whatever man had been out with her so late. There was no note this morning, he observed happily, as he parked his truck in front of the house and marched with springy steps to the door.

He had one pudgy forefinger almost on the bell when he noticed the door was slightly ajar. That was unusual. He decided not to ring the bell and instead gave the brass knocker a polite double rap. He knocked again, louder this time, without getting a response.

"Miss Martin?" he called. "Miss Martin."

He pushed the door open, just wide enough to poke his face inside, and was going to call her name again when he saw the still figure of a women on the living room sofa, just to the right of the foyer. Must have fallen asleep on the sofa, he figured, and he hesitated before entering further. His company had strict rules about putting even one toe into a customer's residence without permission. Now his voice was pitched high enough to rouse even the soundest sleeper.

"Miss Martin, this is Joe. Uh, Miss Martin, are you awake?"

The figure on the couch did not stir. A shiver of uneasy fear pierced Joe Dempsey's heart. There was something about her . . . the way she lay there, so rigid and unmoving. The hell with company rules. She looked . . . he was afraid to say it, even to himself. He pushed the door open and tiptoed in, approaching the couch in the manner of a nervous husband about to waken a bad-tempered spouse.

His lips were just forming the "M" for another try at "Miss Martin" when he saw her eyes. They were staring, unblinking, at the ceiling and the sliver of fear turned into an icy needle. He shook her shoulder, knowing as he performed this instinctive act that it was useless. "Miss Martin . . . for God's sake, Miss Martin . . ."

For a moment, he had a panicky impulse to flee. Let somebody else find the body. He was fat, lonely slob of a bachelor, the woman on the couch was beautiful, and he was an obvious target for questioning if he called the police. He might even lose his job. Wait a minute. Maybe she had died from a heart attack or something. *Natural causes* was the comforting phrase. Gingerly, he looked for marks of violence. For blood or a wound or bruises. All he could see was a slight, almost imperceptible discoloration at the base of her jaw muscles. He felt for her pulse, rather inexpertly, and found none. He swallowed hard, his heart pounding, and he turned away toward the telephone on an end table next to the sofa.

There was no directory in sight and his hand shook as he dialed the operator and asked for the Alexandria police. Conscious that fright and shock had pitched his voice two octaves higher than usual, he gave his name, the address and the circumstances under which he had found the body. He was told not to touch anything and to wait for the police to arrive.

The admonition was unnecessary. Joseph J. Dempsey wouldn't have touched anything in that accursed house with a twenty-foot pole. He managed to phone his company, informing a supervisor what had happened, and requested that a relief driver pick up his truck and continue the route. "I may be here quite a while," he added plaintively, but with a distinct effort to sound brave.

There was nothing to do but await the ordeal of police interrogation. How many times had he watched crime stories on television and chortled in patronizing, superior fashion at the edge-of-panic displayed by nervous suspects. He wondered if his own grilling would be conducted by a detective with, say, Jack Webb's firm but fair technique. He began to compose mentally his answers, his explanations, along with an optimistic resolve to show both calmness and a respectful desire to cooperate. That should impress a Jack Webb/Joe Friday type. Not that he knew a hell of a lot except for finding the body.

He didn't even know, he realized, a hell of a lot about the girl who was on the sofa. A stewardess for some airline, apparently plenty of money if clothes were any indication —that was about it. He could not resist one more peek at the corpse, and it finally penetrated his frightened brain what she was wearing.

Miss Martin had finally donned a negligee. Only not for Joe Dempsey.

He shuddered and went outside to wait for the police.

Detective Lieutenant Robert Balfour Smith of the Alexandria Police Department actually welcomed the call.

For two reasons. He had been working on a case involving the non-fatal stabbing of an unfaithful wife by her husband, and Smith, a widower who still deeply mourned, detested anything with the hue of matrimonial conflict. Also, police headquarters was in the throes of being painted and the lieutenant was allergic to turpentine.

By the time he arrived at 6016, a fingerprint man already was at work, a police photographer was snapping pictures of the body and living room, the Alexandria coroner had just stripped off his coat to examine the body, and a patrolman—the first to get there—was standing by the worried Joe Dempsey, who now reached the unhappy conclusion that Lieutenant Robert Smith looked a lot tougher than Jack Webb and not nearly so understanding.

Actually, the driver was examining the detective through the distorted eyes of sheer nervousness. Smith was big but on the flabby side, with a huge shock of ruffled gray hair and perpetually tired eyes that drooped at the corners like a cocker spaniel's. His clothes were rumpled, but it was a kind of untidiness that seemed to stem more from fatigue than inherent unneatness.

"This the fella who found the body?" Smith asked the patrolman.

"Yes, sir. Name's Joseph Dempsey. He's a driver for Dominion Dry Cleaners."

Smith examined Dempsey, whose face bore the petrified, half-hypnotized expression of a deer trapped by a stalking leopard. "Relax, son, I won't bite you. Just tell me what happened."

"I was going to pick up her cleaning like I always do on Tuesday. The door was open. Ajar, in fact. I called but she didn't answer. So I stuck in my head and that's when I saw her. On the couch. Jesus."

"Did you touch her? Or anything else in the house?"

"No, sir. Well, I did feel her pulse. To see if she was . . . asleep, or maybe drunk. Then I called the police."

"You know her name?"

"Miss Martin. I never did know her first name. Miss R. Martin is all I got on my records."

"Any idea where she works?"

"She's an airline stewardess. I . . . we clean her uniforms. I don't even know what airline she's with."

"Know anything about her boy friends? Ever see any men around here?"

"No, sir. I just pick up her clothes and bring them back."

Smith looked at the body and turned back to the driver. "Ever ask her for a date, Mr. Dempsey? She's a pretty good looking girl. Or was."

"No, *sir.*" Joe Dempsey made the answer as emphatic as possible. "She was a real nice person. Real nice to me. Polite and friendly. But I wouldn't have asked her to go out. I . . . I don't date my customers."

"Company rule?"

"No, sir. My own rule."

"You married, Mr. Dempsey?"

"No, sir. I, uh, go pretty steady with a girl though." That was delivered in a hopeful tone indicating that Joseph J. Dempsey wouldn't possibly have shown a romantic interest toward the figure on the sofa. Smith merely grunted and walked over to the coroner, a slight man with tortoise-shell glasses.

"What do you think, Doc?"

"Strangled. I'd guess several hours ago. Have to wait for the autopsy. If she had anything to eat before she was killed, I can give you an approximate time of death. No sign of rape, by the way, although the autopsy will give us something more definite."

Smith turned back to the perspiring driver. "You say she's an airline stewardess. When you took her uniform out to be cleaned, didn't it have the name of the airline on it somewhere?"

"On the jacket wings, I suppose. But she always took off the wings when she sent out a uniform. She may have told me once who she worked for, but I forgot. I don't fly myself. I guess I didn't pay any attention if she did tell me."

The fingerprint man approached Smith. "I'm about through down here. You might as well start crying into your beer. I got a lot of good prints—about fifty or so. I'll bet most of them are hers, though. She was a lousy housekeeper. The kitchen sink's full of dirty dishes. From the looks of them, they could have been handled by half the population of Alexandria."

"Speaking of dishes," Smith said. "That glass on the coffee table by the sofa. You get that?"

"Yep. Probably was hers. There was scotch inside. I also dusted that bottle of scotch over there. Or what used to be a bottle of scotch. It's empty. Suppose she was a lush?"

"How the hell do I know? Did you use Chem Print on any paper material around here? Such as newspapers, paper bags, and such?"

"Sure did. Great stuff, that Chem Print. I wish we had had it a long time ago. Remember those prints we got off that cardboard box in the Mills burglary? Christ, who ever thought they'd come up with a way to get fingerprints off paper? Well, guess I'll go upstairs and see what I can find in the bedroom and bathroom; those are the only rooms on the second floor."

"Do that," Smith sighed. He walked over to the sofa and gently closed the staring green eyes. The coroner, re-donning his coat, chuckled.

"You always did have a sense of delicacy, Smitty," he said.

"They give me the creeps," Smith growled.

The police photographer came over to announce he was finished. "I've snapped a hell of a lot of corpses," he added with a trace of sadness, "but this babe looks better dead than most broads look alive."

"So I noticed," the lieutenant agreed. "Let me have a full set of what you get."

"Sure. About three o'clock okay?"

"Fine, Leave 'em in my office."

"See you, Smitty." The photographer left, just as a police ambulance arrived to collect the body, carried out under the stares of curious onlookers attracted by the converging police vehicles. Smith watched the removal proceedings with disturbed eyes, hating the degrading sight of the long blonde hair and shapely limbs reduced to an impersonal, lifeless lump under a dung-colored rubber blanket. For him, this moment of a murder investigation was the lowering of a curtain on one act and the simultaneous raising of another curtain on a new act.

"Smitty." The fingerprint expert had come from the small upstairs area. His gloved hands were holding a large, black purse. "Here's her handbag, or one of them. She had about fifteen. God, I never saw so many clothes and accessories. This one was on a dresser, apparently the last one she used. There's a wallet inside with about seventy-five bucks. Doesn't seem to be a robbery case. Plenty of jewelry upstairs and most of it, incidentally, looks like the real McCoy. I took her identification card out of the wallet. Thought you'd want to see it before you started asking questions around the neighborhood."

Smith examined the card.

COASTAL AIRLINES, INC.

Rebel Martin		*78946*
EMPLOYEE'S NAME		EMPLOYEE NUMBER
	118–01–9121	
	SOC. SEC. NO.	

HEIGHT	*5'8½"*	
WEIGHT	*128*	
EYES	*Green*	
HAIR	*Blonde*	*Stewardess*
		EMPLOYMENT CATEGORY

The detective turned the card over. The girl's picture was there, a half-smiling likeness that did not do Rebel Martin justice but still filled Smith with a feeling of hate toward the unknown killer. Murder to him was always meaningless and ugly, regardless of motive.

"The poor kid," he mused aloud. "I hope we get the sonofabitch."

"At last reports," the fingerprint man commented, "Coastal Airlines had about twenty-five thousand employees, eight thousand of them in the Washington area."

"So?"

"I was just thinking, I'd hate to see you start out with at least eight thousand possibilities."

"Give me about twenty-four hours," the lieutenant said grimly, "and we won't."

McDermott knew something was wrong the minute he walked into Operations at National. He could smell an atmosphere of death. He could see tragedy on the faces of the dispatchers, crew schedulers, pilots and stewardesses. His first thought was that a Coastal plane must have crashed and it was Lindsay's, too, as the captain followed Max into the room. The minute he entered, the hushed voices stopped like water turned off at a spigot. It was instantaneous and chilling.

"What the hell's going on?" Jim asked. "We lose a bird? You all look like mourners. Come on, what's . . ."

It was Ray Rusk, the chief crew scheduler, who managed to untie his vocal chords first. He walked up to Lindsay, eyes somber. "I guess somebody'd better tell you, Jim. Rebel Martin was found murdered this morning."

McDermott saw first disbelief, then shock and horror race across Lindsay's face. The tall captain stumbled into the crew lounge, falling blindly into the nearest chair. His hands formed an awning over his temples, forehead and eyes and he began to talk, almost in a rhythmic chant. "Oh, God, no. No. No. Dear God, no. Not Rebel. Oh, my God . . ."

"Easy, Jim," McDermott said, patting Lindsay's shoulder in a futile gesture of comfort. "Anyone know what happened?"

Ray Rusk shook his head. "We just heard ourselves. Mike Hunter called me and she didn't know much except that Rebel's body was found in her house this morning. The police notified Mike it was a definite homicide. She's over at the morgue now identifying the body."

Lindsay's voice choked but he got out the words. "How . . . how did she die?"

Rusk hesitated, then decided he couldn't sugarcoat the answer. "She was strangled, Jim."

"Jesus Christ," Jim said hoarsely, without looking up.

Roger Blake came into the lounge, his normally ruddy face a shade lighter. He squatted down in front of Lindsay and gently took the captain's hands away from his face. "Snap out of it, Jim. There's nothing anyone can do."

"They can find out who killed her." Jim's voice was so low only Blake and McDermott heard him.

"That's in the hands of the police," Blake said. "Come on, let somebody drive you home."

"I can't go home. Not now. I'll crack wide open. The kids . . . Norma . . ."

McDermott thought, this is a hell of a time to start worrying about your family, but aloud he said only, "Come on over to my place. Give you a chance to pull yourself together."

76

"I'd rather stay here. I want to talk to Mike when she comes back. I want to know what happened."

Blake shrugged helplessly. "Okay, Jim. If that's what you want. Would you like me to call Norma? She knows your trip's due in and she might worry."

"I'll call her myself. In a few minutes. She shouldn't hear about this from . . . from anyone else."

It occurred to Max that the little conversation with Norma would take some guts, and he was glad Lindsay hadn't passed the buck. He could not help wondering what would happen now to the marriage. It probably was saved, at least to the extent of retaining a father for the kids, although that would depend on Norma's capacity for forgiveness. He suspected Jim would have to do some crawling.

Blake interrupted his thoughts. "Couple of you stews— How about running up and getting some coffee? About ten cups. Here's five bucks. Goddammit, I'd rather have a triple shot of scotch. What a stinking mess."

"Max." Lindsay's voice didn't even sound like his own.

"Yeah."

"You can find out who did it. You could help the police. You knew Rebel. You knew . . . about us."

McDermott was startled. "Forget it, Jim. Leave a murder investigation up to the pros. You wouldn't want a cop fooling around with your airplane would you?"

"But you were a cop yourself. A homicide detective. You could work with the police. Blake would give you the time off, wouldn't you, Rog?"

Max exchanged glances with the chief pilot, and Lindsay looked imploringly at them both, as if his suggestion carried the possibility of bringing Rebel back to life.

"Negative," Max said, abruptly but not unkindly. "Even if Blake let me, the police would take a dim view of an outsider horning in. No sir. Goddamn, Rog, what the hell are you nodding for? You agreeing with him or me?"

"With him," Blake said, unable to hide his excitement. "Jim may have something. It wouldn't be a bad idea for us to have a kind of unofficial observer in on this. You *were* a cop, Max. The police might go for an ex-detective sitting in on the investigation. You don't have to gumshoe around. Just help as much as you can. In return for which they'd let you in on any questioning. No, let me finish"—McDermott looked as if he were ready to explode—"Christ knows the police will be talking to everyone on this bloody base and maybe the whole system. We could use someone like yourself. As protection for the airline."

"You're out of your mind," Max snapped. "Any self-respecting homicide cop would rather kiss a leper than invite an amateur into a murder investigation."

"You're not an amateur," Blake protested. "You're an ex-cop."

"I'm an ex-baby, too, but that doesn't mean I still wet my pants. In other words, you stupid bastard, I was a cop so long ago I couldn't solve an unidentified fart in an elevator with only two people in it, one of them me. Read me loud and clear, Rog, the answer's negative. And even if I said yes, the police would say no, so forget it."

"Maybe," Blake said with a tight grin. "But Charlie Belnap's got a hell of a lot of pull and I figure he'd go for it."

"I couldn't care less whether Belnap goes for it. I turned in that badge thirty-five years ago and not even the president of this airline is gonna make me put it on again, officially or unofficially."

"Do it for Rebel," Lindsay said desperately.

"I don't owe Rebel a goddamned thing," McDermott said rudely.

"Then do it for me, a fellow pilot. A friend."

"Even if I wanted to," Max said impatiently, as if he were a teacher trying to explain a simple fact to a classroom of dunces, "you guys can't get it through your thick skulls that cops don't like outsiders—not even former cops.

Who the hell do you think I am—Ellery Queen?"

"Well," Blake said in a tone of unshakable decision, "I'm going up to see Gilcannon. Sorry, Max, but if he buys this brainstorm, we'll go right into the old man and leave it up to him."

Mike Hunter's arrival prevented McDermott from continuing what he feared was purely a rearguard action. The stewardess supervisor was a tall, slender woman in her late thirties, pert features accentuated by her pageboy hairdo. She walked right up to Lindsay with a long, rather mannish stride and kissed him gently on one cheek.

"I'm sorry as hell, Jim. How much do you want to hear? How much can you take?" McDermott was thinking, cynically, that from all the sympathy being hosed in Lindsay's direction, the whole base must have known of his plans for marrying Rebel.

"Everything," Jim said.

Mike told him about the discovery of the body by the driver, and the few details Lieutenant Smith had imparted to her. By this time, a fairly sizeable crowd of flight personnel had gathered around them, listening avidly.

"When did it happen?" Lindsay asked.

"They won't know until after the autopsy. Sometime during the night or early this morning. That's all they'd tell me."

"Any sign of criminal assault?" Max rumbled.

Mike glared at him. She had met the check pilot and liked him, possibly because she recognized in that ugly, seamed face the granite personality of a man who was tougher than she. But now she was indignant at what she considered a dumb question.

"If a girl's choked to death," she snapped, "I'd say it was criminal assault."

"Criminal assault is rape," McDermott said simply.

"Oh. Well, I asked the detective in charge that. He said they'd have to wait for the autopsy, but he doubted it. I

. . . I saw her at the morgue, Jim. She didn't look too bad. She had on a negligee and a bra and panties. I don't think she was, uh, sexually molested."

"Thank God for small favors," Lindsay said bitterly. He put his head down again, rubbing his eyes wearily.

"I'm going up to see Gilcannon," Blake announced, evading McDermott's scowl. The two stewardesses sent to get coffee returned, handing out the steaming paper cups. Max gave one to Lindsay, kneeling in front of him as he did.

"Drink it. Do you good. When you finish, someone'll drive you home."

"I can drive myself home."

"You couldn't drive a car ten feet." Max rose and surveyed the crew members who still formed a curious circle around the stunned pilot. "Okay, one tragedy doesn't mean we shut down the airline. Let's leave the man alone for awhile and go about your own business. Not you, Mike." Mike had started to follow the dispersing crowd, but stopped as McDermott drew her aside.

"How much do you know about Lindsay and Rebel Martin?" he demanded, keeping his voice low so Jim could not hear.

"I know . . . well, I heard they were going to get married."

"You know Mrs. Lindsay?"

"I've met her a few times."

"You got a car?"

"Yes. But if you've got any ideas about me driving Jim home, file and forget it, buster. I'm not sticking my nose into *that* little domestic mess."

"He's in no condition to drive himself. I'll admit he should face his wife alone, but if somebody's got to be with him, I'd rather it's someone Norma Lindsay knows—and trusts. Preferably her own sex."

"I said I met her a few times. That doesn't mean she trusts me"

Max grinned, achieving the look of an amiable gargoyle.

"You've got a pretty damned good rep for being den mother to every mixed-up stew on the system, not to mention a few mixed-up pilots. People trust you by instinct. Besides, I've got an ulterior motive, so you're elected and quit arguing."

She started to protest again but curiosity overrode her reluctance. "What's the ulterior motive?"

"I'd like to hear how Jim breaks the news to his wife and how she takes it."

"Both hows, I'd say, are none of your goddamned business."

"Maybe. But that pale facsimile of an airline captain sitting ten feet away from you, with his hands still covering his eyes, is about to come apart at the seams. And that, friend, *is* my business."

Mike looked over at Jim, and then back at McDermott. "I'll take him home. If he'll go with me."

Lindsay did. Apparently, Max reasoned, out of the inherent craving of a male for female sympathy and comfort. He watched the two leave Operations, Lindsay shuffling along with short, uncertain steps, his head down, as if mesmerized by shock. Dimly, Max heard a phone ring and Ray Rusk's answering voice.

"Crew sked, Rusk. Yeah, he's right here. Max, it's Blake."

McDermott picked up the phone, knowing in advance it was bad news. The chief pilot didn't bother with preliminaries. "Max, Gilcannon wants you to come right over to Belnap's office. Hangar Seven, upper level. Just give the receptionist your name."

"I'd like to give you a good boot in the rear," McDermott stormed. "I told you I'm not playing detective for you, Belnap or anyone else."

Blake chuckled. "I told that to Gilcannon and he told it to our president and our president said get your ass over to his office. It's an order, Max."

McDermott uttered one profane four-letter word, loud

enough so that three stewardesses in the adjoining lounge blushed. Ten minutes later, he had reached Hangar Seven, almost at the far end of the airport complex. It was a comparative slum area for the executive offices of a major airline, but McDermott had known Charlie Belnap for years and secretly relished Belnap's insistence on keeping most of his top subordinates at the airport. He was one of the real aviation pioneers, a man who had started Coastal back in the days of airmail biplanes that just managed to stagger over the Alleghenies. On the subject of office space, he had relented to the extent of locating sales and reservations in a downtown Washington building but kept the main executive offices right at National—"close to the action," he liked to explain.

McDermott had heard rumors that the majority of Coastal's brass considered it degrading to work on the second floor of a maintenance hangar, Gilcannon in particular. No one, Gilcannon included, had the moxie to challenge Belnap on the issue, but Max was sure that when Belnap retired or died, the executive offices would be moved downtown.

Hangar or no hangar, Belnap's quarters still looked plush to the Spartan-minded McDermott when the receptionist deferentially ushered him in. The president, a plump little man with twinkling eyes and a face that must have been carved out of raw leather, greeted him warmly. In sharp contrast, McDermott noted, to Gilcannon who rose from a chair with obvious reluctance, giving the impression that a check pilot didn't really deserve such protocol.

"Max, it's been too damned long," Belnap was saying. "Haven't seen you since you flew that Minneapolis inaugural. How've you been? And welcome to Washington. Should have called you in before this, you old goat."

"Charlie," Max said sourly, "when you give with the small talk, it's pure bullshit. Get to the point."

Belnap and Rog Blake laughed, but the faint frown on

82

Gilcannon's face did not escape Max. The executive vice president, he decided, had to be thinking that when Franklin Gilcannon achieved the presidency, heaven help the check pilot who addressed him so disrespectfully. Nor was Gilcannon wearing the only scowl in the room. The second belonged to a big, heavy-set man with eyes that strangely achieved alertness even as they exuded fatigue. Cop, McDermott ruled instantly, although he could not have put into words why.

Belnap introduced him. "Max, this is Lieutenant Robert Smith of the Alexandria Police Department. Lieutenant, this is the man we told you about, Captain McDermott. An excellent investigative background, as I explained earlier. Homicide, like yourself."

"McDermott," Smith acknowledged curtly, with a brief but firm handshake.

Belnap sensed his antagonism. "Well now," he continued hurriedly. "Max, the lieutenant was already here, at my invitation, discussing this very unfortunate tragedy when Frank told me of Captain Blake's suggestion. Namely, as I've already outlined to Lieutenant Smith, we thought it would be helpful to all concerned if a Coastal representative might, uh, monitor his investigation. And with your own police background, Max, I . . ."

"I don't dig the choice of the word 'monitor,'" Smith interrupted. "That seems to imply some kind of nosy interference. We're perfectly capable of running this show ourselves. I have nothing against McDermott here, personally, but let's make it clear right from the start he's strictly ex-officio. He can observe, he can sit in on certain interrogations, but he is by no means to be considered a part of the investigative team."

Gilcannon broke in. "We did not intend . . ."

"Just a minute," Smith said in a tone that amounted to very weary patience stretched to the breaking point. "I think this whole notion of an outsider sticking his beak into police business stinks. Mr. Belnap, if in the last ten minutes you hadn't gone over my head to the chief of police and the mayor of Alexandria, I wouldn't have given Captain McDermott the key to the police department men's room."

"Lieutenant," Max growled, "I think the whole silly idea stinks, too. I'm here under protest. I told Captain Blake the police have a right to resent any outsider horning in on an homicide investigation, including an ex-cop who hasn't worn a badge in so long he's forgotten what number was on it. Ex-officio my ass, Charlie; the phrase is persona non grata, only the lieutenant is too damned polite to use it."

Smith examined him with sudden respect. Gilcannon, who had resumed his seat, jumped up.

"We have no intention of usurping police functions," he intoned unctuously, "but this murder involved one of our best stewardesses, a very beautiful girl, and the papers will be jumping all over it. We, that is, Mr. Belnap and myself, both feel that an official representative of the airline could work with the police to mutual advantage. Aside from McDermott's protecting us on the publicity angle, his own police experience combined with his airline knowledge might be of considerable help to you, Lieutenant."

"To put our needs in plainer language," Belnap said, "what we need, Max, is to have someone around who knows what the hell's happening before it hits the front pages. All you have to do is keep Frank, here, informed."

"It still stinks," McDermott said. "Charlie, you gonna make this an order?"

Belnap inclined his head, reluctantly but firmly.

"Smith, I don't suppose you're willing to tell your chief and the mayor to go screw themselves? It'll countermand that order."

"I see Mr. Belnap's point," the detective said resignedly. "I just want all of you, particularly Captain McDermott, to know where I stand and where he stands. He's to stay out of my hair, sit very quietly in the background, make all the notes he wants, and keep his mouth shut. Do we understand each other?"

"Perfectly," Belnap assured him. "And I'm sure Max does."

Whatever Max was going to say died at the entrance of Belnap's secretary. "Lieutenant Smith, your office is calling you."

"How about some privacy?" Smith requested. "Could I . . . ?"

"Use my secretary's phone in the outer office," Belnap said. "Mrs. Burton, you might as well stay in here, anyway. I've got some dictation coming up."

Smith returned in five minutes, giving McDermott a glance that came close to being a wordless apology.

"McDermott, remember a Captain Bixler?"

Max did, instantly. "Hell, yes. Bix was chief of detectives when I was on the Dayton force. I haven't seen him in thirty years; I figured he must be dead by now."

"Not dead, just retired. I got to know him a few years back when we both went through the FBI school and we've kept in touch. A hell of a good cop. Soon as Mr. Belnap gave me your name, I called Bixler on the chance he might remember you."

"He should," McDermott smiled. "I was the dumbest, greenest, gumshoe he had on his squad."

"That's not what he told me. He said you were one of the best young detectives he ever saw, and he always wondered what happened to you. McDermott, let's go get some coffee and talk. Just the two of us."

Belnap beamed but Max sniffed suspiciously. "I seem to recall a few ground rules you laid down, such as my hiding in the woodwork with only one ear protruding."

"That was before Sam Bixler vouched for you. McDermott, I hate to tell you this but you may be back in the detective business."

5

They drove back to the main terminal building in Smith's car, parking it in a zone reserved for congressmen and diplomats. An FAA policeman immediately approached them, shaking his head vigorously.

"No parking," he called out. "This is a restricted zone."

Smith produced his badge, adding, "We're on official business," which drew from the FAA cop a quizzical look at McDermott's airline uniform.

"It's that stewardess murder case," Smith explained. "Captain McDermott is working with the police."

"Okay, go ahead and stay there. I always thought it was a goddamned shame to let those half-assed politicians use all this space."

"Thanks for the promotion," Max said dryly as they got out of the car.

"Promotion?"

"Now I'm working with you. Apparently you weren't kidding about my being back in the detective business."

Smith shrugged. "I'll level with you, McDermott. You *could* be a big help. I don't know a damned thing about airlines. We don't have anything to go on with that stewardess. And I'd take Sam Bixler's word for it if he recommended an ex-con for police chief."

"I'm not sure I appreciate your sudden one-eighty, but if you think I can help, I'll try. Where do you want to start?"

"With some coffee. And while we walk, I'll ask you a very

87

important question. Did you know that dead girl?"

"Yep."

"Well?"

"Fairly well."

"Enough to tell me about her friends—or maybe I should say her enemies?"

Max considered this carefully. "I can give you some names. Mind you, I said names, not leads."

"That's a start. Where we going for coffee?"

"Snake Pit probably be best. It's quiet and we'd get more privacy."

"Snake Pit? Sounds like a storage space for ptomaine germs."

"It's a little employees' cafeteria on the lower level. Everyone calls it the Snake Pit."

The cafeteria was almost deserted. McDermott and Smith sat at a table as far removed from the other customers as possible, Max noting with amusement that the lieutenant could not help eyeing a pretty United stewardess who was sipping a coke a few tables away.

"Pretty girl," Smith ventured.

"Very," Max agreed.

"Now this Martin girl. Rebel, they called her. That her real name? She was listed as Rebel Martin in her employment folder—Gilcannon showed it to me—but I figure she must have been christened with a little more conventional tag."

"Rebel was her given name."

"Speaking of pretty stewardesses, this Martin babe wasn't just pretty. She was gorgeous. Even dead, she was beautiful. This is about my two hundredth homicide and for the first time in my life I could understand necrophilism. I'm only kidding, McDermott"—Max was frowning—"but I did want to make a point. Anyone with her looks must have had a pot full of boy friends. Right?"

"Very full," McDermott said laconically.

Smith took out a small notebook and a ballpoint pen, Max grinning inwardly at the inscription on the latter: "Courtesy of Sharkey's Funeral Home."

"Would you mind giving me the names of her close friends?" the lieutenant asked. "Male in particular. But also girl friends, gals she flew with a lot who might give us some leads."

"About the latter," McDermott cautioned. "Rebel didn't have any close female friends. She was pretty much of a loner. Frankly, most of her colleagues were jealous of her."

"Figures," Smith sighed. "I'd hate to be a dame competing against a dish like that."

"Furthermore, she didn't fly a lot with anyone in particular. Stews bid trips mostly to fit in with the days they want off, not to fly with friends. Or sometimes they'll bid for trips flown by certain pilots. Rebel did."

"Oh? Would you happen to know their names? Or possibly just one name?"

Max had an impulse to keep Lindsay out of the mess, but erased it instantly. There was no point in hiding anything from the police, and he knew if Smith caught him playing coy or being evasive, Max would have one hell of a time explaining to Belnap why he was off the case.

"There was one," McDermott said. "They were going to be married. Captain Lindsay. James Lindsay."

"You have his home phone and address? I can get them from your personnel office but it'll save time if you know it. He sounds like someone I should talk to."

Max gave him the address and telephone number, but decided it was time to put Smith straight on the subject of Captain Lindsay. "Look, Lieutenant, I wouldn't get any hard-on about Lindsay. I was with him when they told him about the murder. He took it hard. I agree you should talk with him, but I'd personally appreciate it if you'd wait a day. He's shook up."

"Sometimes that's the best time to talk to a suspect,"

Smith lectured. "When they're all shook up. You should know that."

"You can take him out of the suspect category," McDermott said. "We were in Chicago last night and didn't get back here until around ten this morning."

"Oh?" Smith could make that one little word, with the right inflection, sound like an oration of doubt, suspicion and even accusation.

"Aside from the fact that he couldn't have committed murder from a distance of six hundred miles, he really loved Rebel. He told me only last night he was getting a divorce so they could marry."

The sleepy eyes came alive. "Married man, huh? Interesting triangle. Typical but interesting. And how about Miss Martin? I take it from their matrimonial plans she reciprocated his undying affection?"

"For Christ sake," Max growled. "You trying to sound like Philo Vance? Yeah, she reciprocated. In spades."

"Yet you said she had a pot full of boy friends. If she was so nuts about this pilot, how come she swung?"

"Lindsay's married," McDermott said. "Until he decided to get a divorce Rebel figured she had a right to do anything she pleased. What's more, Jim agreed with her."

"Understanding fella, your Captain Lindsay. Very broad-minded. Which brings me back to my original inquiry. Her boy friends. Would you say they were casual? That they just kinda filled in her leisure time when she wasn't seeing Lindsay?"

"The truth is," McDermott said, "the kid was something of a swinger. She told me once she shacked up with damned near every guy she dated. You asked me if they were casual friends. Casual as far as she was concerned, because she was carrying a torch for Lindsay. But I gathered a few of the characters she had on the string were pretty serious about her."

"The names of same would be very much appreciated,"

90

Smith said. "Boy, from what that fella Gilcannon told me, she was the All-American girl type. The kind you'd like to bring home to meet Mother."

Max grunted, "If I could have believed Rebel herself, the name of Franklin Gilcannon was on the list."

The sleepy eyes seemed to stir again. "Oh? This case is getting downright messy. I know Gilcannon is a big shot, McDermott, and I don't relish putting you on any spot, but if we're going to be working together, honesty is the required policy. So what do you know about his relationship with Miss Martin?"

"Part of what I know is first-hand, part is second-hand. The latter comes from someone you can't question—namely, the victim. I couldn't swear how factual it is."

"I don't care if it's fifth-hand," Smith said placidly. "You're an ex-cop. I don't have to tell you I'd settle for a piece of string if we can't find a hawser rope."

"Okay. Rebel told me about Gilcannon the same night she informed me she loved Jim Lindsay. That house she lived in—Didn't it strike you as unusual?"

"Unusual? It's just an old Alexandria house. What's unusual about it?"

"It's too much house for stewardess pay. Rebel told me Gilcannon paid part of her rent. And while I was there, she opened a package with a jade pendant inside; it cost somebody a mint and according to Rebel the donor was none other than our esteemed executive vice president."

"She could have been showing off," Smith mused, without much conviction.

"There was a card with the pendant, signed 'Frank.' Very sentimental, too. Nope, I'd bet a month's pay it was from Gilcannon."

Smith's voice was the epitome of casual innocence. "Incidentally, what were *you* doing at her house?"

"We had just come in from a trip. Lindsay asked me to drive her home."

"You ever slept with her?"

"I came goddamned close. That same night. I was surprised as hell. She had just finished telling me how crazy she was about Lindsay and then went into a very obvious seduction act. Why the look of total doubt, Lieutenant?"

"Frankly," Smith chuckled, "I can't see you turning her down and I can't see her making the offer. You ain't exactly Gregory Peck."

"Well," Max said ruefully, "you'll just have to take my word on both counts. If you want my motive for rejecting heaven, I happen to think Jim Lindsay's a good joe and I couldn't quite get myself into bed with his beloved."

"I don't know if I'd trust an airline pilot, but I'll trust a good ex-cop. Okay, McDermott, let's get to the nitty-gritty. Tell me about the rest of her friends—on the theory that one of them turned out to be the worst kind of enemy."

Max talked for the next half-hour.

The first one he saw, he told Smith, was Bob Denham, the young ramp agent Rebel had described as her secondstringer. Max had taken Betty Roberts to dinner at Normandy Farm, a restaurant about twenty-five miles from downtown Washington, located in the rolling hills of the Potomac hunt country.

While the evening didn't exactly get off on the wrong foot, it wasn't an auspicious beginning. Maximilian McDermott was guilty of only one form of male vanity: after-shave lotions. His newest civilian suit was four years old, his choice of ties showed all the perception of a man afflicted with total color blindness, and he persisted in smoking pipes that screamed for honorable and permanent retirement. But he also was a sucker for any advertisement hinting broadly that wearing a particular astringent was the equivalent of feeding one's date a quart of aphrodasiac.

On this occasion, he had just expended $6.95 plus tax on

92

an item called "Tiger's Fangs," which he had seen advertised in *Playboy*—a typical Madison Avenue pitch depicting a Casper Milquetoast character surrounded by gorgeous women apparently bent on committing mass rape. As the caption so succinctly phrased it: ONE WHIFF OF TIGER'S FANGS AND YOU'RE IN LIKE YOU KNOW WHO. He picked Betty up at her apartment and she sniffed the air the second she got into the Mercedes, her thin nose wrinkling is a disillusioning display of olfactory displeasure.

"What in God's name is that odor?" she asked.

Max winced. " 'Tiger's Fangs.' At six-ninety-five for three ounces, the least you could have done was keep quiet."

"Why should I keep quiet? It makes my eyes smart. Anyway, I love your car, kind of goes with you. Not very good-looking but solid, dependable."

"Mercedes, eighty-five hundred for thirty-eight hundred pounds," McDermott said in a rare attempt at humor. Her praise of the automobile restored his punctured pride, and his mood was further improved when they arrived at the restaurant. Max fell in love quickly with Normandy, a tastefully converted farmhouse on a huge, wooded lot. To the left of the entrance lobby was a cocktail lounge reminding McDermott of English pubs—dark panelled, intimate, with big beer kegs for tables.

"Let's have a drink in here before we eat," he suggested. "Looks relaxing."

"Might as well. It's crowded tonight and we'll probably have to wait for a table."

McDermott gave his name to a hostess and they found a place in the lounge. They had just ordered drinks when Max caught Betty staring across the room. His eyes followed hers, focusing on a table across the room. Rebel Martin was sitting there, with a handsome, wavy-haired youth who must have been her own age or even younger. She was talking and laughing loudly, and even as they noticed her, she took her date's hand and rubbed it against her thigh.

Max growled something under his breath, thinking that it had been only a week since Rebel had voiced her love for Jim Lindsay. It might have been mental telepathy, but Rebel spotted them almost simultaneously. She lurched clumsily to her feet and literally staggered over to their table. Her eyes were that curious mixture of false brightness and dull bleariness that are the twin signals of intoxication. The young man she was with stayed in his seat, although he gave Betty a half-hearted wave of recognition.

"Well, well," Rebel greeted them, her voice slurred. "Our esteemed check pilot and Miss Roberts. Didn't know you two had something going. Guess I should have stayed with you that night in Chicago, Betty."

Max wanted to slap her but settled instead for a comparatively mild reprimand. "I think your date would like you to get back to your own table, Rebel."

Rebel laughed in an ugly, drunken way. "Oh, let the silly bastard wait. He'll get me in the sack soon enough. You two eaten yet? We could get a table together."

The look of disgust in Betty's eyes made the slight shake of her head unnecessary.

"No, thanks," McDermott said in a tone devoid of civility. "From what I just saw, you might slide under the table and start screwing."

"Mr. Morals himself," she sneered. "I guess I know when I'm not wanted." She hesitated, looking at Max as if she were trying to dredge up some kind of explanation or apology out of her alcohol-clouded mind. McDermott could have sworn he saw tears in her eyes, but he decided it probably was a glistening film of drunkenness.

"I'd better get back to lover-boy before he gets jealous," Rebel said. "See you around."

"Would that be a Bob Denham?" Max asked Betty after Rebel left.

She was surprised. "I thought you didn't dig gossip. Yes, that's Denham."

94

"Seems a bit low in the social strata for Rebel," McDermott observed.

"He's been crazy about her ever since she came to Washington. He follows her around like a puppy. Spends every cent he makes on her and keeps telling everybody they're in love and will get married one of these days."

"I would suspect," Max said, "he's got about as much chance of marrying Rebel as I've got of taking Charlie Belnap's job away from him. By the way, our beauty queen is leaving."

Rebel and Denham were walking out of the lounge. They turned right in the lobby instead of left, which would have taken them into the dining room. Apparently they had decided sex was more important than food. Rebel didn't glance back in their direction and Max wasn't sorry.

"There's something about that dame that seems to attract trouble," he said to Betty.

"There's something about Rebel that seems to attract hate," she corrected.

"Hate? I've gathered that anyone she dates goes into a spin and crashes."

"There's that old adage, Max, and it fits Rebel's affairs— a very thin line divides love from hate. The way she plays around, some of her lovers could develop into haters very quickly."

Max nodded but said nothing. He was thinking, for no particular reason, that Bob Denham could easily cross that dividing line.

It was Mike Hunter who pointed out the second of Rebel's lovers. But Max first told Lieutenant Smith about Michelle Hunter herself.

If she had liked McDermott instantly, it was mutual. She was bawdy, yet she possessed an innate sense of dignity— qualities which would have put her equally at home at a truck drivers' beer party or a White House reception. Effervescent and boisterous, yes, but as Max discovered when he got to know her, Mike also was over-sensitive and very easy to hurt. Brilliant, with the vocabulary of a Phi Beta Kappa although she had nothing but a high school education, but also addicted to four-letter words which she tossed around with the natural aplomb of a Marine serving his fourth hitch.

Max respected her for the way she did her job, too. A stewardess supervisor had to combine the personalities and qualities of a tough drill sergeant and a kindly Mother Superior. She and two assistants had one hundred and twenty-five stewardesses under their direct supervision, all highly individualistic girls who refused to stay in the mold that had been their flight training. They were mostly kids in their twenties, expected to show maturity and judgment far beyond the normal capacity of women in that age bracket. That's why Mike personified the ideal supervisor. She understood the inevitable conflict between chronological immaturity and the often ruthless demands of the jet age. She could weigh the human failings of a young girl against the equally serious difficulties of airline operations, and somehow she never let either a stewardess or her company down. She was constantly juggling one against the other, trying to be Strong Boss and Sympathetic Older Sister simultaneously, a trick to be rated as the most delicate balancing act outside of a circus high-wire performance.

As a pilot, McDermott not only recognized but appreciated the schizophrenic aspects of her job, the conflict of trying to be loyal to her girls and Coastal at the same time. He had seen the same collision of interests in the Air Force, where fine commanders tried so hard to walk the tightrope between essential discipline and humane tolerance. In the military, leaning over too far in one direction was labeled over-identification with men under command, and this was the identical danger Mike Hunter had to avoid without destroying both base morale and the only too natural sympathy of one woman for another.

Her eyes were the mirror through which those who really knew her could see her split personality. Brown eyes, set deep in her Kewpie face, as soft, trusting and placid as a doe's until she got angry. Then they took on the deadliness of a cobra's stare, capable of demolishing lies and phony alibis with a single icy stare.

Roger Blake introduced her to McDermott a few days after Max took the route qualification flight with Lindsay, warning him in advance, "Don't be surprised at anything she says."

Her opening line was, "Jesus, you're the homeliest sonofabitch east of the Mississippi," a greeting which positively endeared her to Max. He quickly grasped that her tart tongue, her incessant wisecracking, both constituted a carefully-constructed facade behind which she tried to hide her real depth and sensitivity.

He bumped into her a couple of days later, sitting alone and rather forlornly, he thought, in the Snake Pit. On impulse, he joined her without asking permission.

"Hi," she said, openly pleased.

"You look a bit on the blue side," McDermott said, "but don't bother me with your troubles, I'm in a lousy mood myself."

"I've got a hundred and twenty-five troubles," Mike said wistfully. "If I ever found a stewardess who didn't have at least one crisis a week, I'd resign and give her my job."

"Maybe you get too involved with them" Max suggested.

"Too many of them want me to get involved. I'll start to slap verbal hell out of a girl for a bad passenger letter, and she'll start telling me it was all because she had a fight with her boy friend the night before. Next thing I know, I'm comforting her instead of canning her."

"Stews are no different than pilots, Mike. They either

keep personal difficulties off their airplane or they don't fly."

"I know," Mike agreed, "but some of those kids are so bloody immature. Maybe that's why I get soft-hearted. Maybe we expect too much of them. All I can do is pat their fannies, tell 'em to keep a smile on their puss and stay away from married pilots. Including you, buster. Or aren't you married?"

"Negative, I'm surprised you didn't know. Everyone else in this damned base seems to have gotten a memo on my marital status."

"Occasionally, I fall behind on late gossip. I wasn't prying, Max. It's just that pilots are one of my biggest headaches. We have a few of you apes around who'd lie like Ananias just to get a stew in the sack. Too many of my girls get involved with the bastards and then they're no good to themselves or the company."

"There also are a few too many stews around who get involved with said apes knowing damned well they're married," McDermott growled.

"Granted, I know one I'd like to draw and quarter. She's nailed one of our married captains and the poor cluck doesn't know what hit him. In this case, I'd blame her, not him. The bitch could seduce a saint."

She lit a cigarette and looked at McDermott curiously through a haze of acrid smoke, obviously waiting for him to ask a question. He didn't but she shrewdly sensed that a question wasn't necessary.

"Have you met the Cleopatra of Coastal yet?"

McDermott lit his pipe and blew the smoke right at her. "If you insist on getting into personalities, stop playing coy."

"Rebel Martin. You must have heard of her. You can't go to work for this airline without hearing about Rebel by your second day."

"Yeah, I've heard of her. I met her. And the poor cluck to whom you were apparently referring."

"Bitch describes her, doesn't it? I really feel sorry for Jim Lindsay. Oh hell, I shouldn't be talking about one of my girls like this."

"No, you shouldn't," Max agreed in a matter-of-fact tone. "Seems to me if she does her job on an airplane, that's where your own involvement ends."

Her retort was spit out more than spoken. "I'm not talking about Rebel Martin, stewardess. I'm talking about her as a human being. Which she ain't."

"I never pass judgment on someone I don't know very well," McDermott said cautiously.

"I can," Mike said, and a look of undiluted venom clouded her eyes. "I know her too goddamned well."

Silence hung between them for a black moment. Then Mike shrugged. "I've got to do a ramp check. Walk me out to Gate Four."

It was at Gate Four that they came face to face with the subject of their conversation—namely, Rebel. She had just gotten off a trip and meeting her as she came through the jetway was a well-dressed, older man with a pot belly and straggly white hair out of tune with a rather handsome face. She gave him a dazzling smile and tucked her arm in his as they walked away. Mike made a mental note to remind Rebel that public displays of affection on the part of stewardesses were contrary to Coastal policy.

"She's really something," McDermott sighed. "I haven't seen her with the same guy twice in a row."

"The guy who just met her is really something," Mike volunteered. "Lyle Tarkington of the Taj Mahal chain of dress shops. He's disgustingly rich, also disgustingly nuts about Rebel. If you ever see her wardrobe, about ninety percent of it comes courtesy of Mr. Tarkington. There are times when I wish I had her outlook on life."

"This Tarkington character married?"

"Separated, I think. I seem to remember about his wife filing for divorce six months ago. I've been holding my breath. If she names Rebel as corespondent, I can just see the headlines: 'STEWARDESS NAMED IN DIVORCE SCANDAL.'"

"Well, was Rebel the cause of the breakup?"

"So rumor had it. And with our girl, rumors usually turn out to be a fact."

"Add one and one," McDermott said.

Mike's eyebrows asked the question.

"One more guy who loves her and one more woman who hates her guts."

"Make it one and two," the stewardess supervisor said. "Add me to that list."

Two days later, McDermott recounted to Smith, he saw something he never expected to see: Frank Gilcannon with Rebel in public. Outwardly innocent of course. Gilcannon, Max knew, had to be aware of President Belnap's insistence that Coastal's top executives walk the straight-and-narrow.

When Max spotted them he was munching a cheese-burger at the airport coffee shop. Rebel and Gilcannon were at a table in a corner near a window that overlooked the ramp area, totally absorbed in conversation. She was not in uniform, dressed instead in a smart white suit that accen-tuated her incredible figure. The jacket was cut low enough to approach the borderline of indecency, and the upper moons of her full breasts were plainly visible.

From all appearances, they could have been discussing some cabin service problem but just as McDermott was about to turn his glance away, Rebel slipped off one shoe under the table and rubbed her stocking foot against Gil-cannon's leg. The executive vice president scowled and said something that painted a hurt-little-girl look on her face, like a child scolded unexpectedly for a harmless prank. The look worked its intended magic, for Gilcannon flashed a smile of instant forgiveness. Max was amused. Frank Gilcannon had a reputation for toughness, yet with Rebel he displayed all the rigidity of a melting marshmallow.

Gilcannon was big, with youthful, unlined features and a hawkish nose so pronounced that one got the feeling he could stab out an eye if he nodded too close to somebody's face. Not so youthful was his almost total baldness, a single wisp of sandy hair bisecting the center of his head in such a way that it gave him the appearance of an Iroquois indian. Max wondered again why Gilcannon was playing around with a lowly stewardess; Belnap had fired more than one Coastal executive for what he considered careless morals. Yet, Max admitted, no one looking at Rebel in that suggestively-cut jacket could blame Gilcannon for taking a chance. Even Belnap, at the age of seventy-one, might have drooled a little.

The check captain was gulping down the last of the cheeseburger when Rebel walked by, not noticing him, the subtle, delicate aroma of her perfume lingering in his nostrils. Impulsively, he glanced back at the table where she had been sitting, and mentally shook his head at the sight of Gilcannon, who was still watching Rebel with unmitigated lust written all over his face. Or was it all lust? Max thought he detected something else. A faint suggestion of wariness and doubt. The barest hint of menace.

"That's about all I can tell you," McDermott said to Smith. "She was deeply involved, apparently, with four men. There may have been others for all we know, but somehow I doubt it."

"Four," the lieutenant repeated. "One winner and three losers. I'd like to know if she broke the good news to the runners-up."

Max nodded. "I assume you'll ask them."

"You're damned right I'll ask, along with some other questions. I've also got a few for your friend, Captain Lindsay. It still intrigues me that he knew she was playing around with other guys and he just turned the other cheek."

"Which implies that you don't believe it."

"Let's just say that I'm not convinced."

"Well, I am," McDermott said. "Maybe it sounds screwy, Lieutenant, but I believed both of them. That they really loved each other. Jim's the kind of character who could forgive Rebel because his own conscience was killing him. And Rebel wasn't a bad kid. The morals of an alley cat, sure. But a lot of her sleeping around was because of Jim; she never expected to land him permanently."

"Just when did she land him, by the way?"

"I'm not sure. Fairly recently, I suppose. Maybe in the last week or so. He didn't tell me about it until last night and I gathered it was a decision he had just reached himself. Which means he probably had just gotten around to telling Rebel he'd marry her."

"You ever met Lindsay's wife?"

"Once. I had dinner at his house. About a month ago."

"Did she know all about his affair with the Martin girl?"

"Probably. The atmosphere was thicker than a San Francisco fog. If she didn't know then, Lindsay had to tell her when he asked her for a divorce."

"Not necessarily. He wouldn't have to supply names."

"He's the type who would. But I'll bet a month's pay Norma Lindsay knew the name of the so-called 'other woman' long before divorce was mentioned. Rebel had been out to their house before she and Jim started their hanky-panky. She gave their little girl Debbie a doll and Debbie named it 'Rebel.' I saw the look on Norma's face when the kid was introducing me to that damned doll. Brother, she *knew.*"

"The Lindsays have any other children?"

"One. An eleven-year-old boy."

"Too bad. Maybe now they can all pick up the pieces and

start over again. Your airline gals make for a very interesting gang of predatory females. What do they teach them in stewardess school: how to serve drinks and wreck homes?"

McDermott was nettled. "Look, Smith, Rebel was no more representative of the average stew than Candy was a typical teenager. By and large, they're good kids. Loyal, adaptable, intelligent and they work their asses off in a very tough and important job. And when they finally quit flying, they make good wives, with the lowest divorce rate of any female group in the country. Sure Rebel was something of a slut. But you can find Rebels in any profession, including law enforcement."

"I seem to have touched a raw nerve," Smith apologized. "Sorry, McDermott. I know how mad I get when people over-generalize about cops." He closed a small loose-leaf notebook into which he had been scrawling entries as Max talked. "If you can steer me to the nearest phone, I'd like to call the coroner's office. That autopsy should be done by now."

Max took him to his own office and waited outside, although Smith suggested that he stay.

"I hate eavesdropping on phone calls when I can hear only one end of the conversation," McDermott said. "Brief me when you're finished."

The lieutenant emerged in five minutes, looked around to make sure no airline personnel were within listening distance, then examined Max with the air of a man about to issue a startling announcement.

"Autopsy's finished," Smith said in a low voice. "Things are getting kinda complicated. For one thing, our Miss Martin had enough alcohol in her to stay drunk for two days."

"That's a complication?"

"Could be. The coroner says she must have been so loaded, she couldn't have defended herself against a midget. Which means the killer easily could have been a woman."

"Strangling isn't exactly a female mode of murder," McDermott said. "A dame's more likely to use a gun or even a knife."

"Theoretically. The trouble is, I keep getting a hunch that this case isn't going to fit any normal pattern."

"If you're going to take into account all the women who hated Rebel," Max said cynically, "that suspect list is going to resemble the passenger manifest on a 747. I see what you mean about complications."

"You haven't heard anything yet. It seems Miss Martin was about three months pregnant."

Max whistled. "Pregnant," he repeated incredulously.

"Very. And now I'd love to know the name of the happy father, inasmuch as it might be the same name as the killer. Wonder if Lindsay knew she was going to have a baby. Okay, McDermott we might as well start the real digging. Let's go talk to our first suspect."

"Lindsay? Dammit, Smith, I told you he was. . . ."

"Not Lindsay. Mr. Gilcannon."

Frank Gilcannon originally might have gone for McDermott's participation in a murder investigation, but the moment Max and Lieutenant entered his office, he looked definitely displeased.

"I'm trying to run an airline," he complained, reluctantly motioning them toward a couple of chairs. "I hope you have something important to discuss. Or perhaps you've found out something."

Smith could be deceptively soothing. "Just trying to put some scattered information together, Mr. Gilcannon. I realize you're a busy man and, believe me, we don't like to bother you."

"I'll do anything I can to help," Gilcannon said, cooling off.

"Fine. Suppose you start off by telling us how well you knew Rebel Martin."

Gilcannon's strong face paled. "I knew her. I know a number of our stewardesses."

"As well as you knew Miss Martin?"

"And just what is that crack supposed to mean?"

"It means what it says. Was Miss Martin just another employee or something a little more special? Such as a good friend."

"We were good friends, yes. Not close friends, but I liked her. She was an exceptionally good stewardess. A credit to the airline."

105

"Are you in the habit of giving expensive gifts to your stewardesses, Mr. Gilcannon? Even the exceptional ones like Miss Martin?"

Max could sense the wrestling match in Gilcannon's mind —the conflict between fear of admitting too much and fear of hiding too much in case Smith knew more than the vice president figured he did.

The answer finally came out, propelled by anger. "My gift-giving activities are none of the police department's business. Certainly they are no part of this investigation. What I gave Rebel Martin was between us, an innocent gesture of gratitude on my part, I assure you. I've also done little favors for other stewardesses, not just for Rebel."

"Would you class an expensive jade pendant, accompanied by a rather sentimental note as a 'little favor,' Mr. Gilcannon?"

The executive vice president's face this time flushed crimson. "I'm not going to discuss matters of this sort in front of one of our employees. If this line of impertinent questioning is considered official, McDermott, I'll have to ask you to leave."

"I don't think I will," Max said firmly. "Unless Lieutenant Smith wants me to."

Smith's spaniel eyes hardened. "It wasn't my idea to let Captain McDermott get into the act, Mr. Gilcannon. It was yours and Mr. Belnap's. So he stays in. Now, getting back to jade pendants. . . ."

"I suppose McDermott or some other two-bit gossip monger has been feeding you a bunch of third-hand rumors," Gilcannon exploded. "Rebel must have told you about that . . . uh, my occasional little gifts. McDermott, I won't stand for . . ."

Smith interrupted, glancing at McDermott with a relax-chum-I'll-cover-for-you look. "We found the pendant when we went through her personal effects this morning. Along with a note she had carefully preserved. A note signed

Frank. I sort of put two and two together, so to speak. Neat habit women have, saving all their letters and little love notes. Comes in handy at divorce hearings. Or even murder cases."

"Just a minute," Gilcannon protested. "There are a lot of men named Frank in this town. Perhaps several thousand. Your connecting that pendant to me is a gross, malicious assumption. To be perfectly truthful, I *have* given Rebel little gifts from time to time, but nothing as ostentatious as expensive jewelry. Matter of fact—it just occurred to me—I've heard her mention a Frank something or other, I never bothered to remember his last name. I'll bet he gave her that pendant."

Smith hesitated, unwilling to let McDermott get into trouble with a man who might have a very long, vindictive, memory. It was Max who came to his rescue.

"She might have known a hundred and fifty guys named Frank," McDermott said, "but the one who signed that note was you."

"And how did you deduce that?" Gilcannon sneered.

"Simple. She told me."

Gilcannon appeared to be on the threshold of apoplexy. "See here, McDermott, I've got grounds to fire you for invading the personal life of a superior. Who the hell do you think you are—a punk pilot playing detective? Mr. Belnap will hear about this; make no mistake about it. Why, I'm tempted to . . ."

"Hold it, Gilcannon." The executive vice president paused, the furious words he was about to say colliding with the look of icy contempt on McDermott's seamed face. "If you weren't banging her, you're a sucker, because she was screwing everyone else. And if you were, don't give me any of that 'I'll tell Charlie Belnap' crap because you don't have the guts. And I think you know why."

"He'd have my ass in a sling," Gilcannon breathed. The fight had gone out of him, like air escaping from a punctured balloon. He sighed unhappily. "Okay. I gave her the pendant. So what? I didn't kill her."

Looking at McDermott gratefully, Smith resumed. "Are you married, Mr. Gilcannon?"

"Yes."

"Were you having an affair with the Martin girl?"

Gilcannon gave McDermott such an imploring look, Max felt a little sorry for him.

"Mr. Gilcannon," he relented. "I give you my word— anything I hear in the course of this investigation is off the record, unless it turns out to be a factor in the solution of the murder. Remember, I'm supposed to report directly to you. Those were Belnap's orders."

Gilcannon's face brightened at this reminder, sobering again only when Smith repeated his question. "Were you having an affair?"

"Yes. For about the last year, I'd say. I can't defend my actions. But she was, you know, extremely beautiful. I'm afraid I was a bit smitten. More infatuated than in love. Certainly I wouldn't have left my wife for her. That might have jeopardized my whole career."

Smith examined him shrewdly. "I'm curious to know why you felt it necessary to tell us you wouldn't have left your wife for her. Did Miss Martin ever suggest that you get a divorce and marry her?"

"No," Gilcannon said quickly. "She wasn't the marrying kind. She was perfectly willing to let our . . . our little affair remain status quo. An innocent gift now and then. That's all."

"Her home, Mr. Gilcannon. Do many of your steward-esses have houses all to themselves?"

The vice president looked at them suspiciously. "No. Most of them live in apartments. With one or two room-mates."

"That house of hers is in a fairly high rent section of Alexandria. Would it be possible for her to pay such rent on what a stewardess makes?"

108

"I don't know what rent she was paying," Gilcannon said sullenly. "But she wasn't the first girl to have a place of her own. She probably had some outside income, like some do. From her family, perhaps."

"That personnel record you showed me lists an aunt in Pittsburgh as her only close relative. I believe you told me yourself her parents are dead. The Pittsburgh address, by the way, is not in a particularly affluent area; I know that town pretty well. So I doubt whether the girl's aunt would have been a source of extra dough."

Gilcannon said nothing, his silence a challenge.

"Mr. Gilcannon, I must urge you again to be truthful. I appreciate your admission about the affair. Now I must ask you if you were paying all or part of her rent on that house."

"And where did you dredge up that little tidbit?"

"From me," Max said softly. "And I got it from Rebel."

"That goddamned bitch!" Gilcannon snarled. "She never could keep her mouth shut. I should have . . ." He stopped, suddenly conscious that he was digging a very large hole, and he sighed so loudly it was almost a groan. "Okay, you've got me. Yes, I helped her with her rent. I gave her about fifty dollars a month—sometimes more if she was short of dough. Damn it, Lieutenant, I told you I was infatuated with her. I don't see anything wrong in what I did."

"Nothing wrong," Smith agreed, "unless that fifty bucks a month was blackmail."

Gilcannon's heavy face turned red again. "Blackmail? Why in Heaven's name should Rebel have tried to blackmail me?"

"You told me that leaving your wife for that girl could have ruined your career. The case is only a few hours old and it hasn't taken me long to discover that Rebel Martin wasn't exactly angelic. She let a married man keep her, partially keep her, anyway"—the last revision was in deference to the self-righteous anger flooding Gilcannon's face—

109

"and she sure seems to have been quite a bed-hopper. So I wouldn't put it past a dame like her to bleed you a little. Let's say she asked you to pay part or all of her rent, and out of her everlasting gratitude she promised not to go to your wife or maybe even Mr. Belnap, and confess all."

"There was no blackmail in our relationship. That's the God's truth, Lieutenant." The vice president's anguished denial, Max thought, sounded genuine.

"I hope so, Mr. Gilcannon," Smith said. "But I'm afraid we also have a second possible motive for blackmail. Your paragon of passion, the late Miss Martin, was three months pregnant."

Both Smith and McDermott studied Gilcannon's face, alert for any sign of surprise, fear or guilt. His only reaction, strangely enough, bordered on relief.

"I'm sorry to hear that," Gilcannon said with apparent sincerity. "Is this considered significant? Does it open new avenues of investigation?"

"It opens one up in your direction," the lieutenant said calmly. "I'll have to ask you again: was she blackmailing you?"

"I said no and I'll say it again," Gilcannon snapped. "Why the hell should her being pregnant have anything to do with me? I know damned well *I* didn't knock her up."

"You might have quite a time proving you didn't. But even if you weren't the father, her being with child—to use a delicate phrase—this would make blackmail a little bit more logical, wouldn't it? She still could have accused you of being the father."

"Impossible," Gilcannon said, with such an air of assurance that Max suspected he had something up his well tailored sleeve.

"Impossible?" Smith asked.

"Definitely. I'm sterile. My wife and I have four children. We didn't want any more so about three years ago I had a vasectomy, one of those operations that make conception

110

impossible. And, I might add, Rebel knew it. She never could accuse me of fathering her baby."

"May I have the name of the doctor who performed that surgery?"

"Certainly. Doctor Lakeman. He has an office in Bethesda. I can call him now for verification, if you'd like."

"That won't be necessary," Smith said. "We can do our own verifying. I'd still appreciate your leveling with me, Mr. Gilcannon. It's very possible she was blackmailing somebody and that person killed her. That's why I want to know again, as tough as it is to admit it, if she was blackmailing you because if she was, she could have pulled it on more than one guy."

"She was not a blackmailer," Gilcannon insisted. "Not with me, anyway."

Smith studied Gilcannon's face. "Were you aware that Miss Martin was going to marry one of your pilots?"

The vice president looked momentarily surprised, then dropped a mask of indifference over his features. "No, I was not. May I ask his name?"

Smith glanced at McDermott, who hesitated, then said, "Jim Lindsay."

"I suspected as much," Gilcannon said. "I know she's been seeing him. Too bad. I suppose Lindsay's pretty broken up."

Smith ignored the rhetorical question. "I'd appreciate one last bit of information, Mr. Gilcannon. Can you establish your whereabouts of last night, say between eleven P.M. and six A.M. this morning?"

"Of course. I was home with my family. I suppose you'll have to verify this?"

"It would be helpful," Smith said with a trace of sarcasm.

Gilcannon seemed flustered. "Well, it seems my wife is out of town visiting her sister. But three of my children were home; the fourth is in college."

"How old are the three who were home last night?"

111

"Sue, the oldest, is sixteen. Then there's Jennifer; she's eight. And Tommy's between them. He's thirteen. Frank, Junior, is a senior at William and Mary."

"I assume one or more of them could confirm that you were home all night?"

"I suppose so," Gilcannon said doubtfully. "Actually, Lieutenant, I'd rather you wouldn't ask them unless it was absolutely necessary."

"Oh?"

"I'm not trying to hide anything, believe me. But if you ask my children whether I was home last night, they'd make some connection with the murder. They read the papers, Sue and Tommy in particular. And it's possible they'd, uh, mention something to my wife. It would be most embarrassing to have my family think I'm in some way involved in a murder case."

"I didn't get you involved, Mr. Gilcannon. You marched on stage all by your lonesome, because you were dumb enough to have a girl like Rebel Martin as your mistress. And I'd be remiss in my duty if I didn't establish the whereabouts of every person who knew that girl and who might have had reason to kill her."

Gilcannon paled again. "Does this mean I'm under suspicision?"

"Mr. Gilcannon, in a murder investigation, the Anglo-Saxon concept of justice is turned completely around. Every possibility, or suspect if you prefer, is presumed tentatively guilty until proved innocent. Not in any legal sense, of course, but as a matter of practicality."

"I see. I assure you, I didn't kill Rebel. If . . . if when you talk to my children, if you could phrase your questions in such a way. . . ."

"I'll phrase them as delicately as possible," Smith promised. "By the way, what time did they go to bed last night?"

Gilcannon looked miserable. "Well, Tommy and Jennifer were in bed by ten. It was a school night. Sue stayed up until after the eleven o'clock news on TV."

"So if you had gone out, they wouldn't have been likely to hear you or even know about it." It was a statement, not a question.

"I didn't go out," Gilcannon said with a touch of annoyance.

"Okay, for the time being I'll take your word for it." Smith snapped his little notebook shut. "I appreciate your giving us your valuable time."

"Wait a minute," Gilcannon said, in a way suggesting he had switched from the subservient role of suspect to the masterful personality of an executive. "Have you or are you giving this to the papers?"

Smith smiled. "You mean the fact that you've been questioned?"

"Of course not. I mean about Rebel's being pregnant."

"Any reason why I shouldn't?"

"A very good reason. Makes us look bad. It's embarrassing enough to have one of our stewardesses a murder victim. But the pregnancy bit—well, it doesn't do much for the public image of our cabin attendants."

Smith bestowed upon him a gaze of disdain. "I should tell you to go to hell, Mr. Gilcannon, but McDermott here already asked me to keep the pregnancy angle out of print for a while. I'm doing it as a favor to him."

Gilcannon condescended a faint smile of surprised appreciation in Max's direction, although actually he was no more surprised than the check pilot.

"Thanks for hanging that pregnancy censorship deed on me," Max said as soon as they were outside Gilcannon's office. "I gather you were aiming at scoring some brownie points for me with that particular brass hat."

Smith nodded. "I figured you might be in for some trouble with that joker. My God, McDermott, I wouldn't talk to any of my superior officers the way you did. And I sure as hell didn't expect you to tell him you gave me all the stuff

113

about him and the girl. If Gilcannon turns out to be lily white in this mess, you could be in trouble. I hear he's sort of a crown prince behind Belnap and I don't want you on his permanent shit list."

"It would be just as bad for him to be on my permanent shit list," McDermott said quietly. And the way he said it convinced Smith that the burly check captain wasn't bluffing.

They went to Smith's car, the detective stopping in Max's office long enough to make two calls—one to the main office of the Taj Mahal Dress Shops, arranging an appointment that afternoon with Lyle Tarkington, and the other to a detective colleague asking him to interrogate Robert Denham.

"We'll talk to Denham ourselves later, probably tomorrow," Smith explained.

"Your persistent use of the word 'we' intrigues me," McDermott said. "Look, I've got enough cop left in me to give you all the cooperation you want. But you're putting me on a spot. I'm not sitting in any corner with my mouth shut. I'm spilling everything I know and that includes a fair-sized slug of gossip and rumors. I don't like being a stoolie and, so help me, that seems to be the role I'm playing."

Smith shrugged. "That thought has occurred to me, but I don't have much choice. You got involved with certain people in a hell of a hurry. Key people, maybe. I don't like putting you on any spot, McDermott, but in a way you put yourself there before any murder was committed. You knew the victim, you knew about her own involvements, and you turned into a peculiar kind of gold mine for a dull old plodder like me. I didn't want to let you in on the action, but from the time you told me about that Gilcannon creep, I decided I really needed you more than your damned airline did. You, my friend, are what every homicide dick prays for—a single, central source of valuable information

114

that'll save me days of digging. So, even if you wanted out now, you're all mine until we crack this case. If it'll make you feel any better, I'll pin a temporary badge on you and tell everyone you're my partner, like Sergeant Friday says. Matter of fact, with non-airline types like Tarkington, who doesn't know you from J. Edgar Hoover, that's not a bad idea. I'll introduce you as my partner and you can help me with the questioning."

"It seems I'm hooked," Max grunted.

"You're damned right you're hooked. Who knows, by the time this is all over you may want to work for me instead of Coastal. How much does a—what do they call you, a check captain?—how much do check captains make?"

"I'm pulling down thirty-five grand a year and 'No, thanks' to your offer."

"I just lost a good assistant," Smith said ruefully. "It's too bad they don't pay us in proportion to the crimes we solve. Me, I've been with the force thirty-one years and some lousy government clerks are drawing bigger salaries."

Strangely, he uttered that complaint with no trace of bitterness, stating it as a simple fact that could not be changed by griping. They discussed the hardships and handicaps of being a policeman the rest of the way into downtown Washington, where Smith parked in a lot near the office building in which Taj Mahal maintained its headquarters.

Said headquarters, both McDermott and Smith noted, made Coastal's look shabby. The reception room was panelled in walnut and the spotless, modernistic chairs gave Max the feeling that he was in a luxurious living room more to be admired than used.

A haughty, regal-looking receptionist took their names, with the air of a society matron receiving a delegation from a slum area, and called Tarkington's secretary. Tarkington himself bustled out of his office to greet them, cordially enough with a "welcome-gentlemen-can-I-send-down-for-some-coffee-for-you-it's-an-honor-to-meet-you-both-I-always-cooperate-with-the-police-except-ha-ha-when-I-get-a-parking-ticket." The words gushed unchecked from his mouth so fast that it was only too obvious Mr. Lyle Tarkington was scared to death.

Smith increased his nervousness by fixing Tarkington with a cold, disapproving stare, curtly refusing the offer of coffee. Tarkington escorted them into an office that made the reception room look shabby. He chirped, "Please sit down, gentlemen, and tell me what I can do for you."

"Did you know a Rebel Martin?" the lieutenant opened.

Tarkington's face was a study in tortured uncertainty. "Uh, Rebel Martin, you said? You mean the stewardess who was killed? I believe I heard about it on the radio driving to the office this morning, and there was a story in the early edition of the *Star.*"

"I didn't ask you if you knew about her death. I asked if you knew her."

"Well, uh, yes. Slightly. She was one of my customers. Beautiful girl. Terrible tragedy. I saw her at the airport only a few days ago. I don't know what this world's coming to. All this violence and . . ."

"You say you knew her slightly, as one of your customers. How would you define slightly?"

"She was a very good customer," Tarkington hedged, his pink scalp perspiring.

"Did she have a charge account with your firm?"

"Oh yes. Of course."

"Would you mind letting us see the records. Say her purchases for the past year?"

Tarkington looked sick. "Well, I believe her account was relatively inactive. I don't think you'd get much from it."

"Mr. Tarkington, in the course of investigating her death, we inspected her place of residence. She had a wardrobe that would have made a movie star envious. I'd venture to say that ninety percent of her clothes carried the Taj Mahal

116

label. If her charge account has been inactive, I'd be safe in assuming she paid cash for most of her wardrobe?"

"Yes, I, uh, imagine that would be the case."

"Mr. Tarkington, my partner here has been checking with some of Miss Martin's closest friends. He was told that you made her a gift of her wardrobe or most of it. Is that true?"

The dress tycoon gulped. "Well, she was such a beautiful girl and stewardesses don't make much money. I suppose that on some occasions, I'd let her have some clothes at a substantial discount. Virtually for nothing, you might say. Of course, these were items we used in modeling and so forth. Clothing we normally would not market on the retail or even wholesale level. Slightly damaged or soiled in many instances."

"You say she paid cash for this. I assume you'd have a record of those transactions, these items sold to her at what you described as a substantial discount."

Beads of sweat glistened on Tarkington's forehead. "Inasmuch as I'm the owner of this company, the transactions were between the two of us. When I saw something I thought she'd like, an item we couldn't sell for various reasons such as soilage, I'd let her know and she'd give me the money. There weren't any records."

"Oh?"

"Of course not. Why should there be? There's nothing illegal about not keeping records of such, uh, personal business deals."

Smith reached into the breast pocket of his jacket, drew out a fat cigar and lit it in what had to be a deliberately rude gesture of disdain for both the swanky surroundings and disbelief in Tarkington's answers.

"Did you have business dealings with other customers, Mr. Tarkington?"

"A few. It's not unusual to . . ."

"Suppose we cut out this ring-around-the-rosy stuff. Were

117

you shacking up with Miss Martin, if you'll excuse my use of the colloquial?"

"I was not," Tarkington said with indignation so feeble that it was totally ineffective.

Max suddenly stepped in. "Your wife sued you for divorce about six months ago, didn't she?"

"That is correct." Tarkington was examining McDermott curiously, half grateful that the "partner" had halted Smith's line of questioning and half-fearful at what McDermott might be getting at.

"As Lieutenant Smith said, we've questioned several of Miss Martin's friends regarding her background. It was common knowledge around her airline that she was the reason for your wife's requesting a divorce. You've been seen meeting her flights on more than one occasion. This isn't a picture of platonic friendship, Mr. Tarkington—a multi-thousand dollar free wardrobe, a divorce action and a relationship pretty much out in the open."

"Rebel wasn't named as a corespondent," Tarkington said desperately, lunging at this argument with the eagerness of a drowning man who has just spotted the only piece of driftwood within a radius of fifty miles.

"Not officially, perhaps, but was she or wasn't she the chief factor in your wife's seeking a divorce?"

"And," Smith broke in, "there's no use in evading the point because we can ask your wife the same question."

"Rebel was the reason," Tarkington said. "Unfortunately, after Valerie and I separated, Rebel wouldn't marry me. There was never anything really serious between us. I've been seeing her from time to time, taken her to dinner occasionally. As a matter of fact, I think I should tell you that my wife and I have discussed a reconciliation. Nothing definite as yet, but you might say it's in the works. So I bore no grudge against Rebel, and I assure you I had nothing to do with her death. I was extremely fond of her. She . . . she

118

made me feel young again. Virile. I'm fifty-seven, gentlemen, and it was flattering to have such a beautiful girl even
halfway interested in me."

"Or in your products," Max muttered, drawing a glance
from Smith that was part reproach, part admiration.

Smith resumed. "All right, Mr. Tarkington, another question. Can you establish your whereabouts last night and
early this morning? Particularly from around midnight to
six A.M."

"I was in my apartment, asleep. I have my own place for
now. My wife still lives in our home."

"Would you have any means of verifying this?"

"I'm afraid not. I wasn't sleeping with anybody that could
swear to my being at home, I'm sorry to say."

"Where is your apartment, Mr. Tarkington?"

"Prospect House, in Arlington."

"Self-service elevators, I suppose."

"Yes."

"How long have you lived there?"

"Almost six months."

"Is there some kind of reception desk in the lobby? One
that's manned all night?"

"Yes. I think I see what you're driving at. The night receptionist would have seen me going out."

"You keep your car there?"

"Yes."

"Parked outside or in a garage?"

"The garage." Tarkington's face fell, anticipating Smith's
next question.

"But you could go from your apartment to the garage
without anyone seeing you?"

"I suppose so. But I swear, I didn't go out last night or this
morning. Not until eight, when I left for my office."

"For the time being I'll take your word for that. Now
then, did you know Rebel Martin was pregnant?"

119

Tarkington's reaction, like Gilcannon's, was one of honest relief.

"Well," he said almost cheerfully as if the revelation automatically cleared him of all suspicion, "I certainly know *I* couldn't be the father."

"And on what do you base this firm conclusion?"

"We, uh, well, to put it bluntly, Rebel always made me take . . . precautions the few times we indulged in, ah, relations. At my age, it was something of a compliment."

"Always, Mr. Tarkington?"

"Those occasions were few enough to permit no lapse of memory," Tarkington assured him with a wistful kind of smile. "And believe me, nobody could forget such an occasion with Rebel."

"Did you and your wife have any children?"

"No, I'm sorry to say."

"May I ask why?"

"Valerie never wanted any."

Max asked, "Did Miss Martin tell you she was pregnant?"

"No, she didn't. It comes as a complete surprise."

"When did she tell you she wouldn't marry you?" Max pressed.

"Oh, not more than a couple of months after my separation."

"In other words, four months ago."

"That's right."

"But you kept seeing her."

"Yes, occasionally."

"When was the last time?"

"I met her at the airport last week. We went to dinner."

"And she said nothing, then or previously, about her being pregnant?"

"Absolutely nothing," Tarkington said, somewhat virtuously.

"There's a ray of sunshine in all this for you," McDermott said. "If someone hadn't bumped her off, you probably would have wound up supplying her with maternity clothes."

"I consider that an insult," Tarkington flared, with his first show of spirit.

"I'll apologize for my partner," Smith said wearily. "Mr. Tarkington, did the Martin girl ever try to blackmail you?"

Tarkington looked genuinely puzzled. "Why on earth should she blackmail me? I already told you how generous I've been."

"Well, speaking hypothetically, let's say she changed her mind about not marrying you. Let's say that after she found out she was pregnant, she told you it was your baby and you'd better marry her or else. Now you've said you and your wife were going back together. Or might. So the girl's pregnancy—again hypothetically, mind you—the girl's pregnancy could have spoiled all your reconciliation hopes. That's what I mean about blackmail."

"It wouldn't have been blackmail, lieutenant. If Rebel had told me I was the father of that baby, I would have married her the second my divorce became final."

"Very decent of you," Smith said wryly. "Especially since you had every reason to assume you couldn't have been the father."

"True," Tarkington admitted with a slight smile. "I suppose I would have spent the rest of my life wondering if I really *was* the father. But I don't think it would have made any difference. As God is my witness, I would have married her, even with, uh, certain doubts."

"Your attitude, under the circumstances, is commendable," Smith said caustically. "However, the self-sacrifice would have been unnecessary, inasmuch as Miss Martin had planned to marry one of Coastal's pilots." He searched Tarkington's face, as he had Gilcannon's, and was rewarded by the same look of momentary surprise.

"I would have been very happy for her," Tarkington said

121

with an obvious effort at sincerity. "I assume he was the father?"

"I wouldn't know," Smith said. "By the way, I'd like your wife's address and phone number."

Tarkington, unruffled by the abrupt change of subject, wrote the information down on the back of a business card, handing them to the detective with the admonition, "You might try calling her first, Lieutenant. She's usually out in the afternoon."

"Thanks, McDermott, let's go."

The detective and the pilot stopped off for a beer and to compare notes before proceeding to Smith's next interrogation target—Mrs. Tarkington, he had decided.

"Last one of a long day," he added. "We can resume first thing tomorrow morning. Pick you up at your place—River House, I think you told me."

"Yeah. By the way, when you got the autopsy report showing pregnancy, did you also get an approximate time of death?"

"About four A.M., give or take thirty minutes each way."

"From food decomposition."

"Right. Incidentally, the fingerprint boys struck out. They must have found thirty different sets of prints around that house. Most of them on dirty glasses, dirty dishes and dirty furniture. She was a lousy housekeeper."

"So I remember from my only visit. Maybe one set will turn into something."

"I doubt it. And I suppose you remember your police lessons; you can't get prints off human flesh."

"Maybe some nut did it," Max said doubtfully. "A burglar or mental case."

"Possible, but there isn't a bloody clue along those lines. No sign of any jewelry missing. She had about seventy-five bucks in a purse that was on her bedroom dresser in plain view. The coroner said there was no evidence of rape; she hadn't had intercourse within the previous twenty-four

122

hours, which for that babe must have been a minor miracle. Nope, it all points to someone she knew, someone she knew extremely well. Someone she brought into that house or let come in and stay long enough to strangle her at a very ungodly hour. I still got a hunch that her being pregnant is the key."

"That pregnancy business bugs me," Max said.

"Why? Girls get pregnant all the time."

"Not savvy girls, and Rebel was savvy. There's no excuse for an unwanted pregnancy in these days of the Pill. Anyone as promiscuous as Rebel would have known better. It doesn't make sense."

"It would make sense," Smith suggested, "if she wanted to get pregnant."

"Her wanting to wouldn't make sense. Add up the guys she was dating seriously. That ramp agent, Denham, is a young squirt who doesn't make enough to have kept someone like Rebel in cosmetics. Tarkington's not a very likely father and I think he was telling the truth about marrying Rebel if she asked him to. Gilcannon was just a sugar-daddy and he sure as hell wasn't any marriage prospect. Also, I'll bet that sterility operation will check out. Lindsay? Well, Rebel might have wanted to have his kid but you said she was three months gone and three months ago she didn't know Jim would marry her."

"Which still could point to blackmail as a murder motive. Not for dough, but for a marriage she might force a man into. Or make his life so miserable that the father would do anything to shut her up. She wasn't too far along for an abortion, by the way. Incidentally, do your stewardesses go to some kind of a company doctor? I'd like to know when she found out she was pregnant. There was the name of a Doctor Philbine on a bottle of prescribed medicine in her bathroom. I'll have to locate him."

"Philbine? Hell, that's Coastal's own doctor. He wouldn't do you much good. If he's the one who examined Rebel, she

123

would have been grounded five minutes after the examination. He'd have to report a pregnancy to her supervisor immediately."

"Meaning Mike Hunter."

"And Mike would have told you about it right off."

"Suppose the Martin kid didn't know she was pregnant."

"After three months? I doubt if she would have self-diagnosed it as an ulcer."

"You're right," Smith sighed. "Well, finish your beer and we'll go see Frau Tarkington."

"A wise choice," Max grinned. "At least you can't ask her if *she* was the father."

"At this point, I wouldn't be surprised at anything. I wouldn't even be surprised if *you* knocked that gal up. That would be funny as hell, McDermott—you turning out to be my best suspect."

"Like you said," McDermott agreed amiably, "nothing should surprise you. By the way, Lieutenant, my first name is Max."

The detective looked pleased, as if McDermott had paid him a compliment.

"My friends call me Smitty," said Robert Smith, holding out a pudgy hand.

A phone call established that Mrs. Lyle Tarkington was at home, willing, though obviously not eager to receive the police. The address was just off Foxhall Road, in an exclusive residential area. They battled gathering rush-hour traffic to get there, both speculating en route that Valerie Tarkington probably was a washed-out, discarded wife in her late forties or early fifties.

She turned out to be a tall, voluptuous, stunning woman with long black hair worn in a fashionable upsweep. Her legs would have made a chorus girl envious and there wasn't a wrinkle on her neck or face. Languid, with a throaty voice and the walk of a stalking panther—that was Tarkington's estranged wife and McDermott silently conceded that it would have taken a Rebel to give her any competition.

She welcomed them with an air of amused boredom, as if she thought they were boys playing at cops and robbers. Smith actually seemed in awe of her, accepting her offer of coffee eagerly, like a child invited in by a neighbor for a piece of cake.

"Very kind of you, ma'am," he said politely, when a uniformed maid put a steaming cup in front of him. Max, who gruffly spurned the coffee, half-expected him to drink it with one pinkie outstretched in the manner of a man being served high tea.

"You said on the phone you wanted to talk to me concern-

125

ing that murder I just read about in the *Star*. That stewardess."

"Yes, ma'am. We've already talked to your husband. He
knew her and . . ."

"Very well," she interrupted, her dark eyes flashing
anger. "The slut broke up our marriage."

"So we understand," the lieutenant said in what for him
was almost a tone of sympathy. "We also understand from
your husband there's a reconciliation in the offing."

"Lyle said that? He's being terribly optimistic. He asked
me to reconciliate, but I haven't made up my mind yet."

Smith coughed as he took too big a sip of the hot coffee,
apologized, and resumed his questioning. "You understand,
Mrs. Tarkington, we must ask some personal questions in
anything like a homicide case. Forgive my . . ."

"Perfectly all right, Lieutenant. A policeman's lot is not
a happy one, or something along those lines. Ask me whatever you want." Then, as Smith beamed pontifically, she
added, "And I'll decide whether I want to answer."

Her calm impertinence seemed to shake Smith loose
from his deference. Now he was himself again, inspecting
her from under those sleepy lids for a full thirty seconds, a
look so coldly critical that her own composure wavered
momentarily.

"Did you ever meet Miss Martin?"

"No."

"Do you know where she lived?"

"I haven't the foggiest. In an apartment, I suppose."

"Did your husband say he was in love with her?"

"In a disgustingly juvenile way, he implied as much."

"He asked you for a divorce or was it the other way
around?"

"The divorce was my idea. Lyle wanted to have his cake
and eat it, too, if you'll pardon an overworked cliché. He
had the idea he could still have me as his wife while he
played around with that whore as long as he wanted."

126

"Did he tell you he'd fight the divorce or any legal actions along those lines?"

"No. He said it was possible that a man could want two women, that he still loved me and had given me all the material things in life, and that we should be adult about the whole thing and give him time to get his paramour out of his system."

"I take it your reaction was not what you'd call sympathetic."

"You're goddamned right it wasn't sympathetic." The two men inadvertently started as the profanity spurted out of the regal mouth. "I told him I wasn't sharing a husband with anyone, least of all a flying prostitute."

Out of the corner of his eye, Smith saw McDermott's nostrils flare and he said hastily, "Now, we know all stewardesses aren't prostitutes, Mrs. Tarkington, so I don't think that remark was . . ."

"They are as far as I'm concerned. I've watched them flirt with male passengers and ignore all the women on board."

Max waded in, ignoring Smith's pleading look to curb his temper. "Your opinion of stewardesses in general is of absolutely no importance. Your opinion of Miss Martin is. You called her a flying prostitute. I take it your husband told you quite a bit about her—obviously her profession, for example, even her name."

"Lyle told me everything about her and about them. He apparently thought that complete honesty would soften my attitude. He confessed he was giving her clothes. He even told me when he had been to her house. He used to lie about it, at first, but when he came home stinking of cheap perfume and his mouth all chewed up by the damned nympho, then he had to openly admit the affair."

Smith's mouth was open but McDermott beat him to the punch. "You say he told you he had been to her *house.* How did you know she lived in a house? You said you assumed she lived in an apartment."

127

Mrs. Tarkington wasn't the least bit flustered. "Don't try to trap me, Mister. I used the word house simply as a place to live. Synonymous with apartment, if you insist on making a federal case out of a matter of pure semantics. Perhaps I should have said brothel; it would have been more appropriate." She examined her long, scarlet fingernails with an insolence that reminded McDermott of a spoiled Persian cat languidly preening itself.

Smith resumed. "You're quite sure you never met the victim, Mrs. Tarkington? You had no idea where she lived?"

"Quite sure, Lieutenant."

"Were you at home last night and early this morning—up to, say, six A.M.?"

"No, I wasn't."

"And where were you?"

"I suppose you insist on knowing."

"I do."

"I was screwing with a friend of mine. I won't give you his name." Her handsome, arrogant features were as deadpan as if she had told them she had been at a flower show.

"I'm afraid you may have to give us his name, Mrs. Tarkington."

"He'd be most embarrassed," she said with a low, throaty laugh.

"Not nearly as embarrassed as you if you don't supply the name."

"Very well. Harmon Downey."

"And where might we contact him?"

"He's a trial lawyer. He has offices in the National Press Building."

"Is Mr. Downey married?"

"None of your damned business. The only thing you have to know is whether I was with him, I assume, at the same time the murder was committed."

"Where were you and this Downey character conducting your assignation, Mrs. Tarkington?"

128

"I didn't know you detectives knew such big words, Lieutenant."

"Okay," Smith sighed. "Where were you screwing?"

"In the corner display window of Garfinckel's Department Store at 14th and F Streets," she said coolly.

Smith closed his notebook in a gesture of surrender and started to rise, but McDermott motioned him back. The pilot's heavy lips were compressed into an angry slit and the scar on his face was blood-red, like a fresh wound. Even the haughty Valerie Tarkington felt a throb of fear as he spoke, each word coated with contempt.

"Listen to me, you supercilious bitch, and listen carefully. A girl is dead, and how she died is of vastly more importance than how she lived. From now on, when an investigating officer asks you a question, you'd damned well better answer it straight and fast and never mind those smart-ass wisecracks. Once more: where did you shack up with Downey?"

"In his apartment," she answered, trying to sound defiant and succeeding only in sounding considerably meeker.

"Thank you," Max said. "Smitty, let's go, unless you've some more questions."

"Just a minute," Mrs. Tarkington said, her voice restored to a semblance of its former self-assurance. "I want you both to know I'm going to protest to your superiors about the way this man"—she nodded at McDermott—"talked to me. I'm still Lyle Tarkington's wife and he has considerable influence. No lousy, two-bit cop is going to call me a bitch."

"Supercilious bitch," Smith corrected her. "Feel free to protest, Mrs. Tarkington. I have a strong feeling you'll be wasting your valuable time."

Once outside the Tarkington's plush Georgian home, however, Max regretted losing his temper.

"She can't do anything to me," he told Smith while they

were driving back to the airport, "but a joker as loaded as Tarkington could raise hell with your brass."

"Forget it, Max," the lieutenant reassured him. "Frankly, you were a little out of line but she isn't going to cause me any trouble. I didn't insult her; you did. And my brass already has okayed your little part in all these shenanigans. Jesus, that's some dame. She's cool enough to commit murder. Tarkington must be out of his mind. I'd rather reconciliate with a piranha. Wonder where he got the guts to cheat on her in the first place."

"I seem to have read somewhere that a lot of men wind up cheating on over-domineering wives. It's a defense mechanism. Supposed to give a guy back his self-respect or even his manhood."

The detective chuckled. "I'll leave the Freudian angles to you. I'm more curious to have your reaction on that slip of the tongue she pulled."

"Her reference to Rebel's living in a house?"

"Yep. You jumped on that real fast. Think it was significant?"

Max rubbed the late afternoon bristle on his jaw. "Maybe. I wouldn't be surprised if she knew Rebel a hell of a lot better than she let on. She may have been to that house. She's the kind of woman who wouldn't be afraid to confront a mistress. But a murderess—. It doesn't add up, Smitty. For one thing, I doubt if she really cares enough about her husband to get him back via a murder route. I got the distinct impression she's enjoying herself, as that alibi would indicate. She's got friend Tarkington right where the hair is short; he's panting to come back now, and she's just toying with him. Talk about having your cake and eating it. If she goes ahead with a divorce, she'll take the poor bastard for everything but his underwear. And if she lets him come back, he won't dare leave for the bathroom without her permission."

"She's cold-blooded enough for that to be a motive,"

130

Smith mused. "Gets rid of the other woman and puts her husband down on his hands and knees. Speaking of the husband, how do you rate Tarkington as a suspect?"

"Not very high. No motive, for one thing."

"Unless you buy that blackmail theory I keep clinging to."

"You're really hooked on that," Max grumbled. "For one thing, you keep assuming the father and the killer are the same person. That's not necessarily true—in fact, there might not be any connection between her pregnancy and her death. Me, I'm more hooked on a jealousy motive. Somebody so ape over her, he goes off his rocker when she tells him she's gonna marry Jim Lindsay."

Smith shook his head. "From what you've told me, there's a good chance she never had time to break that news to the also-rans. Anyway, Gilcannon and Tarkington apparently didn't know about her marrying that pilot. They both seemed surprised."

"Surprise is a very easy emotion to fake. I've still got a hunch she told somebody, thereby signing her death warrant."

"Denham, maybe?"

"Maybe. You planning on talking to him tonight?"

Smith shook his head. "No. I've got to meet with the press back at headquarters and I'll have one of my boys see Denham. Incidentally, you'd better go along with me for that press briefing. That's what Belnap wanted you in the act for. Make sure I protect your airline's image."

McDermott scowled. "What are you going to tell them?"

"The usual crap. We're checking into a number of leads. We have very few real clues, which'll make me look like Sherlock Holmes if we crack it later. And no mention of the pregnancy."

"If you'll promise me you'll keep that last promise," Max said, "I think I'll go home."

Smith sighed in total weariness. "Might as well, Max. I'll

pick you up at eight tomorrow morning. Like to go out and talk to the Lindsays, the captain in particular."

The lieutenant arrived on schedule, greeting Max with a laconic "Hi" and wordlessly handing him, as he climbed into the car, a sheet of paper easily recognized as an informal investigative report. McDermott had filled out many of them himself, he remembered with an unexpected twinge of nostalgia. It had been laboriously typed with two fingers, if the quality of the typing was any indication, reminding Max of his own hunt-and-peck police colleagues who so typically hated filling out any forms other than applications for retirement.

"Report on Denham," Smith explained, and Max managed to read it despite Smith's rather jerky driving style; the detective operated an automobile as if he had a grudge against it.

Memo to Lt. Smith:

Subject's name Robert Denham, age 26, never been married. Employed by Coastal as ramp agent for 3½ yrs. Said knew victim very well, dated her frequently, that they planned to be married someday when his financial situation improved. Claimed deceased had no known enemies and was "very well liked by everyone." In very next breath described her as wonderful person who was misunderstood and that a lot of people were jealous of her. His demeanor was sad and he talked so low at times I had to ask him to repeat his answers. Said he and deceased never quarreled and had a "perfect relationship." Claimed he did not see her night of murder, that he went bowling with his regular team, watched tv when he got home, and went to sleep around 1:30 A.M. Said he watched most of a program called 'Night Gallery' and then the news and Dick Cavett. Gave me the plot of two episodes on 'Night

Gallery' and the names of three guest stars on the Cavett show. These checked out. Got huffy when he was asked if victim had any other boy friends. Admitted knowing she went out with older men she cared nothing about, and that he was one she loved. Got a bit dramatic and said he wanted to be left alone in room with killer when we found him. No tears shed, tho, and subject seemed composed tho naturally upset about murder. Denham's address, phone number and other data are in Martin file.

Gillespie, Sgt. APD.

McDermott handed the report back to Smith, who gave a quizzical side glance, apparently waiting for a comment. He got one. Max was staring straight ahead, his almost perpetual scowl creasing his battered features.

"I've got a nasty habit of reading between lines," McDermott said. "For example, did you get the impression from this report that Denham was putting on a phony act of sorrow?"

"Somewhat. That what you got out of it?"

"I did. Remember, I saw Lindsay come apart after they told him Rebel was dead. This Denham kid seemed to be hamming it up a bit for police benefit."

"Maybe he's not the type who cries easily."

"Neither is Jim Lindsay, but it didn't help him much. Hell, Smitty, I wouldn't be surprised if Rebel's death was a load off Denham's shoulders. She was way out of his strata. I don't buy his not knowing she had the moral code of a Gestapo agent. I'll bet what he feels right now is mostly a sense of relief. Not that he's happy she's dead, but that the murder ended a relationship he knew was hopeless and didn't have the courage to break off himself.

"Unless," Smith suggested quietly, "murder was his way of breaking it off."

"That's pure theory."

"Theory is all we have right now. But I could make a very

133

strong case for Denham's being our boy. Let's assume she could have pulled the proverbial wool over his eyes, but only up to a very recent point. Either he finds out Rebel's been making a fool of him or she gets around to telling him she's gonna marry a pilot. Either way, something could have snapped. Denham realizes he was being bled, lied to and hoodwinked by a tramp. Hell hath no fury like a man who finds out he's been a sucker. And that seems to describe our lovesick Mr. Denham. Sucker. You know something, Max; I wish I had known this Rebel. Women like that fascinate me. I hate 'em but they fascinate me. They can make a guy believe they're telling the truth even when he knows it's a lie, just because he wants to believe it. Take Lindsay. I may be naive, but I suppose an airline captain isn't exactly stupid or weak. Yet he lets himself get involved with a, a— well, I said it before—with a goddamned tramp. Tough to figure."

"Sex is pretty strong motivation." Max reminded him. "You saw Rebel dead. I saw her alive. Let me put it this way, Smitty: if you were investigating a murder and she was a prime suspect, all she would have needed was one of those 'let's go to bed' looks and you couldn't have asked her another question."

"I'm too old to be bothered by dames like that," Smith laughed.

"Nobody was too old for Rebel. She could have given Methuselah an erection."

They drove the rest of the way to the Lindsay home in relative silence, each occupied by his own thoughts, with conversation limited generally to McDermott's uncertain directions. Smith finally found the house despite the directions, prompting a comment to McDermott that "I hope you're better at navigating a plane than you are locating a simple address."

Lindsay himself came to the door, evidently unsurprised at their visit.

134

"I kind of expected to see you today," he said to McDermott as he invited them in. He gave Smith no more than a cursory glance and Max was convinced the captain knew he was a policeman even before they were introduced.

"Jim, this is Lieutenant Smith of the Alexandria police. He wants some information from you and he'd also like to talk to Norma briefly. Is she home?"

"She went to leave Debbie at the day nursery. Be back any minute. Lieutenant, where would you like to talk? Here in the living room or maybe my den would be more private."

"Living room's fine," Smith said.

They accepted Lindsay's almost pleading offer of coffee, McDermott silently noting the over-eager hospitality that afflicts the average citizen about to be questioned by the police. He sat next to Smith on the couch, facing Lindsay, and it seemed a million years ago that he had been there, holding Debbie on his lap. Smith's dry voice shattered his thoughts.

"Captain, I understand that you were in Chicago on the day prior to Miss Martin's murder. You stayed in Chicago that night and did not return to Washington until approximately four hours after the body was discovered."

"Correct," Jim said calmly. His eyes were tired and his face a bit drawn, but Max thought he had snapped back considerably from the previous morning.

"Do the pilots of each flight room together when they're out of town?"

"Negative. We have our own rooms."

"Where did you stay on this particular trip?"

"The O'Hare Inn. That's where our crews always stay."

"Would you mind giving me a rundown on what you did in Chicago that night? Have dinner with anybody?"

"Max and I ate together, at the Inn. I suppose you'd like the rest of our timetable."

Smith nodded.

"We finished dinner about eight and talked for God knows how long. I had trouble falling asleep and took a mild sedative; it must have been around midnight. I conked out —well, maybe about an hour later. That's all I can tell you. I met Max in the lobby the next morning and we flew back to Washington." He swallowed hard in his first show of emotion. "I heard about Rebel right after we landed."

"McDermott here tells me you were pretty shaken. You should also know he's considered part of the investigation. He's given me considerable information on Miss Martin and the people she knew best. Including yourself. I don't want you to think harshly of him for violating any confidences."

Lindsay's response was stiff. "I never would. It was me who suggested he might be of some help to the police."

"Good. Then I don't suppose you'd mind confirming some of the things I've been told about you and Miss Martin. You were in love with each other and you intended to divorce your wife so you could be married."

"That's right." For some reason, Jim avoided McDermott's eyes and stared directly at the detective.

"Your wife was aware of all this?"

"She was."

"Are you still planning to get a divorce, in view of what's happened?"

"I don't know. I honestly don't. We talked a little about it last night, but both of us were too upset to reach any decision. Norma, my wife, has been absolutely splendid. Any other woman would have sent me packing by now and I would have deserved it. I can't answer your question right now. I hope Norma and I can work things out, at least for the children's sake."

"Captain Lindsay, you'll have to forgive my frankness. As I must tell any apparent principal in a murder case, there's no room for delicacy or tact. Did you decide to marry Miss Martin because she was pregnant, presumably by you?"

136

Lindsay's jaw hinged open like the bottom of a steam shovel.

"I didn't know she was pregnant," he said hoarsely. "Now . . . where did you?"

"The autopsy disclosed she was about three months pregnant. You didn't know that? She didn't tell you?"

The look of abject misery that had been on the pilot's face the day before had returned, so starkly that his whole body seemed to shrivel. "She never told me. I had no idea. That poor, poor kid."

"When did you tell Miss Martin you were getting a divorce and that you'd be free to marry her?"

"About a week ago. Six days, to be exact." Jim's voice was two octaves lower than when the questioning started. "We were in Salt Lake City on a layover. I told her then that Norma had agreed to a divorce. I reminded her that the settlement terms would be stiff because of the kids, but that if we loved each other we could make a go of it. She cried, but it was a happy kind of crying. Now, I wonder if it was crying out of relief. I guess she never dared tell me about . . . about having a baby. Not while she wasn't sure I could marry her. I don't know why she didn't tell me that night."

"Perhaps I can suggest a reason. But you might not enjoy hearing it."

"I wish you would."

"Maybe she didn't want to tell you because she wasn't sure you were the father."

Smith might have punched Lindsay in the mouth. Max saw the pilot's jaw muscles tighten in that curious reflex of his. But Lindsay had his own brand of courage under this fresh stress.

"That is very possible," the captain said quietly. "I suppose that's the only logical explanation. But she should have known it wouldn't have made one bit of difference. It could have been my kid. God knows, I still would have married her."

137

Smith heaved an incredulous sigh. "And yet you also knew it could have been someone else's. You're being quite noble, Captain. After the fact, of course."

McDermott could not squash a stab of resentment at Smith's nastiness, but Lindsay's response never came close to a rebuke. "I think you're confusing honor with nobility, Lieutenant. I wouldn't have put a girl I loved through the embarrassment of blood tests to determine fatherhood. I would have accepted that responsibility myself, inasmuch as there was a very good chance I was the father."

"Are you telling me you didn't give a hoot that she slept with other men?"

"I cared a lot. I'm only human. But I had to look at it from her standpoint. I've told Max all this. Just two nights ago I explained it to him. She loved me but I was married. So I had no right to insist on her fidelity. She knew I had to go home to a family and to a marital bed. She knew I didn't stop having relations with my wife. She was a very proud, independent girl and I'm completely convinced that in her own mind she wasn't cheating on me. She would get lonely and pretty discouraged about our future, and she drank. Probably too much, at times. Under all these circumstances, she ran around, I repeat, ran around; I didn't say sneak around. That's to her credit, Lieutenant. She never lied to me. I think the fact that she didn't tell me about the baby is proof that she loved me. She could have beat me over the head with that pregnancy and forced me into a nasty divorce. No, it makes a great deal of sense that she wouldn't or couldn't tell me right away. And I love her all the more for that."

In spite of himself, Max felt like applauding. Even the dour Smith relented.

"That crack I made about being noble, Captain," he said with a grudging kind of grace, "I apologize. But damned if you're not."

Lindsay said nothing, and Smith resumed.

138

"Again, I must ask you to put up with some intimate questions. When you had intercourse with Miss Martin, didn't you take any precautions against pregnancy?"

"I assumed it wasn't necessary. Rebel told me she took birth control pills. I never doubted her word. I know some girls get careless about pill schedules and I suppose she did, particularly if she was drinking heavily."

Max interjected, "Jim, mind if I ask you something?"

"Of course not."

"Do you know if Rebel told anyone about your getting married?"

Lindsay rubbed his jaw thoughtfully before answering. "I doubt it."

"Why? After all that waiting, she'd be ready to include it in her cabin PA. She'd certainly tell other stewardesses. And maybe some of the other guys she's been dating. In the latter case, to break things off and burn those bridges behind her."

"I asked her not to say anything to anyone, for the time being. Not until Norma and I were officially separated."

"But you're not sure she kept quiet, are you? Hell, Jim, a newly-engaged female looks around for the nearest megaphone."

"No, I'm not sure. But she knew how I felt. I wasn't proud of the affair. It was bad enough with the whole damned airline knowing about us. I didn't want the gossip vultures feeding on the separation or divorce bit—not until it actually happened."

"And you told her this?"

"In no uncertain terms. She promised not to say anything to anybody."

"Well," McDermott snapped, "she didn't keep her promise."

Lindsay flushed. "How do you know she didn't?"

"Mike Hunter knew you were marrying Rebel. She told me, just before she took you home."

"She was guessing," Lindsay said weakly. "Just guessing. She heard some rumors and . . ."

"Bullshit. If you didn't tell Mike, Rebel must have. And if Rebel told one person, she probably told others, including the sonofabitch who strangled her."

Smith broke in, rather testily. "Just a minute, Max. Let's keep the theorizing between ourselves."

Max ignored him. "Quit kidding yourself, Jim. Just think back to yesterday morning, chum. In Operations. You were getting drowned in sympathy. I saw two stews crying and they weren't shedding tears for Rebel; they were looking at you. Every man and woman in that room felt for you—as a man who lost a fiancee, not just a friend. In other words, your plans to marry Rebel were no secret and I'd sure as hell would like to know who took the news so hard, they went off their rocker."

Lindsay looked sick. "You think somebody killed her out of jealousy?" Because we were going to be married?"

Smith snorted. "That's McDermott's theory, but he's a long way from . . ." Whatever he was about to say was never finished, because at this moment they heard a car pull into the driveway and a few seconds later, Norma Lindsay entered, sad-eyed, her face drawn. McDermott could not decide whether she was composed or merely listless as Lindsay performed the perfunctory introductions and then left her to wait in his den.

Smith questioned her with almost courtly gentleness and tact, as if he were afraid the slightest harsh remark would jostle her into hysterics. Whether from the lieutenant's delicacy or her own inner strength, she remained calm as she confirmed what her husband already had told them. Yes, she had agreed to a divorce. No, it was too early for reaching any conclusions about changing those plans. Yes, she had known about Rebel for some time but up until a week ago she had hoped for the sake of the children that Jim eventually would give up Rebel. Naturally, she was home with

140

Kevin and Debbie when the murder was committed. "Where else would I be?" she said disdainfully.

"One last question, Mrs. Lindsay," Smith concluded. "Did you hold any resentment against Miss Martin?"

Her answer was unemotional in tone, but Max sensed the spleen that poisoned every word. "I hated her. What wife wouldn't? With all the eligible men around, she picks a happily married man with a family as her target. Jim didn't have a chance. And, as it turned out, neither did I."

"You seem to put most of the blame on her and not your husband," Smith remarked.

Norma Lindsay smiled sadly. "Most men are weak where fidelity is concerned, while most women are strong. Of course I blame Jim to some extent. But I also have sympathy for him and a certain understanding of what he's been going through. I have none for Rebel Martin—not even now, when she's dead."

"You're a remarkable woman, Mrs. Lindsay," Smith said with enormous sincerity. "And, in spite of what happened, I've got to admit Captain Lindsay is a remarkable man."

"I know that. That's why I think . . . I hope we can stay together." Her eyes moistened and her mouth quivered. "Although it will never be like it was."

Smith snapped shut his ubiquitous notebook. He dreaded a woman's tears, and what made the atmosphere even more uncomfortable, as he confided to McDermott as they left that troubled home, was his admiration for Norma Lindsay.

"She's a rarity, a lady with both guts and compassion," the lieutenant said.

"Also a capacity for unadulterated hate," Max observed.

"How the hell do you expect her to feel about that Martin broad—grateful?"

"Nope, but I'm thinking you could add her to the distaff list of suspects, if you buy insane hate as a motive."

"She's about as insane as I am," Smith said. "Speaking of this distaff side, how's about a run to the airport?"

"Sure. Who'd you like to talk to?"

"I'd like to see this Mike person. Mike Hunter—that the name?" Max nodded. "Thought I'd sound her out on anything she might have heard from her stewardesses."

McDermott grinned, albeit doubtfully. "Okay, but all you'll get from Mike's girls is what you've been hearing since the murder: Rebel knew a hell of a lot of females who aren't wearing mourning bands."

Max was wrong. Smith got more than that from Michelle Hunter. He got two more suspects.

Mike made an instant impression on the tough old detective, although McDermott was not quite sure in what direction.

They walked into her office just at the moment she was on the telephone, conning some Coastal official into a newer typewriter for her secretary.

"Thanks, Luther," she was bellowing into the mouthpiece as they entered. "You'll get your reward in Heaven because I'm not about to give it to you in bed." Smith looked a little bewildered.

No introductions were necessary; the lieutenant and the stewardess supervisor had met in Rebel's apartment the morning of the murder. Smith and McDermott sat down in a couple of shabby, nondescript chairs and out came the detective's notebook.

"Miss Hunter," he began, "I . . ."

"Call me Mike," she beamed. "Everyone else does."

"I don't like to get too informal during an interrogation," he said in a mildly rebuking tone. "Now then, Miss Hunter, I was hoping we could pick your brain, so to speak, about any possible enemies Miss Martin might have had among your stewardesses."

"For God's sake," Mike protested, "are you telling me she was killed by a woman?"

"It's very possible. I don't see any harm in telling you that the autopsy showed an alcohol content in her blood level which added up to extreme intoxication. In other words, she was stoned, smashed and bombed. Which, in turn, means her killer could have been a woman. That's why I'd like to know if she had any real enemies among her flying associates."

"There are one hundred and twenty-five girls at this base," Mike said cautiously. "I doubt if you could call any of that one hundred and twenty-five Rebel's friend, but I wouldn't class a single one as an enemy. Not enough to commit murder. That includes me."

The shaggy eyebrows went up to half-mast. "Oh? You didn't like the deceased either?"

"I sure as hell didn't. I'm sorry she's dead, but don't list me among the mourners."

"How many of your girls would you say disliked Miss Martin with your apparent intensity?"

"Four or five, I suppose. Maybe more. Those who had legitimate reasons for jealousy."

"And what would you say was a legitimate reason for jealousy?"

Mike Hunter lit a cigarette, and both men saw her hands tremble almost imperceptibly as she groped for words that would be informative without being too incriminating. It was as if she were tiptoeing through her vocabulary. "Rebel had a habit of moving in on . . . on somebody else's property. She seemed to take special delight in dating guys who were supposed to be serious about another stew. Then she'd drop the bastard like he had a social disease. I saw enough female tears shed in this office to refloat the *Titanic*. Among the tears shed were my own, but I couldn't call Rebel in and lower the boom. I've got this thing about conducting vendettas for personal reasons. I'd have given three months' pay to catch Rebel in some rules violation, but the stuff she pulled was never a no-no in a stewardess manual."

143

"I take it," Smith said, "that you were one of her so-called victims."

Tears welled up in Mike's brown eyes. And she swallowed hard before she spoke. "I'm a thirty-two-year-old spinster. Never even wanted to get married. Up until about eighteen months ago. Then I met a man. A widower who ran a couple of gift shops. Hell of a wonderful person. We started dating and I flipped my wig. He asked me to marry him and I accepted. It was about this time that Rebel walked in here one night while my guy was waiting for me to finish work so we could go out to dinner. She wanted a pass or something, I don't remember exactly. But I do remember she seemed blue and lonely and I wound up asking her to join us."

"And she did," Smith said with an air of sympathy. "This providing the equivalent of a tiger being invited to join a herd of innocent deer."

"Tiger is right. She ate my guy up alive. He hardly looked at me the whole evening. After dinner, we drove Rebel home first and then back to my apartment. My guy begged off coming up, said he had a headache. When he kissed me goodnight, I might as well have been kissing a fag just going through the notions. I started drinking and the more I drank, the madder I got. I finally went downstairs, got in my car and drove over to Rebel's house. I listened outside her door. I knew she was with some man. I could hear . . . sounds. I knocked on her door. She finally opened it. She was wearing just a robe, nothing underneath. Tried to get rid of me, said she had company, but I pushed the door open, shoved her aside and walked in where I could see her living room. There was my guy, sitting on the couch, in his underwear. His face was smeared with so much lipstick, he looked like he was bleeding. They both started to stammer out some kind of inane apologies but I turned right around and left. That was the last time I ever spoke to him. It also was the last time I ever saw him."

144

"I'm sorry to open old wounds," Smith said, "but we might want to talk to this man. Could I have his name?"

The tears glistened brighter but the voice was still steady, although lower. "It won't do you any good. He died of a heart attack a couple of months later. I always thought that bitch screwed him to death."

Smith cleared his throat—nervously, McDermott thought. "Miss Hunter, as you know, Miss Martin was killed between three-thirty and four-thirty A.M. yesterday. Were you home at the time?"

"Home in bed, alone, as usual."

"Could anyone verify that?" Smith sounded almost eager to have Mike supply an alibi, but she shook her head.

"I guess I'm a suspect," she said with no trace of rancor or fear. "I didn't kill her. I'd swear that on a Bible but I don't suppose that's good enough."

"Kind of wish it were," the lieutenant said unhappily. "If the status of suspect frightens you, it may help to know you're getting one hell of a lot of company. Look, you said there were four or five other girls in sort of the same boat as you. The ones whose guys she moved in on. I'd appreciate their names."

The supervisor thought for a moment, chewing on a pencil stub and managing to look like a little girl as she did. "Four's all I can think of offhand, but three of them aren't here anymore. Diane Porter transferred to LA over a year ago. Karen James is based in San Francisco. Let's see, I think Barbara Norgard got married about six months after Rebel broke up her engagement to another guy. She lives in Phoenix and has two kids. I can think of only one who's still flying and is based here."

"And her name?"

"She couldn't kill a sick ant," Mike assured him.

"Her name?"

"Betty Roberts."

McDermott silently hoped his face didn't betray concern

although he tended to agree with Mike's appraisal of Miss Roberts' homicidal potentiality.

"Before I leave, I'd like her home address and phone number," Smith was saying. "Also, would you happen to know the name of Miss Martin's personal physician?"

"No," Mike said. "I can ask around. Some of the girls might know. Or maybe she left the name around her house somewhere."

"Nothing like that in her effects," Smith said. "We'll have to keep looking. Miss Hunter, frankly I'm trying to locate her doctor, if she had one, because the autopsy showed she was three months pregnant."

"Whew!" Mike blurted. "Finding the father might be tougher than finding the murderer."

"They could be the same," Smith said as he avoided McDermott's eyes. "Do you think your airline doctor might have examined her recently?"

"He'd have to report a pregnancy to me immediately. I've had no such word from Doctor Philbine."

"So Captain McDermott told me. But is it possible Doctor Philbine might know what physician Miss Martin was going to on the outside?"

"Could be. Let's ask him." She got Philbine on the phone and was told promptly that the airline doctor had no idea whom Rebel might have consulted medically.

"I guess that's about all for now," Smith said. He started to rise but McDermott stopped him.

"Mike," Max asked, "when you drove Lindsay home yesterday, how did he act when he saw his wife? And how did she take the news?"

"I wouldn't know," the supervisor replied. "He thanked me for driving him home and said he wanted to see his wife alone. So I left."

"Dammit," McDermott scolded, "I told you I wanted to know their reactions. That's why I asked you to drive him home and see in the first place."

146

Mike was nettled. "What the hell was I supposed to do—carry him up his front sidewalk? He didn't invite me in and I have this little hang-up about going in where I'm not wanted."

"Okay, okay," McDermott sighed. "It wasn't your fault."

Smith was curious. "Why'd you want to know how they acted, Max?"

McDermott's brows furrowed. "Smitty, I'm not quite sure. Maybe subconscious suspicion about the grief a man shows in a murder case. I guess the cop in me wasn't as dormant as I thought."

"Jim walked up that sidewalk toward his house like a man being led to his execution," Mike recalled. "If that was an act, he deserved the Academy Award."

Smith closed his notebook, thanked Mike Hunter, and suggested a Snake Pit cup of coffee to Max.

"That Hunter dame—she's more my type than the Rebel Martins," the lieutenant said with an air of over-the-hill wistfulness as he sipped the brew. "If she ever confessed bumping off that girl, I'd swear I'd testify it was justifiable homicide. Then I'd turn in my badge and try selling insurance or something."

"Nice gal, Mike," Max agreed. "Incidentally, so is that Roberts kid she mentioned. I can't see her as a murderess."

"At this point," Smith sighed, "I'd be willing to question old Belnap himself. You know the Roberts girl?"

"Yep."

"Well?"

"Fairly well."

"Think it would do any good to talk to her?"

"I doubt it. But don't take my word for it."

"I won't. I won't even take your word for Captain Lindsay. For example, I've got a man checking at the phone company. Finding out if any calls to the Martin house were made from Chicago the night of the murder."

McDermott was startled. "From Chicago?"

147

Smith eyed the check pilot amusedly. "Yeah, from Chicago. Because I'd like to know if your undaunted captain might have been making sure the Martin girl was going to be home all night just in case he dropped in."

"Where the hell do you think Chicago is, Smitty—across the Potomac?"

"I know where it is. About seven hundred miles away. Also, only about ninety minutes away by air. You may be a great pilot, but you're a bit rusty as a cop. What I want from you is a list of flight schedules covering every airline that operates between Washington and Chicago."

"I think you're nuts," McDermott said.

"Probably, but I still think it was very possible for Captain James Lindsay to have flown back to Washington that same night, commit the murder, and return to Chicago in time to take out his own trip."

McDermott borrowed an *Airline Guide* from Operations and took it back to the Snake Pit, where Smith was waiting. The detective shook his head sorrowfully as soon as Max opened the thick volume, with its small type and voluminous symbols, abbreviations and codes.

"It's pure Greek," he mourned. "I'll leave it up to you. Look for two things—a flight that leaves Chicago for Washington after eleven P.M., when Lindsay says he went to bed, and whether there's a flight out of Washington that would put him back to O'Hare in time to meet you in the lobby of the motel at eight A.M."

"Coastal doesn't have anything matching that timetable," McDermott said. "I know that ORD-DCA schedule by heart."

"And what's 'ORD-DCA' mean?"

"ORD is the airline code for O'Hare. DCA is Washington National. IAD would be Dulles. BAL is Baltimore's Friendship Airport."

"Why ORD? I'd think OHA would be more logical. And IAD for Dulles—it's ass backwards."

Max explained, with an unintentioned air of superiority. One seldom gets a chance to feel superior to a police officer. "ORD is the abbreviation for Orchard. I think Orchard was the name of the farm on which O'Hare was built. Dulles used to be DIA, for Dulles International, but the FAA found out there was another airport somewhere overseas that

149

used DIA for a symbol, so they just changed the letters around. I'd like to have a buck for every DIA baggage tag the airlines had to throw away when they changed the code."

"Dammit," Smith frowned, "we'll have to check all three airports—National, Dulles and Friendship. Although maybe we could skip Baltimore. It would be too long a drive from Friendship to Alexandria."

"We probably could skip Dulles, too," Max suggested. "Lindsay parks his car at National. Our Washington-based crews don't fly trips out of Dulles."

"So, if he flew back from Chicago to see his girl friend, he'd use his own car to get to her house. With a taxi or a rental car, there'd be too much chance of identification. Okay, what other airlines besides Coastal are possibilities?"

McDermott was perusing the *Guide,* squinting at its tiny type. "I think we've got something, Smitty. United has a Chicago-Washington 727 trip at twelve-forty-five A.M. Last of the night. Arrives National at three-fifteen A.M."

"Yeah. It's twelve-forty-five Central and three-fifteen Eastern."

"That three-fifteen would get him into Washington in plenty of time to go calling on Miss Martin. How about a return trip?"

"For Christ's sake," Max protested, "you've got him indicted already. You're going on nothing but . . ."

"Keep your pants on," Smith said placidly. "I'm not saying Lindsay pulled this off. I'm just trying to see if he could have. Look for a flight that would get him back to the motel by eight."

McDermott returned to the *Guide* and immediately spotted a line of type that fascinated him in spite of himself. "Here it is—and the only one. American has a 727 trip leaving National at six-thirty A.M. That's only five-thirty

150

Chicago time. Arrives O'Hare—let's see, I need a damned magnifying glass for this stuff—arrives O'Hare at seven-ten A.M. Which gives him forty minutes to get from the terminal to the O'Hare Inn by eight. It's a great theory, Smitty. But it stinks."

"Why does it stink? Because Lindsay's a fellow airline pilot? Because you can't visualize another captain involved in a murder case?"

"No," Max snapped. "Because it has more holes than a ping-pong net. Starting with the biggest hole of all, he'd be leaving himself wide open for identification by a regiment of witnesses. Ticket agents. The stewardesses on both flights. The driver of the courtesy bus that the motel runs to the airport."

"Well, that's a point," Smith acknowledged. "Do you guys wear your uniforms on layovers, like when you go out to dinner?"

"Not usually. It's customary to bring a business suit along in case we want a beer or a couple of drinks. A pilot caught drinking in uniform would be crucified."

"Did Lindsay wear his uniform when you went out to eat that night?"

"No, he wore a suit. So did I."

"I figured he'd need to be out of uniform if he wanted to get by potential witnesses unnoticed. You wouldn't happen to have a picture of him, would you?"

"Personnel would. Maybe public relations. Are you . . .?"

"Yep, I am." Smith answered the question before it was asked. "I'm going to have some prints made and shoot them out to Chicago. My Windy City compatriots can show them to whatever persons might have come in contact with Lindsay on either of those two flights. We can do the same thing here. And take that dying-cow-in-a-thunderstorm look off your ugly puss. I gather you still detect an unpleasant odor from my theory."

151

"Hole number two," Max enunciated. "The timing is too tricky and too dangerous. He'd have to be crazy to take the chances involved. One little mechanical delay, a weather problem, maybe a hangup by air traffic control—his whole timetable's shot to hell. Everything would hinge on both flights departing and arriving on schedule, which in the airline business is a very risky assumption."

"It will be very easy to check out both flights for the morning in question," Smith reminded him. "The weather was very good that day. I'll bet they were on time."

Max ignored him. "Hole number three. You know we had dinner in Chicago that night. Well, we both went to our rooms right after we had that long talk about Rebel. Lindsay called me around midnight. He wanted me to go to the bar and have a beer. Said he couldn't sleep and wanted to talk some more. He was all wound up about Rebel and his divorce plans."

"You interest me. Proceed."

"I bowed out. I was too sleepy. He said he understood and apologized for waking me. So let me ask you something, Smitty: would a guy planning to sneak back to Washington to commit a murder on a split-second schedule, a schedule that would give him a perfect alibi, would such a guy bother to invite me down to a bar only forty-five minutes before the last flight he could take to make his alibi work?"

"Hmmm," Smith said.

"The hell he would. He had absolutely no way of knowing I wouldn't accept. I could have said yes as easily as I said no, and there would have gone his whole scheme."

"Well," Smith began tentatively.

"Hole number four. Also five. He's an airline pilot, not a damned actor. His grief was real. And his wife confirmed the divorce story. Can you still be serious about suspecting Lindsay?"

152

"Not very," the lieutenant said. "But I'm still going to send out his picture."

Rebel Martin's funeral was the next day and the elements, as they so often will, contributed to the inevitable gloom of burial services. It rained, not heavily, but in a cold, steady drizzle that reminded Max of something he had once read: rain at a funeral is God's own tears.

A half-dozen stewardesses were there, led by Mike Hunter, who had made the funeral arrangements after talking to Rebel's aunt in Pittsburgh. The relative decided not to come after Mike informed her Rebel had no life insurance as such; a policy with the airline paid off only if she had been killed in a crash.

Coastal paid the funeral bill. Typically, Mike had taken up a collection among the stewardesses for flowers and the pilots chipped in for a wreath of their own. There also was a large spray from Jim Lindsay, who came to the funeral alone, wearing sun glasses despite the dark, dreary day. Bob Denham was there, solemn-faced but, as McDermott carefully observed, displaying no sign of outward grief. Most of the pilots who showed up clustered around Lindsay as if they hoped their proximity would give him strength. The stewardesses present looked properly sorrowful although, as Max found out later, Mike virtually had ordered their reluctant presence. One was Betty Roberts.

And then there was Lieutenant Robert Smith, strangely dignified and even dapper in a freshly-pressed blue suit that showed through a battered raincoat from which two buttons were missing. He sat next to McDermott at the brief church service, nudging him as the minister, who didn't know Rebel from Raquel Welch, intoned that "The Lord's will has taken from us a friend and flying colleague, unfortunately in the prime of her so useful, helpful and honorable Christian life."

"Didn't anybody brief the padre?" Smith whispered.

"Most eulogies are fiction," Max whispered back. "At my funeral, they'll probably tell how even-tempered I was."

The detective and the check captain stood together at graveside, Smith's sleepy eyes peering at the circle of mourners as if trying to spot some sign of giveaway behavior.

"Which one's Denham?" he muttered, and Max pointed to the young man whose handsome face was frozen into what he apparently hoped was unmitigated sadness but which managed to convey only an expression of grimness.

The last prayer was uttered and Max, the lieutenant waddling behind him, stopped enroute to his car to talk to Mike Hunter.

"For someone who bore no love for the deceased," McDermott observed, "you sure took a lot on your shoulders."

Mike nodded at Smith. "Someone had to do it," she said quietly. "I didn't want Jim Lindsay to see her buried as if she had no friends."

"It was very decent of you, Miss Hunter," the lieutenant put in. He started to say something else, but at this moment Lindsay walked up to them and kissed Mike on the cheek.

"Mike, I understand you made all these arrangements for Rebel. I'm not much for words, but I want you to know I'll never forget this. I know you didn't like her, so I'm doubly grateful."

For once in her life, Mike couldn't propel even one word out of her mouth. She nodded rather awkwardly and Jim, hesitating momentarily as if he wanted to say more to her, finally turned to McDermott. "Thanks for coming to say goodbye to her, Max. You, too, lieutenant." He paused again, looking at each of their faces. "Well, I . . . I guess I'd better get home."

He strode away, shoulders slumped, a sight uncomfortably reminding Max of that first layover in Chicago when the check captain had watched Lindsay walk so slowly, dejectedly, down the motel corridor.

"Poor guy," Mike said.

"Yeah," Smith said in a tone that somehow inserted a touch of cynicism into agreement. "Max, how about leaving your car at the airport and driving a couple of places with me?"

"Sure, where we going?"

Smith gave Mike Hunter a sorry-but-this-isn't-for-your-ears look and she took the hint. "So long, Max. Lieutenant. Let me know if . . . if you find out anything." She reverted to her old saucy self. "Or don't you confide in suspects, Lieutenant?"

"I'll make an exception in your case," Smith said with rare gallantry. He watched her tall, lithe figure as she walked away toward her car. Max chuckled.

"You could always ask her to dinner and question her further," he said archly.

"Go to hell. I'm old enough to be her father. Max, I've arranged to see that Denham boy at his apartment. It's his day off. But first, I want to stop at the Martin house. Thought you'd like to tag along."

"I would. What's cooking at Rebel's house?"

"I've got two men over there trying to find the name of the doctor who might have told her she was pregnant. There has to be some scrap of paper around. Maybe some odds and ends of phone numbers she wrote down, numbers we could check out. The prescription labels were a dead end; they're all from that Doctor Philbine."

Max was puzzled. "What could a doctor tell you, except that he examined her and told her she was going to have a baby?"

155

Smith glanced at him with that look of hopeless resignation all veteran cops bestow on colleagues who ask stupid questions—the same look, McDermott ruefully confessed to himself, that Max often gave young copilots who asked stupid questions.

"Maybe," Smith said, "she told him the name of the father."

"Not likely," Max argued. "A girl in her spot wouldn't volunteer that information even to a doctor. It's none of his business and no reputable physician would even ask."

"True. But the departed was a very unusual person. God knows what information she might have volunteered. To anybody. That's what makes this such a lousy mess."

Smith's two subordinates had pretty well torn Rebel's house apart by the time they arrived.

"She wasn't much of a note-writer," one of them grumbled to the lieutenant. "We've been through every drawer in the damned place. No sign of a stray number. We looked through that little pocket phone directory again, the one we found in her airline purse. Every name and number in there was a stewardess, pilot or some other person with Coastal. Her hairdresser. A few stores. That's it. She must have used the regular phonebook whenever she wanted to call somebody whose number she didn't know, and she apparently never wrote it down again for future reference. There's no use checking the phonebook. There must be three thousand doctors in Northern Virginia alone, assuming she went to a doctor in Virginia."

"We wouldn't have to check all doctors," Smith said. "Just obstetricians."

An inspiration hit McDermott. "Wait a minute, Smitty. She may have marked up the regular telephone directory. Put marks by numbers she used and couldn't remember. Didn't you ever do that? When you're too lazy or busy to transcribe a number, you make a little mark by the name, in the directory itself. Or you circle or underline the number. I do it myself all the time."

"Get the phone book," Smith ordered. "We'll check *physicians* in the yellow section."

On the third page, under physicians, they found it. Rebel had circled the name of "Dr. John Decker, gynecologist." Smith scribbled down the address and phone number, bestowing on McDermott a look bordering on fraternal affection.

"I keep thinking, Max, you're a better cop than you are a pilot," he remarked. "Come on. We'll go see this Decker."

"What about Denham?"

"He's been ordered to stay home all day. We can drop in on him anytime."

Max actually was glad to get out of the house. While they were sitting in Rebel's cluttered living room, pawing through the phone directory, he had the uneasy feeling he could hear her husky voice and smell her perfume, the memory of the latter even stronger than the musty odor that seemed to have been sprayed into this place of death.

Dr. John Decker turned out to be a slender, graying man with a brusque manner but a quick, pleasant smile. Smith had phoned him to make sure they could see him that same day. The doctor at first had pleaded a waiting room full of patients but instantly relented when the detective mentioned, "It's about that stewardess murder case."

Now they were in his private consultation room, the doctor sitting behind an old but magnificent oak desk and lighting a pipe. "As I told you on the phone, Lieutenant, I don't have any patient named Rebel Martin. I assume you think the girl came to see me under a fictitious name."

"Right. She had circled your name on the phone book."

The doctor nodded. "If she wasn't married, the chances

are good she wouldn't have given me her real name. Would you happen to have a photograph with you? I saw the one in the newspapers. She looked vaguely familiar but I couldn't swear it was the girl I'm thinking about."

Smith handed him an eight-by-ten glossy he had taken from Rebel's personnel file. It took Decker only a minute to bob his head in rueful recognition.

"That's her," he said. "I'll get her folder."

The doctor returned, carrying a brown manila medical file which he opened and examined briefly. "The name she gave me was Mrs. Ruth Marvin. She said she had missed a period and believed she was pregnant. I gave her a thorough examination and told her she was right."

"You sure as hell were," Smith said. "The autopsy showed a fetus about three months old. Did she display any emotion? Was she perturbed or upset? Any tears?"

"She didn't bat an eyelash," Decker said. "I'm afraid I made the usual polite remark about hoping her husband will be happy with the news. The minute I said it, I felt like a fool. I don't know why, but I just had the feeling right from the start that she wasn't married. She didn't gush or babble like the usual young wife who thinks she's going to have a baby. In fact, she didn't say a word through the whole examination. Rather cold-blooded about it, I thought."

"When you mentioned her husband, what was her reaction?"

"A very curious reaction. I think I remember her exact words. She said something like, 'Thank you, Doctor, but I don't think he'll be very happy about this. I am, but he won't be.' She smiled when she said it, but there wasn't any humor in that smile."

"What was the date you saw her?"

Decker glanced back at the folder. "Seven weeks ago, yesterday."

"Tell me, Doctor, isn't it unusual for a woman to assume

158

pregnancy after missing only one period? I'm no expert on the subject, but I thought you couldn't really tell for a couple of months."

"Normally, yes. Yet I've known some women to sense pregnancy immediately after conception. It's an almost mystic kind of intuition. I might add, Lieutenant, in most cases I wouldn't tell a patient she was definitely pregnant on the basis of missing only one menstrual cycle, even if the tests showed positive. This girl, however, had every pregnancy symptom known to medicine. Some morning sickness, starting a few days after her period became overdue. Breasts very tender. Definite pelvic swelling. Plus the fact that while I was taking her medical history, she told me that her cycles were extremely regular—every twenty-eight days—and always had been. Actually, she came to me because she was one week late on what would have been her next period. Because of this past history, and the examination itself, it was my best medical judgment that she was indeed pregnant and I decided to tell her right then."

McDermott asked, "Had she been your patient for long?"

"The day of her appointment was the first time I laid eyes on her. I asked her if anyone had referred her to me and she said no, she merely picked my name out of the phone book mostly because my office was close to her home."

Smith was disappointed. "It's too bad she told you she was married. We were sort of hoping she might have let something slip about the father. Maybe not the actual name, but some clue, some hint, some indication. I take it you can't recall her saying anything like that."

Decker looked at the contents of the manilla folder again. "She listed her husband's name here. From what I know now, it obviously was fictitious. She said he was self-employed and worked at home, the same address she provided as her own."

Smith's sleepy eyes were suddenly alive. "What was the name she gave?"

"Robert Marvin."

Robert Denham lived in a small apartment in Arlington and welcomed them with the alacrity of a man being paid an official visit by an Internal Revenue Service auditor.

"I've already talked to the police once before," he said testily. "I don't know what else I can tell you. I'd rather forget the whole thing, including Rebel."

"Oh?" There was that two-letter symbol of skillfully blended disbelief, sarcasm and cynicism. "I should have imagined you'd have difficulty forgetting a girl you loved and planned to marry."

Denham's eyes fell under Smith's direct gaze. He was silent. The lieutenant's voice took on a note of friendly consolation. "Look, Mr. Denham, I get the impression you feel a kind of relief now that she's dead. Isn't that true?"

"I miss her very much," Denham insisted, but without conviction.

"Level with me, Denham. It'll help us solve this case. We know what kind of woman she was. You aren't shedding any tears are you?"

Denham's handsome, clean-cut face contracted in a spasm of bitterness.

"No, I'm not," he said. "Now that she's gone, it's just like waking up from a nightmare. Now I can tell myself what I didn't have the guts to admit before . . . before she got killed."

"And what was that?" Smith said gently.

"That she didn't really love me. That she used me. That she'd sleep with other men and then would lie about it. And I'd swallow the lie because I was too afraid to believe the truth. I'd swear, if I had actually caught her in the sack with someone else, she could have alibied her way out of it. I kept rationalizing that she must love me or she wouldn't have paid any attention to me. She could have had any guy she wanted. But down deep, I knew she was just toying with me. Christ, how could I have been so blind?"

"An interesting question, Mr. Denham. Why *did* she pay attention to you? From a purely materialistic standpoint, you didn't have much to offer on your salary. Yet she did see you, and you've even stated publicly you planned to marry her. Perhaps you're being a little too modest. Or shall we say you were being a bit over-optimistic about marriage. Indulging in some wishful thinking when you told people you and Miss Martin had serious intentions?"

"Up until very recently I actually thought she'd marry me, someday," Denham said, and there was a note of wistfulness in his voice, as if he were suddenly remembering the Rebel he had courted and loved.

"She said something to you shortly before she was murdered, something that demolished your matrimonial dreams?"

"Yes."

"When was this?"

"I'd rather not say. It doesn't make much difference, does it?"

"You're a poor judge of what makes a difference in a murder investigation," Smith said tartly. "When did she break the no-marriage news to you?"

"I'm not being stubborn, Lieutenant. I just don't want to talk about something that still hurts like hell."

Smith shifted gears. "Suppose I break some additional news to you, Mr. Denham. News that may hurt like hell. Miss Martin was three months pregnant. Any chance of your being the father?"

Robert Denham smiled, although it was more of a grimace. "That's not news. That's what she told me when she said she'd never be able to marry me."

The spaniel eyes raised, escorted by the "Oh?"

"God, it was just like she kicked me right in the face. I remember that, for a second, I thought maybe it's my kid and she'll have to marry me. In fact, I even assumed it must be mine. So I said to her right off, 'Rebel, don't be afraid. I'll marry you.' And she laughed at me. Goddamn her black soul, she laughed at me."

"Okay, Denham. Tell me right now, buster. When was this? You tell me right now or you'll be at police headquarters in fifteen minutes charged with suspicion of homocide. Talk!"

Denham's eyes filled with tears and he blinked. He looked imploringly at the lieutenant, then at McDermott, a trapped animal facing an executioner. "If I tell you, I'll be held anyway."

"So you lose either way. Talk, dammit."

"It was the night she was murdered."

"What time did you see her. And when?"

"At her house, about midnight."

"You told Sergeant Gillespie you watched a program called Night Gallery and the Dick Cavett show. You gave him the plots of both Night Gallery episodes and the names of Cavett's guest stars."

"Of course I told him. I actually did watch Night Gallery right after I got home from bowling. But when I heard Rebel was killed, I didn't want to get involved in a murder I had nothing to do with. I just looked up the Cavett show in the advance tv listings; they had the names of the guests. Christ, lieutenant, I was trying to firm up an alibi."

"Did you go over to her house without being invited, or did she expect you?"

"I called her during a commercial when I was watching Night Gallery. She sounded a little drunk and said she didn't want to see anybody. But I hadn't been with her for a week or so and I talked her into letting me come over for a little

162

while. I said I just wanted to talk to her. She'd been drinking but she wasn't completely bombed. Her eyes were blood-shot but it wasn't from booze. She'd been crying. I . . . I made a pass at her and that's when she told me."

"About the baby?"

"She said she couldn't . . . couldn't let me make love to her anymore. She said she wasn't fit for a nice guy like me. That's when she told me she was pregnant. When I offered to marry her, she laughed. She said I was a good kid but . . . she said it wasn't my baby she was gonna have so I might as well get out of her life. And that she was going to marry someone else."

"Did she tell you whose baby it was?"

"No. I asked her. She laughed again. She said, 'Wouldn't you be surprised?' Then she changed all of a sudden. Got real affectionate and apologetic. Said I . . . she said I always had been a good bed partner and wouldn't I like to make love to her again as a kind of . . . farewell. I wanted to hit her. I felt nothing but dis-gust. Right then and there I fell out of love with her. I started to leave and she threw her arms around me. Said I didn't have to go so long as I didn't stay more than an hour or two. She asked me again to go to bed with her. That's . . . that's when I hit her."

"You hit her?"

"I slapped her. With my open hand. All she did was laugh, kind of crazy like. Mean. She said to get the hell out of there, because someone else was coming in a couple of hours. So I left. I was sick inside my guts but not for long. It's like I told you before. When I heard she was dead, all I felt was relief. A kind of gratitude that I didn't have to worry about her anymore. Worry about those other guys all the time. All the goddamned time. I used to wake up in the morning wondering who she had been to bed with the night be-fore."

"Why didn't you tell this to the officer who questioned you after the murder?"

"I was afraid. So I just said I was home all the time. For an alibi."

"That's not much of an alibi," Smith said. "It's no alibi at all unless you can prove you were home."

"I can't even say for sure I was at home," Denham muttered. "After I saw Rebel, I drove into downtown Washington and went to a bar. It was about 1 A.M. I drank until the bar closed an hour later. I must have had at least six or seven straight bourbons and I got pretty plastered. I don't even remember driving home. The next morning, there was a ticket on my windshield. I was so bombed that I parked the car practically on top of a fire hydrant around the corner from my apartment."

"A parking ticket?" Smith was frowning.

"A parking ticket." Denham laughed but without mirth. "How about that, Lieutenant? A parking ticket and here I am about to get arrested for murder. For all I know, I drove back to Rebel's and strangled her. Because I can't remember anything from the time I left the bar until I woke up the next day. So help me God I don't think I killed her. I couldn't hurt her. I just can't remember anything after the bar."

"Do you have that ticket with you?"

Denham was mystified. "The ticket? Sure. It's in my pocket. Here it is. I haven't paid it yet."

Smith took the ticket, examined it and handed it over to Max. "Look at the time," he said.

McDermott looked. It was an ordinary summons issued by the Arlington County Police Department. The patrolling officer, a J. Cornish, had logged the time of ticketing Denham's car, identified as a 1968 Chevrolet convertible, at 3:45 A.M.

"Denham," Smith said soberly, "how long would you say

164

it took you to drive from your place here over to Miss Martin's house?"

"I never made it in less than twenty minutes, even late at night. Usually twenty-five or maybe thirty."

Smith handed him back the ticket. "I suggest you pay it, son. It's a very valuable ticket. It may save you from getting booked for first degree murder. Mind if I use your phone?"

"No, sir. It's right over there."

Smith dialed a number. "This is Lieutenant Smith, Alexandria homicide. I want to contact one of your boys, a Patrolman Cornish. He wouldn't be around, would he? Yeah, I figured he's on the lobster shift. Look, would you call him at home and have him call me immediately at this number, 365–2306. Got it? Yeah, I know he's probably asleep but this is important. Thanks, I'll remember you in my will."

The return call from Cornish came through in less than 10 minutes. Smith himself answered. "Cornish, do you remember ticketing a 1968 Chevvie convertible the morning of the fifth? Right, Tuesday. The ticket you made out read 3:45 A.M. The car was parked in front of a hydrant on 34th Street. Dammit, I know you can't remember every car you ticket. But this one may have been driven by a suspect in that stewardess murder. Did you see it again that morning? Think, Cornish, think. Atta boy . . . you sure? You drove by again a half-hour later and it was still there? Yeah, that's a pretty damned good reason for going back to check it. You've been a big help, Cornish. Sorry I had to bother you. Goodbye."

Smith hung up and shook his head at the white-faced, puzzled Denham. "Like I said, son, be thankful for that ticket. Also, be thankful for a cop who's apparently afraid of his wife. Cornish said he got to thinking about your car after he made out the ticket. His brother-in-law drives a red Chevy convertible, same year as yours. Cornish figured if he gave his wife's brother a ticket, he might catch some hell at home so he drove back to see if the car had blackwall tires. Yours are whitewalls. Cornish evidently heaved a big sigh of relief and drove on, thereby establishing a fine alibi for you."

"I don't quite get it, lieutenant," Denham said. "I'm grateful for the alibi, but . . ."

"The ticket was made out at 3:45 A.M. The car was still there thirty minutes later. You couldn't have killed Rebel Martin between the hours of 3:30 and 4:30 if your car was parked around the corner from here between 3:45 and 4:15. The worst I can do to you is book you for drunken driving but I'm a little late. So I'll just ask you one more question and, if you have the right answer, I'll kiss you. When Miss Martin suggested that farewell love session, provided it didn't last for more than two hours, did she say what future visitor prompted her to set a rather unromantic time limit?"

"Well"—Denham hesitated as he prodded his memory—"all I seem to recall is that she said something about expecting company later. I was so mad at her I didn't ask her who. I suppose that's what you'd like to know?"

"I sure would," Smith grumbled. "Whoever it was, killed her. Max, I think we . . ."

Max interrupted. "Denham, what was the name of that bar you were in?"

"Tim's Tavern, on Pennsylvania Avenue. I go there now and then."

"Thanks. Okay, Smitty. That's all I wanted to ask."

Smith opened up on him as soon as they got in his car. "Okay, Max why did you have hot pants about that bar?"

"For Christ's sake," McDermott exploded, "what the hell kind of detective are you? Aren't you going to check his alibi?"

"His alibi is the parking ticket, and a damned good one it is, too."

"Not if he didn't really get drunk."

Smith shook his head in the manner of a father trying to be patient with a backward son who asks dumb questions. "You're getting at something, but I'm too thick to grasp it."

"Smitty, we're letting this guy off the hook too easy. Remember, he called our attention to that parking ticket, which turned it into his alibi. You grabbed at it right away, but, if you hadn't, I'll be that somehow he would have gotten you to look at it. So let's suppose he never went near a bar. Suppose he deliberately parked his car next to a hydrant so it would get a ticket, went over to Rebel's by some other means—a borrowed car or a taxi—killed her and then fed us an act about not remembering anything. He lives alone. He had no way of establishing that he was at home when the murder was committed except through something crazy like that ticket."

"Wait a minute," Smith cautioned, "the ticket was no good to him unless the time corresponded to the murder. He'd have no way of knowing when a police car would come around."

"The hell he wouldn't. Aren't patrols run pretty much on schedule?"

"Well, yes."

"So he could have observed those patrols for a few nights. He'd know within five or ten minutes when it was due to pass his corner, where he parked. He couldn't have anticipated that cop coming back to see if it was the brother-in-law's Chevy. But that was so much gravy. The ticket still gave him something of an alibi which he'd need, and the officer's accidental curiosity made it more plausible."

Smith looked doubtful. "What you're saying Max, is that if Denham committed the murder, it had to be premeditated. To observe a police car on its rounds, for example, so he could set up the alibi. Which is why I can't buy it."

"Why can't you buy it?"

"Because if that police car hadn't come back, the alibi was too thin. Besides you're arguing against yourself. You've

167

been saying for two days that jealousy was at the bottom. Jealousy is more likely to be the trigger for an impulsive murder, committed in a fit of blind rage. And that dame apparently could have pissed off a saint. Denham described her as a mean kind of drunk, and a mean drunken woman could force almost any man into violence. Nope, the more I think about it, the more I'm convinced the murder wasn't planned. Somebody went to her house that night, not too long after Denham left. He found her stoned and in that state, she teased or insulted him or goaded him into murder."

"You're probably right," Max said reluctantly. "And I do seem to be arguing against my jealousy theory if I keep suspecting Denham. But I'd still check that bar."

"Oh, I'll check it," Smith assured him. "Although the fact that he readily supplied us with the name is another argument against you. It would have made more sense for Denham to claim he was too smashed to remember where he got drunk. If he faked the bar angle, he wouldn't have given us its location. It would be too easy to check."

"Okay, you've talked me out of it, temporarily. But I'm still curious about Rebel's using his first name for that doctor's file—Robert Marvin. If she was panting to marry Jim Lindsay, why didn't she list the supposed husband as Jim Marvin? The odds were all in favor of that baby being Jim's."

The detective shrugged. "The odds were all in favor of her not really knowing whose baby it was. She might have used Denham's first name subconsciously, out of spite. Because he was the one she'd be least likely to marry and it would have been a kind of joke to use his name. Anyway, Max, Denham said one thing which intrigued the hell out of me. Catch it?"

"That Rebel was expecting company later," Max guessed.

"It's not unreasonable to assume the murderer phoned her that night to make sure she'd be home, alone, so he could set up an appointment with her."

"So what? You can't trace a local phone call."

"No, but I can trace a long distance call. Such as one a certain airline captain might make from Chicago if he wanted to be sure his lady love would be waiting for his loving arms. Or hands."

At Smith's urging, Max returned to his flight duties that afternoon.

"I've just got some old-fashioned, dull digging on tap for the rest of the day," the lieutenant had told McDermott. I'll give you a fill-in tonight. How about having supper with me? Say around six."

They arranged to meet at a downtown restaurant and McDermott spent the rest of the day giving a young captain an easier six-month checkride than the pilot expected. He was a quiet, competent, no-nonsense airman whose proficiency McDermott tagged as above average in the first fifteen minutes, and Max found his mind wandering back to the murder. He still leaned toward Robert Denham as the prime suspect, as he explained to Smith that night.

They were eating at Costin's, a steak house in the National Press Building which was the detective's favorite dining spot.

"I struck out, all the way down the line," Smith said dispiritedly. "And so did you. Tim's Bar recalled seeing Denham most vividly. I talked to the night bartender, who said Denham's a fairly regular customer and usually a nice kid. But on the night in question, he said Denham slopped up nine straight bourbons and they had to throw him out when the joint closed. The bartender said he was a mite belligerent and he couldn't see how the hell he could have driven home without getting picked up. So he *was* stoned and his parking by that hydrant was about as deliberate as a hiccup."

169

"That's my strikeout," Max said. "What about yours?"

"Lindsay's supposed phone call from Chicago to the Martin house. He didn't make one. Whoever kept that date with her after Denham left, assuming Denham's innocent, must have been a local character. Also, I drew a blank on his picture. We sent a print to Chicago via wirephoto and between the Windy City boys and our own guys, we must have talked to at least twenty persons. Nobody saw anyone vaguely resembling Lindsay that night or the next morning. Doesn't mean too much on the American flight to Chicago. The plane was full and the chances were against anyone remembering a single passenger unless there was something outstanding or unusual about him. United's twelve-forty-five A.M. to Washington, the one he'd have to take if he wanted to commit the murder, had only fifteen passengers. Somebody should have recognized his picture if he had been on the plane, particularly the stewardesses. But no soap."

"That Denham still bugs me," McDermott mused.

"Why? His alibi is pretty tight."

"Yeah, but he's so damned much more logical than someone like Gilcannon or Tarkington—or Lindsay, if you've still got your suspicions. The first two are respectable businessmen. Jim's a professional airman, almost a businessman himself. That doesn't mean they're not capable of murder under enough provocation or pressure. But you'd have to put the word theoretically in front of capable, and that's too hazy. Now Denham—well, maybe it's undemocratic to establish a correlation between social or economic stratum and willingness to murder, yet it would make more sense in his case. He hasn't the educational or financial background that would give him the stability to resist a temptation to kill."

Smith looked both puzzled and amused. "How's that again?"

170

"I mean, men like Gilcannon, Tarkington and Lindsay would have too much at stake to get nailed on a murder rap. Even if one of them wanted to kill somebody like Rebel, they'd have to consider the possibility of being caught. They'd weigh their careers against the risk, and they wouldn't be likely to accept the risk. Which leaves Denham as the more likely possibility, simply because he'd never debate the pros and cons."

"Nobody killing on impulse weighs pros and cons," Smith said soberly.

"Granted, but of the four men, Denham's the best bet to lose his cool. His motive is the strongest. He admitted he found out Rebel was playing him for a sucker. That she was going to marry someone else, presumably the guy who got her pregnant. That's sufficient emotional stress to push him into murder. He was mad enough to hit her. He told us that."

"He also parked by that damned hydrant," Smith reminded.

"I almost wish he hadn't," Max smiled mirthlessly. "Let's order."

They continued the discussion throughout dinner, returning to McDermott's suspicions concerning Denham.

"He's a strong possibility, if the murder were committed in a split second flush of uncontrollable rage," Max insisted.

Smith remained doubtful. "Any man who really loved her was capable of homicide, once the love turned to hate. She could have taunted or threatened whoever was in the house that night to the point of strangling her. That could mean Tarkington or Gilcannon or anyone else. And I don't quite agree that men like them couldn't commit murder because of the risk. Go back to my blackmail theory, Max. Take Gilcannon, for example. If the Martin girl had been blackmailing him, he wouldn't have been weighing a wrecked career against the risk of the electric chair. He already would have been threatened with ruin and then he'd have to take the risk."

"Possible blackmail is strongest in Gilcannon's case," Max conceded, "but it isn't nearly as strong with Tarkington and it's non-existent with Lindsay and Denham too, for that matter. How the hell could she have been blackmailing a ramp agent who only wanted to marry her? So we're back where we started, with a pile of unanswered questions. Why was she murdered? Did pregnancy supply somebody with a motive? Was the motive jealousy, hate, rejection or blackmail? God, what a jumble."

A voice broke into their conversation. "Good evening, gentlemen, or is it more relevant these days to say good evening, fuzz. Why aren't you both out solving murders?"

It was Valerie Tarkington, sleek and perfectly-groomed, standing by their table and smiling rather nastily. Smith started to rise, noticed that Max had remained seated with a glare of pure disgust on his face, and sank back.

"Any developments, Lieutenant?" she asked with false politeness.

"Nothing major," the detective mumbled.

"Too bad. I almost feel like confessing—and then withdrawing the confession because you couldn't prove it in a million years. Good night, gentlemen." She verbally italicized the last word as if it were an insult.

She sailed away, joining a tall, well-dressed man who had preceded her past their table.

"Goddamned Lucretia Borgia," Smith growled. "If that Martin babe had been done in with poison, I'd arrest that snotty broad tonight."

"You ever check out her story?"

"I did. A very illegitimate assignation but a very legitimate alibi. I had to drag it out of her lover-boy. It was like mining coal with a nail file. And Gilcannon's doctor confirmed that sterility operation. By the way, I also talked to the Roberts girl. She spoke very highly of you. She also didn't have a thing to tell me except that she was on a

172

layover in Nashville when the murder was committed, and she said something very interesting about her boss."

"Boss? You mean Mike Hunter?"

"None other. The Roberts kid was pretty nervous when I started questioning her, so to put her at ease I mentioned it must be nice to have a supervisor like Miss Hunter. She agreed and then she blurts out that a lot of girls were scared of her. I asked why, and she said Miss Hunter can be sweet until she loses her temper. 'A very short fuse' was the way she put it."

Max was annoyed. "A short temper on the part of a stewardess supervisor isn't what I'd call significant," he snapped. "If I had Mike's job, playing nursemaid to a bunch of temperamental females, I'd be short-fused myself."

"I didn't say it was significant," Smith soothed him. "I said it was interesting. Anyway, I can't see that Hunter gal as a killer. For one thing I liked her, which is a lousy reason for a cop to eliminate a suspect. More to the point, she told us that larceny job Rebel pulled with her boy friend took place eighteen months ago. I can't quite see her brooding over it for a year and a half and then committing sudden murder. Unless . . ."

"Unless what?" McDermott prompted.

"Unless she brooded about it so long, that she did a very careful job of planning a homicide."

"She doesn't strike me as the type for premeditation," Max said. "She'd have been more likely to slap the hell out of Rebel right after she lost her fiancee. I'm surprised she didn't."

"Frankly, so am I. Dammit, Max, I'm stumped. I think I'll call every one of them down to headquarters, where the atmosphere is less conducive to lying. Maybe somebody'll crack under a good grilling. Here take a look at this."

He handed McDermott a sheet of paper. Max read it carefully.

173

SUSPECT	MOTIVE	ALIBI	PROBABILITY
TARKINGTON	Rejection Possible blackmail Jealousy Pregnancy	None	Doubtful unless can uncover more definite motive
GILCANNON	Blackmail or Jealousy	Apparently not at home: not definite	Same as Tarkington
LINDSAY	None	in Chicago	Absence of motive and presence in Chi makes unlikely
DENHAM	Rejection Jealousy Played for sucker	Strong evidence if he at home	Strongest motive of all male suspects but alibi must be shaken
HUNTER	Revenge Jealousy	None	Unlikely because of time lapse between incident creating hatred and the murder.
V. TARKINGTON	Jealousy	With friend	Motive not in keeping with strong character
N. LINDSAY	Jealousy	At home with children	Very strong motive No apparent opportunity

Max handed back the summation. "You covered the situation very well. In other words, you're flying blind, to use an aeronautical phrase."

"No bright ideas?"

"None. You've either got to pry a confession out of one of them or start concentrating on the assumption that somebody else killed her. A maniac. Maybe a man or woman with reason to hate her but a person you or nobody else knew anything about."

Smith shook his head. "We've been picking up a hell of a lot of wild characters for questioning—known sex perverts, guys with criminal records—you know, the typical flotsam and jetsam that go with a murder case. We even questioned one nut with a reputation for accosting stewardesses at airports. He's been arrested eight times. A burglar is out, as you already know. We've released every person we've questioned. Not the slightest hint of involvement. We've talked to all the neighbors and we drew a complete blank. Nobody saw or heard anything out of the ordinary. We've gotten absolutely nothing from our usual corps of informants. There's one possibility and I hate to even consider it: she might have gone out after Denham left, picked up some psychopath at a bar, taken him home and there went the ballgame."

"Negative," Max said. "Remember, Denham claims she was going to see somebody later. I'll give you fifty-to-one odds that date was with her killer."

"Probably. But that doesn't mean the killer's name is on that list you just read."

"It sure doesn't look like it," Max fretted. "Incidentally, Smitty, I'm a little surprised you included Norma Lindsay."

"Strong motive, the strongest of anybody's," the detective explained. "The Martin dame was not only ruining her marriage but threatening her kids' future and security. I don't mind telling you I was very interested in Mrs. Lindsay. I even had my boys question about half the neighborhood. I wanted to know if anyone might have been baby-sitting for her until the wee small hours. But I struck out there, too. There was no indication she ever left the house. If she got a sitter, we don't know where. I even checked the professional sitter services."

"She might have left the kids by themselves," McDermott suggested. "Kevin, their boy, is a pretty mature youngster for an eleven-year-old."

"Now you don't believe that anymore than I do. Mrs. Lindsay didn't strike me as the type of mother who'd leave a kid that age home alone with a virtual baby. Hell, Max, she also didn't strike me as the type who'd commit murder. Only reason I put her on the list was the motive."

It was the next morning that Norma Lindsay's alibi fell apart.

9

McDermott was just leaving for his office when the jangle of the telephone halted him at the door. He assumed it was Smith, who after their dinner together had been undecided on the program for the following day. Instead, the caller was Mike Hunter.

"Max, something's come up. I didn't know whether to call Lieutenant Smith so I thought I'd better tell you. It may not mean anything but I wondered . . ."

"Goddammit, Mike," Max snapped. "Get to the point."

"Well, it's Kay Baxter, one of our stews. Do you know her?"

"No." Max knew he was being abrupt but the propensity of a woman to drag out a conversation irked him. And he had a funny feeling in the pit of his belly. A premonition, maybe.

"Max, she was in my office just now, getting fitted for a new winter uniform. I chewed her out a little for signing in five minutes late for a flight the other day. The morning Rebel was murdered. She said she was sorry, then she told me why she was late."

"Tell me," McDermott rasped. "And tell me fast."

"Kay said she overslept because she was sitting with the Lindsay children the night before. She said Norma Lindsay didn't get back to the house until after four A.M."

"Jesus Christ," Max breathed. "Mike, hold that girl in your office if you have to padlock her to your desk. I'll call

Smith and we'll be there in twenty minutes."

"She's got a flight to Nashville in another forty minutes," the supervisor complained. "Look, Max, I don't want to get Mrs. Lindsay in trouble. It's probably her own business why she was out so late and . . ."

"Get a reserve stew to work Baxter's trip," McDermott barked. "That's an order, Mike. If that stew isn't waiting for us in your office, I'll ream your butt with a shovel." He hung up before Mike had a chance to say anything more.

McDermott and Smith arrived at Mike's office almost simultaneously. The detective motioned Mike out, ignoring her hurt look, and faced Kay Baxter. She was a pretty girl with red hair, a sweet face and an air of poise and maturity that just fell short of masking her nervousness.

Smith took off. "Miss Baxter, what time did Mrs. Lindsay phone you for this sitting job?"

"It was quite late, either just before eleven or shortly after. She apologized for calling so late but she said something important had come up and that she had to leave the house for a while. She said she had tried to get one of her regular sitters but couldn't."

"Had she ever called you before?"

"No, but she said she had heard that I sat for pin money occasionally and that she took a chance I was free."

"Did Mrs. Lindsay say it was an emergency? Did she seem upset?"

"No, she was quite calm. I turned her down at first. I explained that I had a trip the next day and needed my sleep. She apologized again but said it was very important and she'd pay double my usual fee. I still didn't want to go, but she then said that I'd be doing Captain Lindsay a favor, too. She said he was on a trip or she wouldn't be imposing on me. Golly, that clinched it. I'd do anything for Jim Lindsay, so I said I'd come."

"What time did you get there?"

178

"About eleven-forty-five. She left as soon as I arrived. The children were asleep."

"What was she like when you arrived? Nervous? Distraught? Tearful?"

"No, she was like she had been on the phone. Very calm, very pleasant. I thought she seemed a little tense but that didn't surprise me. It must have been something out of the ordinary or she wouldn't have needed a sitter at that hour. For a moment, I thought . . . well, never mind. It's impossible."

Smith pressed her. "What did you think, Miss Baxter? I just want you to know what you're telling us may be extremely important, so don't hold back on anything."

"I thought maybe she was going out to see . . . to have an affair with another man. But then I knew it couldn't be that. Not if she was married to someone like Captain Lindsay. And, anyway, if she had been planning some hanky-panky, she never would have called a stewardess so she could get out of the house. That would have been . . . ."

Smith interrupted impatiently. "What time did Mrs. Lindsay return?"

"I was asleep on the couch when I heard her open the front door, so I automatically looked at my wristwatch. It was ten minutes after four. She said she was sorry to be so late and gave me twenty dollars. I told her it was too much but she said I deserved even more."

"And what was her state then? Still outwardly calm?"

"Well, not exactly." Kay Baxter was choosing her words very carefully. She obviously had deduced she was being questioned in some connection with Rebel Martin's murder. "She was calm enough, but her eyes . . . well, they looked as if she had been crying."

"She didn't tell you where she had been? What was the nature of this emergency, this business she had to take care of in the middle of the night?"

"No, sir. And I didn't ask."

"Thank you, Miss Baxter. You've been a big help and I appreciate it."

She stood up to leave and then her female curiosity, so beautifully held in check, got the best of her. "You wouldn't want to tell me what this is all about, would you?"

"You'll probably hear all about it eventually," Smith said. "When you go out, ask Miss Hunter if she'd step in here."

Mike didn't step in. She shot in, but Smith raised one hammy paw to halt the questions that were ready to burst forth. "Hold it, young lady. I'll fill you in later if there's anything to tell you. Meanwhile, I'd be grateful if you could phone the pilots' office or whatever you call it and find out if Captain Lindsay is at home or flying today."

Mike shot back out, closing the door behind her. Smith turned to McDermott and the sleepy eyes were also sad. "This may be the big break, Max, but damned if I'm happy about it."

"Neither am I," Max said glumly. "What the hell, Smitty, it's still circumstantial. If she did go to Rebel's around midnight, she must have arrived when Denham was there. What was the coroner's estimate of the murder time?"

"Between three-thirty and four A.M., with a thirty-minute margin either way."

"That stewardess said Mrs. Lindsay got home at four-ten. She would have had to commit the murder at three-thirty or earlier to get home by ten minutes after four. That's cutting it real close."

"Coroners hate to climb out on limbs," Smith said cautiously. "Ours is no exception. That thirty-minute margin of error he gave himself could mean that the murder took place as early as three A.M., which would have given Mrs. Lindsay plenty of time to get home when she did."

They sat in uneasy silence for a couple of minutes, until Mike Hunter returned to inform them that Captain Lindsay was not on a trip and presumably was at home.

He wasn't, however. Norma Lindsay met them at the

front door, clad in a simple frock, her pert face slightly smudged. She looked, McDermott thought, about as much like a murderess as the Mona Lisa.

"Jim's not here," she greeted them. "He took the children to a Walt Disney movie."

"We'd like to talk with you, not your husband," Smith said with formal politeness ringed by the cold steel of police authority.

"Please come in," she invited, and her own voice also was perfect politeness ringed by the cold steel of a woman placed suddenly on her guard.

Inevitably and typically, she offered them coffee which both refused, sensing it would prolong the agony. Smith even cleared his throat before starting the interrogation, and Max knew the detective was experiencing one of those moments when a cop hates his job.

"Mrs. Lindsay," the lieutenant began, "why did you lie to us when you told us you were home with your children during the time Miss Martin was murdered?"

She sat there, hands folded primly on her lap, a strange little smile flecking her lips. "Because I knew if I told you the truth, it would be misinterpreted. Also, I did not want my husband to find out what I had done."

"And exactly what *did* you do, Mrs. Lindsay?"

"I went to see Rebel."

"To kill her?"

"No, to talk to her."

"What about?"

"My husband. Their affair. Our children." Her low, steady voice rose slightly on those last two words.

"Suppose we start at the beginning. What time did you arrive at Miss Martin's house? And how did you know she'd be home?"

"About twelve-thirty. I just took a chance."

"Had you ever been there before?

"No, but I looked up her address and . . ."

181

"Her phone was unlisted," Smith said with a touch of sharpness.

"I didn't mean I looked it up in the phone book," Norma Lindsay said patiently. "Jim has a list of all the pilots and stewardesses based here—their phone numbers and addresses."

"And you had no trouble finding her house?"

"No. I know Alexandria fairly well."

"Why did you decide all of a sudden to pay her this visit? At such a late hour when you weren't even sure she'd be home. Why didn't you try to see her in the daytime, or the next morning, or next week? Why was it so necessary to see her that very night, to the extent of calling in an emergency baby sitter?"

"I guess Kay Baxter must have told you," she said.

"We would have found out anyway," Smith said. "But you haven't answered."

"Jim was away on a trip. Everything seemed to be coming to a head. I had been thinking about . . . about things all day. I wanted to talk to Rebel before he got back. I suppose I was desperate. I knew I wouldn't sleep unless I saw her. It was an impulse but yet, not really. It had been building up for hours. I called Kay Baxter, because I didn't want to use my regular sitters or any of the neighbors. Going out at midnight would have meant some raised eyebrows and a lot of questions. I told Kay I had tried to get somebody else but that wasn't true."

"All right, Mrs. Lindsay. So you got there about twelve-thirty. And you went right in?"

"No. I started to ring her doorbell but I heard a man's voice inside. I went back to my car which was parked just a few feet away from her house. I sat there for about a half-hour until I saw the front door open. A man came out and he went across the street and got in his own car. When he drove away, I rang her doorbell. She . . ."

"Just a minute, Norma," Max interrupted. "Did you get

182

a good look at the man who came out? Did you know him or could you give us any kind of description?"

"I never saw him before. It was dark and I didn't get much of a glimpse of him, but he seemed rather young. Tall with a crew-cut, I think."

McDermott and Smith exchanged glances. "Denham," the detective commented. "That just about clears him. Provided, Mrs. Lindsay, that Rebel Martin was alive when you entered her house. You did get in, I assume?"

"Yes. She was surprised to see me. At first she hesitated, then when I asked if I could come in, she just nodded."

"Go on."

"She invited me to sit down. She obviously had been drinking. Her voice was fuzzy and her speech blurred. I didn't waste time on pleasantries. I told her I knew all about their affair, that Jim had asked me for a divorce and that I had agreed. I said that if it was just Jim and myself involved, I'd step out of the picture willingly. But I reminded her of my children. That a divorce would affect their future far more than it could any adult. That they loved their father. So . . . so I asked her if she'd get out of Jim's life for their sake."

Her voice cracked. Smith took a faded, frayed but clean handkerchief from his pocket and gave it to her, his face coated with sympathy. She wiped her eyes and clenched her small fists around the now slightly soggy cloth.

"I'm sorry," she said simply.

"Mrs. Lindsay, believe me, I'm well aware that this is an ordeal. But a woman has been killed and regardless of what kind of a human devil she was, I'm going to find out who killed her, so that person can be punished according to the law. Would you like a few minutes to compose yourself?"

She gave him a look of pure gratitude and his gruff kindness seemed to inject her with fresh emotional strength.

"She said she was sorry it had happened. That she had tried to keep from falling in love with my husband, but she

183

couldn't help herself. She said she was sorry for the children, too. That she wasn't a bad person, only very mixed-up and lonely for a man like Jim. Then . . . then, that's when she told me."

"Told you what, Mrs. Lindsay?"

"That she was going to have a baby. That she knew Jim was the father. And that was the main reason she couldn't give him up. That her own child as well as mine were involved. She cried. I honestly felt sorry for her. But I asked her again to think of two living children, not just an unborn one. I told her we would pay for an abortion or would pay all her medical expenses if she wanted to have her baby. Then I got desperate."

"Desperate? In what way?"

"I offered to raise her baby as if it were our own. That if she loved Jim and wanted their child to have a good home, this would be the best solution for all concerned. I said we would adopt the baby and give it our name."

"That was pretty drastic, Mrs. Lindsay. And what was her reaction to this offer of adoption?"

"Up to now, she had been decent and kind. Then she became angry. She laughed, almost hysterically. She said nobody would ever get her baby and nobody but Jim would help her raise it. She ordered me out of the house. Then . . . then I guess I goaded her. I couldn't help it."

"What do you mean, you goaded her?"

"I told her Jim didn't really love her, not the way he loved me. I said their own marriage would break up eventually because he'd always have a guilt complex for what he had done to his family, particularly Debbie and Kevin, let alone me. She became furious. She called me a damned liar. She slapped my face and then fell face down on the couch and started sobbing."

"She slapped your face," Smith repeated. "Did you strike her back? Was there any further physical violence?"

"No. I didn't kill her if that's what you're getting at."

184

"Did you leave after the slapping episode?"

"Yes, I left her still face-down on the couch, still crying. God forgive me, I hated her right then as I've never hated anyone in my life. Yet I couldn't help feeling sorry for her again. I hated her but I couldn't have killed her."

"Did you notice the time when you left?"

"No, I'm afraid I didn't."

"Well, you went into her house when this man left. That must have been about 1 A.M. How long would you say you stayed?"

"I have no real concept of the time. I lost track. I suppose it was about an hour at the most. Probably less. Perhaps about forty-five minutes."

"So the latest you left her house was 2 A.M., maybe even a bit earlier?"

"Yes."

Max broke in again. "Norma, while you were there—and before she became angry—did Rebel say anything about your having to leave because she was expecting company."

"No, she didn't. She might have expected somebody though. She looked at her wristwatch a couple of times, rather impatiently. I didn't think anything of it. I knew it was late and she wasn't happy I was there."

Smith resumed. "Mrs. Lindsay, how long would you say it takes to drive between your home and Miss Martin's residence?"

"At the most, about a half-hour."

"And what time did you return home?"

"Shortly after 4. I looked at my watch before I walked in my front door. I felt sorry about the sitter. She was a stewardess and I knew she had to fly the next day. Or rather, that day."

"Can you account for the fact that it took you nearly two hours to drive a distance that normally would take a maximum of 30 minutes?"

"Yes. I sat in front of Rebel's house and cried myself. I

must have been there for about five minutes. Then when I started to drive home, my mind was foggy and I was driving almost by instinct. I kept thinking of Jim and the children and what Rebel had done to all of us. I wasn't paying attention to driving. I must have taken a wrong turn because I found myself going in a wrong direction. I wasn't even quite sure where I was. I stopped for gas at an all-night station and the attendant got me oriented again. By that time, I had been on the road for nearly an hour and it took me another hour to get home."

"Do you remember what service station you stopped at?"

"I don't know the name of the station. It was Exxon. I had my own Exxon credit card."

"Do you remember what street the station was on?"

"Seminary Road."

"Do you still have a receipt for the gas you bought? The carbon copy you get when you use a credit card?"

"I suppose so. I usually put them in my purse or in the glove compartment."

"Would you mind getting your purse? And if it's not there, Max will check the glove compartment."

She returned with her purse and pawed through it unsuccessfully.

"Look in the car, Max," Smith said.

"Is it locked, Norma?"

"No."

Max went out to her car and came right back, handing Smith a piece of flimsy paper on which the name "Sopher's Exxon Station, Seminary Road, Arlington, Va.," had been stamped.

"Same date as the morning of the murder," the lieutenant noted. "May I keep this, Mrs. Lindsay?"

She nodded. Smith closed his notebook, but made no move to rise. "Mrs. Lindsay, I think the moment of truth has arrived. I don't have sufficient evidence for an arrest and this little piece of paper may furnish you with an alibi of sorts. But let me speak frankly. You had every reason to kill Rebel Martin. You admit seeing her shortly before the time of her death. There was overt physical contact between you —only on her part, according to you, but to a suspicious old cop like me it would be only too natural for me to assume you'd strike her back. Or maybe strangle her. This murder is going to be solved sooner or later. If you're guilty, it would be best for you if you told us without further delay, because I'm going to find out anyway."

"I didn't kill her," Norma said firmly.

"I hope you're telling me the truth. We'll check out this service station story, and I'll be in touch."

"Lieutenant," she said, "gas stations get a lot of customers. Suppose no one remembers my stopping. What then?"

"It isn't likely, not at that hour of the morning. Besides, you were lost and whatever attendant waited on you should remember your asking directions. It wasn't that long ago. But you won't be completely off the hook, Mrs. Lindsay, even if he confirms your story."

"I won't?" Her voice was calm, but there was an overtone of fear.

"No, you won't. Because let's say you got to that gas station around three. You still could have turned around, driven back to Alexandria, choked a drunken girl to death, and arrived back home by four-ten."

"Hold it," Max protested. "It took her nearly an hour to get from Rebel's to that gas station. How the hell . . ."

"It took her an hour because she didn't know what she was doing and she got lost. It wouldn't have taken her an hour to go back to Miss Martin's, not from Seminary Road to where the girl lived. Not if she had her wits about her and knew exactly what she wanted to do. Say twenty minutes at that time of night. The murder itself could have been accomplished in five minutes."

Norma was listening to this flurry of debate with interest,

187

but an expression of dullness, almost resignation, settled over her pretty face. She looked at McDermott as if searching, yearning for a word of reassurance which couldn't be given to her. He knew Smith's theoretical timetable was razor-thin, but it was nevertheless possible. The detective stood up.

"If you haven't told me the truth, Mrs. Lindsay, there's still time. I shouldn't take sides, but if you're the murderer, there isn't a jury in the world that wouldn't pity you. Cooperation now would weigh in your favor."

She didn't bother to answer. She merely shook her head and looked at them, directing her question to Max as well as Smith. "Are you going to tell Jim all about this?"

"No," Smith said. "What you did, if that's all you did, is a matter between husband and wife. But if I can give you a word of advice . . . ?"

"Please do."

"Tell him anyway. He'll understand."

"Perhaps," she said. "Or maybe he'll think what you do."

"And what do I think?"

"That I killed her."

Smith's eyes burned into hers. "I'll ask you again. Did you?"

"No. I swear I didn't."

The lieutenant sniffed unhappily, but Max could not tell whether Smith was being reluctant to accept her word or reluctant to persist in his suspicions. All the detective said was, "Thanks, Mrs. Lindsay. I'll be talking to you again after we check that gas station."

They found the Exxon station easily enough and obtained the name and address of the night attendant from the manager. The attendant, a young, clean-cut Negro with an intelligent face, showed no resentment at having his normal sleeping period disturbed. And he definitely confirmed that Norma Lindsay had stopped for both gas and directions, about three A.M.

188

"I couldn't help but remember her," he told them. "She was a pretty little thing and she seemed awfully embarrassed about being lost. I thought at first she might have been drinking, but there wasn't any liquor on her breath and she didn't act drunk. Upset, maybe, but not drunk."

"Well," Smith said en route back to the airport, "that tears it. I believe her story, but I keep wondering if it's just because I want to believe her."

"If she's telling the truth," Max said, she seems to have taken Denham off the hook, unless he went back after she left."

"With the alibi he's got, it's too far-fetched. But I think I'll have another talk with him. And all the others. Do you want to sit in on my third degrees?"

"Yep, I do," Max answered ruefully. "Dammit, Smitty, I never thought I'd get this involved."

"Once a cop, always a cop," the detective laughed. "Incidentally, stay out of the questioning. It'll be at headquarters and there'll be a few of my associates present. I don't want them to know how deeply I let you get involved."

"If you crack it," Max promised, "believe me, you can take all the credit."

Smith didn't crack it, in a week of gruelling interrogation that started with a string of perverts, alcoholics, petty criminals and those occasionally suspicious characters who get picked up for minor offenses and find themselves being grilled on the slightest possibility that they might have been connected with a major crime.

Nothing.

Ditto from informants who might have overheard something or been given a lead on the slayer's identity.

The same from Joseph Dempsey, the man who found Rebel's body, questioned anew for nearly two hours before he finally convinced Smith he was telling the truth.

One by one, the lieutenant interrogated every man and woman on the suspect list he had shown McDermott, quizzing them mercilessly in the formidable, frightening atmosphere of a police interrogation room.

He hammered away at Lyle Tarkington's desire to marry Rebel and her subsequent rejection. He received in return Tarkington's repeated and plaintive assertion that "So help me God, I never really wanted to marry her, I still love my wife."

He dueled with Valerie Tarkington so angrily that Max could almost hear a clash of swords. She taunted him with sly hints that she *might* be guilty, but she always stepped back from the brink of confession by reminding him of her well-established alibi.

He handled Frank Gilcannon with a modicum of deference, solely for McDermott's benefit, but his questioning still was ruthless as he tried again and again to force an admission that Rebel had blackmailed him. Gilcannon's denials were as strong after ninety minutes of sparring as they were at the start.

He had Robert Denham on the grill for nearly three hours, the youth emerging white-faced and shaken but still insisting that when he left Rebel Martin's house, she was alive. He even handled Mike Hunter roughly, cruelly telling her to "knock off that goddamned wisecracking" when she cheerfully suggested they have dinner together "after my confession." She left his office in tears, like a child spanked for something she hadn't done, and never noticed the miserable self-accusing look on Smith's face as she walked out.

He questioned Jim Lindsay for more than an hour, dwelling mainly on the hypothetical timetable that would have allowed the pilot to make an early morning round trip between Chicago and Washington. The captain merely kept looking at him in wonderment that Smith could deem him capable of so intricate a plot, and he also kept reminding the lieutenant that "I loved Rebel—can't you get that through your damned skull?"

190

And finally, Smith used Norma Lindsay like a verbal punching bag, alternately shouting, wheedling, coaxing and sneering until her proud facade of calmness collapsed into the sobs of a woman who had lived under tension for too long. But while her pride and self-possession cracked, she refused to reach the breaking point of confession. Jim, waiting for her outside Smith's tiny office, took one look at her tear-stained drawn face and glared accusingly at Max as well as Smith before he put his arm protectingly around her thin shoulders.

At the end of the week, the lieutenant dropped in at McDermott's apartment, poured himself a double shot of bourbon, and tossed in the figurative towel.

"There are no more leads," he said. "No clues. Nothing to go on. I still think that one of the seven persons most closely associated with Rebel Martin killed her. The Tarkingtons—and I wish I could pin it on that Valerie bitch—Gilcannon, Denham, Mike Hunter and the Lindsays. I swear one of them did it, but God knows which one and how. Five of them have alibis ranging from ironclad to reasonable. Tarkington and Miss Hunter couldn't establish their whereabouts, but I don't have enough evidence to hold either of them for five minutes. Crud, Max, I don't have any evidence against the other five, for that matter. Any suggestions?"

"None," Max said. "Except to wait and see if anything breaks open."

Ten days later, it did.

Roger Blake had called McDermott in, asking him to close the door behind him, and Max was bothered by the serious look on the chief pilots' normally friendly face.

"Got a favor to ask, Max."

"Name it."

"Give Jim Lindsay a special checkride. Throw the book at him."

McDermott frowned. "Any special reason? He's not due for his six-months check for another three or four weeks."

"I know. But two copilots have told me very privately they're afraid to fly with him. They said he's goofing off, he's taking too many chances, and he's a monster with every crew he flies with—cabin as well as cockpit."

"He's had a lot on his mind," McDermott reminded Blake. "Considering what happened, a personality change was inevitable. Temporary, I hope, but inevitable. Besides, you know pilots. A few of them can be juvenile delinquents until they draw a check ride. Then they put on halos the size of an engine cowling."

"Lindsay's no delinquent and never has been. Not until now, anyway. Something's wrong and I figure you could find out."

"You're the chief pilot," Max growled. "Check him yourself."

"The sun will set in the east before I give a checkride as good as yours. Jim likes you, Max. And he trusts you. He might put that halo on with me, but he wouldn't with you. Nobody does."

Max smiled thinly. "Okay. Can you get me an airplane and when?"

"Tomorrow morning, 0700. Ship three-thirty. It's not due to go out on schedule until ten. That gives you three hours to shake him down. Or up."

"Three-thirty," McDermott repeated. "Funny."

"What's funny about it? Just another 727."

"The numbers were stuck in my mind. Three-thirty was supposed to be the hour when Rebel was killed."

He hadn't seen Lindsay since Norma's questioning at police headquarters, and he was shocked at the captain's appearance. Jim looked twenty years older and his eyes were a mirror to his tortured memories. Once so clear, warm and alert, they now wore a film of perpetual sadness. His hair was a noticeable shade grayer and he kept rubbing his temples with one hand, a thumb on one side of his forehead and a middle finger on the other.

"Headache?" Max asked as they stood at dispatch, signing the trip clearance form.

"A little. Eyestrain, I suppose. Although I gather you're not checkriding me for my eyesight, are you?"

"Nope. And you know damned well why you're being checked. Don't start holding it against Blake, Jim, or against me. You're a potential crash flying someplace to happen and we're gonna make sure it never happens."

"Even if you have to ground me," Lindsay said.

"Even if I have to ground you. And I'd ground my best friend if I thought safety was involved. You know that already."

"Yes." Lindsay put resignation and maybe surrender into that single word.

McDermott flew the right seat, with a youngster named Eddie Tolman serving as flight engineer. Max knew him as a savvy kid, due to start first officer training in another month. Tolman usually was addicted to a certain amount of verbal horseplay but today he seemed cowed by the atmosphere in the cockpit, if not strained then strangely unsettled, like the dull, indecisive pain of a toothache.

As he had promised Blake, McDermott threw the book at the Captain. Emergency descents. Stalls and stall recovery. An ILS approach with one engine out. No-flap approaches. Simulated engine fire with shutdown and restart. Smoke evacuation drill. Electrical failure drill. Hydraulic failure drill. A half-dozen ILS landings at Dulles, where traffic was lighter.

In no case could he fault Lindsay. The captain's performance was flawless, if surprisingly mechanical. At times, he seemed to be fighting the 727 instead of flying it, trying to dominate it rather than coordinate with it. Technically, Lindsay was above average and yet Max had the uncomfortable feeling he was checking out a robot. He knew this was not the old Jim Lindsay but he could not precisely define the difference.

They were at thirty-one thousand feet over Morgantown, West Virginia, when McDermott made the final mark in the *"above average"* column next to an item labeled "oxygen mask drill," shook off the uneasy premonition he was cheating on Blake by giving Lindsay the high grade, and told the captain to head home after contacting the Washington Air Traffic Control Center at Leesburg, Virginia.

"Roger, Coastal Training. We have you in radar contact. Descent to flight level one-seven-oh and maintain heading of one-one-five."

Max, handling the radio while Lindsay continued to fly, acknowledged. "Coastal Training, leaving three-one-zero."

He knew Lindsay had heard the descent clearance but the captain made no effort to push forward on the yoke.

"We're cleared down to seventeen, Jim," McDermott snapped.

Lindsay nodded, and finally pushed the 727's snout down. McDermott watched the altimeter unwinding. The needle began to nudge seventeen thousand feet and Max told the Center, "Leveling off at seventeen."

"Coastal Training," the controller ordered. "Maintain one-seven while we reroute some traffic below you."

"Roger," Max said, then took a startled look at the altimeter. They had passed seventeen thousand and the nose was still pitched down.

"Jim, you've gone through seventeen. Get the hell back up there."

Lindsay did not answer.

15,000. Nose still down, and the ISVI needle—Instant Vertical Speed Indicator—was picking up momentum.

"Lindsay, for Christ's sake pull up!" McDermott roared. "We'll hit somebody."

The captain's eyes were riveted on the instrument panel, staring at the ISVI as if mesmerized. It was reading six thousand feet per minute, the maximum figure at which it was pegged. Max dimly heard the flight engineer, panic creeping into his voice, bleat, "Captain McDermott, is he sick?"

"Goddammit, Lindsay, pull back on that yoke!"

11,000 feet.

A loud clicking sound invaded the tension. A sound like a monster cricket flying around unseen in the cockpit. The speed warning clacker had activated, an automatic alarm as they neared Mach 1—the speed of sound.

9,000 feet and the 727 shuddered and bucked. High speed buffeting as the speed warning clacker sounded like a hundred castanets.

Lindsay's eyes were bulging crazily. McDermott reached for the throttles to chop power but with his right hand the captain slapped Max's big paw away.

"Get the hell away," he said hoarsely.

5,000 feet. No more time.

Max, in what seemed like one swift motion, unfastened his belt and shoulder harness, rose up and hit Lindsay flush on the jaw. The captain's head rolled to one side and his eyes closed. McDermott fell back in his own seat, cutting power to zero thrust and pulling the speed brake lever as the airspeed fell off. They were at fifteen hundred feet when he stopped giving the 727 its head and eased back on the yoke.

They landed a long thirty minutes later, Lindsay conscious again, fingering his swollen jaw and staring straight ahead without speaking. Eddie Toland, his face white, kept looking at Jim as if he were some kind of freak. McDermott taxied the 727 to their assigned gate and shut down the engines.

195

"Go into Operations and keep your trap shut," he ordered the flight engineer. "Just tell Blake to meet me in his office in five minutes. Don't tell him anything else and don't talk to anyone else."

"Okay, Captain McDermott." Toland left, visibly shaken, a score of unanswered questions imprinted on his face as he closed the cockpit door. McDermott waited briefly to make sure the flight engineer was gone, before turning to Lindsay.

"Jim, I don't know how you did it or exactly why, but you killed Rebel."

Lindsay closed his eyes. His jaw tightened in the so familiar sign of inner stress. He sighed heavily, like a tired old man.

And then he nodded.

McDermott hustled Lindsay into Blake's office, slamming the door shut behind him. Jim slumped into a chair, sitting there quietly like a little boy who has been told to stay put while his parents performed some chores elsewhere.

"What the hell's wrong?" Blake demanded. "Is Jim sick? Tolman wasn't making sense. He seemed all shook . . ."

Max didn't let him finish. "He told me on the plane he killed Rebel Martin. I'm going to call Lieutenant Smith. Watch Jim and make sure he doesn't try anything. I don't think he will because he's either in a state of shock or he's damned glad to get that murder off his chest."

"Use my phone," Blake gurgled in dismay. "My God, it isn't possible. How did he do it? He was in Chicago that night."

Max ignored him and dialed Alexandria police headquarters. His skull was pounding with a sudden sickish headache. "Give me Lieutenant Smith, Homicide." Please, Smitty, be in.

"Smith, Homicide."

"Smitty, Max McDermott. Meet me at my apartment as fast as you can. Don't ask any questions now. Just get the hell over there."

It was typical of Smith that he merely said, "I'll be there," and hung up. Max turned back to look miserably at Lindsay, cognizant of why he had told the detective to meet him at the apartment. He knew he should have held Jim in Blake's

197

office until the police arrived, or even turned him over to the temporary custody of the airport police. But his own airman's heart had resisted allowing the ignominy of an arrest before Lindsay's own colleagues and friends.

"Smith's meeting us at my place," Max addressed Blake. "I'd appreciate your coming along." He studiously avoided saying aloud what he was thinking—he was afraid Jim might try something dramatic, like jumping out of a speeding car—and Blake understood immediately.

They beat the lieutenant to McDermott's apartment by five minutes, Lindsay sitting between them without saying a word. Even Blake, crawling figurative walls with unsatisfied curiosity, could not find it in his heart to ask Max anything.

When Smith entered the apartment, his sleepy eyes instantly absorbed, digested and analyzed the untold story. "This our boy?" he asked, nodding in Jim's direction but addressing the question to McDermott.

"I'm afraid so. Smitty, you've already met Captain Blake. I asked him to be here, if that's okay with you."

"No objections. Captain Lindsay, I have to inform you of your rights. You . . ."

"Skip it, lieutenant," Lindsay said. "It isn't necessary to hand me all that legal guff. I know you won't violate any of my rights. Just let me get everything out in the open. Max, you suppose I could have a drink before I spill my guts?"

"Bourbon okay?"

"Fine. Make it straight." Lindsay actually chuckled, but in a wry, sad kind of way. "Funny, but I guess this is the last drink I'll ever have. Unless they give liquor out as part of the condemned's final meal."

Blake looked worried. "Jim, maybe you'd better get a lawyer before you talk."

"I'll get a lawyer for the trial," Lindsay said calmly. "Not that it'll do me any good. A combination of Clarence Darrow, Edward Bennett Williams and Melvin Belli

198

couldn't get me out of this. Because I'm guilty."

McDermott returned with a stiff shot. Lindsay gulped it down with one swallow. "Okay, Lieutenant. I'm ready. Where do you want me to begin?"

"Begin with the how," Smith said.

"Well, you guessed it a long time ago except you couldn't crack that alibi. You had my timetable absolutely correct. I took that United flight to Washington under an assumed name, drove to Rebel's house, got there just before four A.M. killed her, drove back to National, caught American back to Chicago, changed into uniform in my room and met Max in the lobby that same morning."

"You sure took a lot of chances," Max said. "Your timetable left no margin for the unexpected."

"Sure," Lindsay agreed. "I knew the slightest delay would ruin the whole plan. Weather, for example. If either American or United had a mechanical delay I was in trouble —American in particular. But remember, I'm an airline captain. I was fairly certain of the weather. I checked the long range forecast three days before I decided to pull this off. If there had been any question of a weather problem, I would have postponed everything until the next Chicago layover when the weather outlook was better. As for a mechanical, that was just a pretty good calculated risk—again, one that only an airline captain would take. I'm a 727 captain, and I know better than anyone else what a reliable bird that plane is. And I knew American and United both have fine maintenance. I didn't have any reason to expect a fouled-up timetable and that's the way it turned out. I even took air traffic control delays into consideration. I figured a United flight that left close to midnight, and an American flight that took off before seven A.M., would beat the heavy traffic."

"How did you know Miss Martin would be home?" Smith asked.

"Simple. I called her that afternoon before I left for Chicago. Gave her a song and dance about a checkride in the wee hours after I got back, which wouldn't be unusual. I told her Norma didn't know about the checkride and thought I'd still be in Chicago. I said I'd stop in on the way home from the airport about four A.M. because I wanted to talk to her. And she promised she'd be home."

"When you flew to Washington and then back to Chicago, weren't you worried about somebody identifying you later on, after the murder? You must have known we'd look into that angle, once we thought of the theoretical possibility of that early morning roundtrip. Nobody at United or American, including the stewardesses remembered seeing you on either flight. We showed your picture to every person who might have had contact with you."

"I'm surprised you didn't think of the obvious, Lieutenant. A disguise. As simple as that. I had a fake mustache I bought at a novelty store. And I cut one of my son's Halloween wigs into something that gave me a bushy hairdo. I assume the picture you had of me was in uniform, with my cap on? I thought so. My disguise was crude but effective."

"You supplied an even more effective device to throw us off," Max said. "That call you made to me around midnight, at the O'Hare Inn. When you asked me to have a last beer in the cocktail lounge. I couldn't figure out why you'd risk having me accept the invitation. I could have said yes just as easily as I said no."

"I knew you wouldn't accept," Lindsay said laconically.

"Oh?" Smith asked. "What made you so sure?"

Jim aimed a tight smile at McDermott. "Max, remember when we were in the restaurant and I told you I thought I saw Rebel across the room?"

Max nodded.

"The oldest dodge in the world. You turned around and looked. And while you were trying to find Rebel, I dropped a half-strength Mickey into your coffee. Not enough to

200

knock you out, but enough to make you sleepy. I had tried the stuff out on myself several times. I found out exactly how much I could give you to make you drowsy without suspecting I had drugged you. I knew when I called you at midnight, you'd be so groggy you would have declined an invitation from the President of the United States. Even if you had said yes, I would have merely delayed going through with the murder until the next convenient opportunity, when all the odds were in my favor again. And I would have used the drug on whatever copilot might be with me. I drugged you because you happened to be there. I thought up the business about a Mickey because if anyone came up with me as a suspect, regardless of my being in Chicago when the murder was committed, I needed one more alibi and that midnight invitation—just before United left—supplied it. A psychological alibi, so to speak. Between that and the disguise, I was sure I had covered up my tracks."

"Ingenious," Smith said, but not in the tone of a compliment. "Now that you've given us the how, I'd like to have the why. You professed to be madly in love with Miss Martin. You were divorcing your wife to marry her. You were the only one to grieve openly. Yet you killed her."

Jim laughed scornfully. "Love her? My God, I didn't love Rebel. At the end, when I decided I had to kill her, I hated every rotten bone in that beautiful bed-hopping body of hers. Infatuated, yes. For a long time. But I finally came to my senses—right around the time you came to the base, Max. I was planning to murder her then. I had to, don't you see? She was trying to blackmail me into a marriage I never really wanted."

Smith looked positively triumphant and Max grimaced. "Blackmail?" the detective repeated.

"The worst kind of blackmail. Using the life of an unborn child to force me into marriage. Yes, I lied to you. I knew all about that baby. Rebel told me just before I took that route check ride with you, Max. She said I had to marry her because I had to be the father. I couldn't deny the possibility, but I reminded her she had been sleeping with other men. Then she told me that she had deliberately tried to get pregnant by me. That she never took precautions when we made love. She said she wanted to have a baby by me because that was the only way she could get me to marry her. At first, I begged her to get an abortion. I refused to marry her. I said I didn't want to break up my home, my family. She just laughed and said if I didn't get a divorce to marry her, she'd go right to Charlie Belnap and tell him the whole story. And she threatened to tell Norma everything, too. God, I was desperate. So desperate—well, you know the rest."

"We don't know everything, Jim," McDermott said. "You said Rebel threatened to tell Norma about the affair. Yet when I had dinner at your house that night, a blind man could have seen the tension. Norma must have known."

"About the affair, yes. But not about the baby. I had admitted sleeping with Rebel but I told Norma I was going to break it off. That I wanted to keep our marriage going. I had already decided that murder was the only solution. A perfect murder, I thought. The kind that only an airline pilot might plan because an airman lives a life of calculated risk."

"Your wife told me she knew Rebel was pregnant," Smith said. She also told us she visited Rebel the night of the murder—apparently just before you got there. Were you aware of that visit?"

A look of pain cruised across Lindsay's features. "Yes, I knew about it. She told me after you questioned her, the day I was at the movies with Kevin and Debbie."

"Then when did you tell Mrs. Lindsay about the baby?"

"A couple of days after Max had dinner with us. Norma couldn't understand why I was still seeing Rebel after I had promised to end the relationship. I finally broke down and

202

told her the whole story, about the blackmail and everything."

"Did your wife know you were planning a murder?"

"No, but she knew I was the one who did it right after it happened."

"You confessed to her?"

"I didn't have to. She never got the courage to ask me. But she knew it, as surely as if she had been in that room watching me strangle Rebel. The intuition of a wife who sees her husband reach a state of total desperation."

"That was quite a little act of grief you staged," Smith observed. "Just one more little gimmick that threw us off. You were supposed to love her and there went any motive."

"Act is all it was, but up to a point," Lindsay said quietly. "I guess it was easier than you might think, because I was so emotionally exhausted to begin with. In a way, I *was* grieving. After I killed her, I was sorry I did it. She was so damned beautiful. I remember looking at her on that couch, her eyes wide open. All the hate drained out of me. All I could think of was how she made love, how many times she had told me she loved me. And I suddenly realized how desperate she was, too. Desperate for me. Desperate enough to kill a marriage and a family, just as I was desperate enough to kill to protect a marriage and a family. In a sense, I suppose there wasn't much difference between us. I was as evil as she, from the start of the affair to the murder itself. Yes, I showed grief. Because I felt grief. The act I put on wasn't all phony."

"That's not the only act you staged," Max said. "The hand-holding in taxi-cabs. Shacking up with her on layovers. Defending her publicly on more than one occasion. All of this *after* you wanted out of the affair. Yet you kept it going in plain view of everyone, especially me."

"It was part of the plan, Max. Aside from using that Chicago layover as the unbreakable alibi, I had to create an image of a man in love. I also had to keep Rebel away from

203

Norma, particularly from telling my wife she was pregnant. So I pretended I was hopelessly in love with Rebel. I even pretended with Rebel, to keep her from blabbing about that baby, and about my being the father. I'm sorry I had to use you, Max. I had potential murder in my mind the day you first flew with me. The minute I heard that business of your being an ex-cop, I decided to make you part of my alibi. That's why I kept insisting you had to be in on the investigation. I knew you liked me and that without ever meaning to, you'd try to protect me. And you did. Especially with that phone call when I asked you to have that nightcap at the motel. I was almost positive that eventually, if you were working with the police, you'd bring up the illogic of that call."

"Well," Smith said, "I guess that wraps it up. I . . . ."

"Not quite," McDermott rasped. "Jim, I've got two more questions. The first is, have you any proof you flew back to Washington that morning?"

Wordlessly, Lindsay fished in his wallet and took out a well-creased, worn carbon copy of an airline ticket. Max examined it and passed it to Smith.

"United 732, Chicago-Washington, the date of the murder." Smith read aloud. "American 543, Washington-Chicago the same day. The departure times of both flights coincide with what he's told us. And the name on the ticket is E. Bramley. How'd you pick that nom de plume, Captain?"

"Ernest Bramley was the name of my first flight instructor. He died about five years ago. I don't know why I used it; maybe because I knew he was dead."

Max said, rather impatiently, "The last question, Jim. Your confession. We were licked. Smitty here was at the end of his rope and I wasn't any help. All of a sudden you decide to tell all. But not with any normal prosaic confession. No, you had to damned near prang a five million dollar airplane with two of your fellow pilots aboard"—out of the corner of McDermott's eye he saw the startled look on

Blake's face and heard Smith whistle—"and if I hadn't slugged you, we'd all have bought the farm. Why you confessed doesn't bother me nearly as much as the way you told me you were guilty. A goddamned Hollywood hack couldn't have written a cornier finish."

"What do you mean, he almost busted up an airplane?" Blake demanded. "What the hell happened on that checkride?"

"He passed that checkride like he was born in a 727," Max said. "We were heading for home and had just been cleared to a lower altitude and Jim kept the nose down. Right through our assigned altitude. After the speed clacker sounded, I cold-cocked him and took over. We started down from thirty-one thousand and I didn't pull out until we were below two thousand. I repeat, Jim, why the suicide dive?"

The captain lowered his head, unwilling or unable to meet McDermott's eyes. There was a long, uncomfortable moment of silence before he answered and when he did, it was in a low voice, bare of inflection, as if he were reciting a story under hypnosis.

"I don't know, Max. I didn't plan to confess. I thought I had gotten away with the proverbial perfect crime. I can't tell you what happened in that plane. Maybe it was because you were in the right seat. You kept giving me orders to do this or do that. I guess in the back of my mind, you weren't a check pilot anymore—you were a cop. It seemed like every order you gave me on flying the plane was a question about the murder. I heard the descent clearance, but when I put the nose down, something inside me snapped. I couldn't move the yoke. All I could think of was Norma and the kids, and that they'd be better off without me. I didn't think of you or Tolman. I just wanted to die. In a plane. I'm glad you slugged me. For your sake and for Tolman's. Not for mine."

Smith, if a man could look stern and sad simultaneously, managed this incongruity. "Captain Lindsay, I'll have to take you down to headquarters and book you for first degree murder. You may make one call to your lawyer and then I'd appreciate your dictating the confession to a police stenographer."

Lindsay stood up, straight and tall. A shaft of sunlight caught the four burnished gold stripes on his uniform jacket. He looked, Max thought with a stab of pain and pity, like the personification of the perfect airline captain. Only now he was just another admitted murderer.

"I'm glad it's over," Jim said softly. "I'm ready."

Mike Hunter came over to McDermott's apartment a few days later, after Lindsay had been arraigned and slapped into jail to await trial. She was on one of her typical crusades, this time a "let's do something for Jim's family" campaign.

"I figured," she told Max over a couple of drinks, "we could line up some stews and maybe even pilots for baby-sitting so Norma can see Jim more often without worrying about the kids. Or maybe raise money for his lawyers. I know we can't let him down."

Max was touched. "I think the best thing we can do for him is make sure Norma's taken care of after he's sentenced. It's not a bad idea to collect some dough for his attorneys. It would mean that much more for his family when the roof caves in."

"Does he have any chance at all, Max?"

"About as much chance as I'd have landing a 727 with both wings gone. He'll be lucky to escape the chair. He wanted to plead guilty on a second degree murder charge but the prosecutor wouldn't buy it. So Jim's lawyer talked him into pleading not guilty by reason of temporary insanity. I gotta hunch he'll have Jim swear he went there that night for just plain sex and then killed Rebel in a fit of temper when she refused to let him off the hook. But I can't

206

see any jury going for that story. His whole plan was too premeditated. Nobody's going to go to all that trouble for a piece of ass. Like I said, he'll be lucky if he's not burned."

Mike had an immediate mental image of Lindsay strapped into an electric chair and shuddered. They were still discussing a fund-raising program when the doorbell rang. McDermott went to the door and was pleasantly surprised to see the homely, tired face of Lieutenant Robert Smith, who looked over Max's shoulder and saw Mike.

"Hope I'm not intruding. I was in the neighborhood and decided to drop in and say hello. I never did get a chance to thank you for all your help, Max."

"You're always welcome, Smitty," Max said cordially. "What are you drinking?"

"Make it a scotch and water. Hello, Miss Hunter." Smith delivered the last three words gingerly, as if he was wondering whether she held the ordeal of that last interrogation against him. But she said "Hi" with a pixie grin and he slumped into McDermott's only easy chair, where he sat sipping the drink Max had mixed quickly.

"Glad it's over?" he said to McDermott.

"In a way. I'm not glad the way it turned out. I'm a crusty old sonofabitch, Smitty, but it hurts like hell to see a professional airman become a lousy killer. And I still think it belongs in the category of justifiable homicide."

"There's no such animal as justifiable homicide except in self-defense," Smith remonstrated mildly. "Not if you believe the Sixth Commandment."

Max nodded in reluctant agreement. "I've still got a few doubts."

"Doubts? That he's guilty? You heard him confess—to a cold-blooded, carefully planned murder."

"Not whether he's guilty. I suppose he is. But I keep wondering about that dive he took at the end of the checkride. That deliberate suicide attempt. It just doesn't fit, Smitty. It's way out of line with the kind of person he is.

207

Sure, he was capable of killing Rebel, that's obvious. But not me or an innocent flight engineer."

Smith snorted. "He said he was out of his mind when he pulled the dive. And for that matter, it's possible the suicide attempt was as premeditated as the murder itself, to buttress a temporary insanity plea. If he was clever enough to plan that girl's death with an almost perfect alibi, he was clever enough to stage a grandiose suicide try—fake but scary enough to show he was slightly off his rocker. And he knew damned well you'd push the right panic button in time to keep from crashing."

McDermott shook his head, more in puzzlement than in disagreement. "That alibi. It wasn't almost perfect, Smitty, it was completely perfect. You weren't within five thousand miles of cracking that case. And yet, very literally, out of our beloved wild blue yonder comes his suicide attempt. He tries to kill himself and two others and makes this totally illogical act the springboard for his confession. And so help me God, Smitty, that's a why which nobody's really answered."

Mike Hunter was staring at the two men, her silence a reflection of her ability to sense when someone should stay out of a conversation.

"There's no unanswered why, Max," Smith said patiently. "His conscience caught up with him, just as he told you. He's not an evil man. He's an intelligent, sensitive human being and he wasn't the type to carry a murder inside his guts for very long."

"If he could kill Rebel to keep his family together, he could have kept his guilt hidden. His motive for not confessing would have been as strong as his motive for murder. The confession means ruin and disgrace for Norma and the children, exactly what he was trying to prevent when he killed Rebel. A confession was illogical and so was the way he confessed."

"That's the way *you* feel," Smith philosophied. "A man's

208

conscience is highly individualistic. Only each individual can tell when he reaches a breaking point. A tough old bird like you could have walked around forever with the knowledge of murder inside you. But not Lindsay. He had to confess."

"By nearly killing two more people? Where was his conscience when he shoved that nose down and almost screwed a beautiful airplane into the ground?"

"Well," Smith said, "you might figure he was off his noodle in the plane, but very, very sane when he planned the murder. It sounds simple to me. You're trying to read between the lines and there's nothing to read."

"Yeah," Max muttered. "I suppose what's bothering me is my own split personality."

"Split personality?" Mike asked.

"Exceedingly split. The cop in me says the case is closed. But the pilot in me keeps asking questions."

"Holy cow," Smith said with open exasperation. "You're the one out of your mind, Max. You don't have . . ."

Whatever the detective intended to say was interrupted by McDermott's telephone. Max answered it, cupping the mouthpiece as the caller identified himself.

"It's Kevin Lindsay," he told Smith and Mike. "This is Captain McDermott, Kevin. Is anything wrong?"

The boy's voice was hair-close to tears. "I didn't know who else to call, Captain. None of the neighbors are home. It's my mother. I think she's . . . she's sick."

"Do you know the name of your family doctor, Kevin? I'll come right over but meanwhile you should call him."

"It's not that kind of sick," the boy said in a choked voice. "I'm scared, Captain McDermott, she keeps talking funny and she doesn't know Debbie or me."

Smith got them to the Lindsay home in fifteen minutes, by the simple process of calling a squad car which met his own car two blocks from River house and escorted them with full siren. It took only one horrified look at

Norma Lindsay to know what had happened.

She was sitting on the living room couch, her eyes peculiarly bright and almost wild. She seemed to have aged ten years. And she kept repeating, over and over again, in a mesmerized litany, "Mother, throw the doll away. I don't like it. Mother, throw the doll away. It's a bad doll . . ."

At her feet was the little doll Debbie had christened Rebel. Its head had been twisted off.

Mike stayed with the children, hustling them down to the rec room in the basement while Smith summoned an ambulance and notified the family doctor to meet Norma at the hospital. Kevin had remained sufficiently calm to provide the physician's name, although Debbie's tears were shaking his own self-possession. When the ambulance arrived, Norma Lindsay was led away without protest, still mumbling about the doll.

"I guess Lindsay deserves to be told," Smith said. "Be best if you were the one. Poor bastard, I keep feeling sorry for him. I guess she just cracked up under the strain. You make any sense out of that doll bit?"

"A little," Max said. Smith had been using the phone in Jim's den, and McDermott was staring at a gold plaque on the wall.

AIR LINE PILOTS ASSOCIATION
ANNUAL SAFETY AWARD

Presented to
CAPTAIN JAMES LINDSAY
of Coastal Airlines
for his research into the effects of
clear air turbulence on swept-wing aircraft
and the development of
safer procedures for combatting this hazard.

210

Max turned around and grabbed the lieutenant's arm. "Smitty, I'll see Lindsay but I want you there when I talk to him."

The detective looked unhappy. "You don't need me to break this kind of news. I don't have any stomach for scenes like this."

"I have a different kind of scene in mind," Max said grimly.

Smith started to argue but the intensity on McDermott's face stopped him. "Want to see him in his cell or my office?"

"Office."

The lieutenant made one call before they left. Within a half-hour, they were facing Jim Lindsay—much thinner and pale, obviously glad to see McDermott but puzzled at the unexpected visit and the summons to Smith's office.

"Family okay?" was his first question, Smith sneaking a sorrowful look in McDermott's direction.

"The kids are fine," Max said. "Norma's under the weather. And I want to talk to you about her, Jim."

"What's wrong with Norma?" the pilot asked.

Max didn't answer. He gazed directly into Lindsay's eyes. "It's time for the truth, chum. You didn't kill Rebel."

Dimly, Max heard Smith catch his breath.

"You're crazy," Lindsay snapped, with a show of his old left seat command authority.

"I don't think so. I've even figured out what happened. Or would you rather tell us yourself?"

"I've already told you. What the hell are you trying to pull, McDermott? What about Norma?"

"I'll get to Norma in a minute. First, I'd like to tell you a little story. Maybe it's fiction, but I don't think so. You *were* going to kill Rebel. You really did concoct that whole wild plot. Everything you confessed to was true—but only up to a point. You worked out that business of establishing an unshakable alibi. You actually did slip me a mild Mickey to make sure I'd be too sleepy to meet you in the bar. You did fly to Washington early that morning, disguised, and then back to Chicago in time to take out your own trip. But you didn't kill her. You just tried your damnedest to make us believe you did. You even went and faked that insane suicide dive to make a confession more believable through its very drama. *You didn't kill Rebel, Jim, but you confessed to the murder because you're taking the rap for someone else. And there's only one person on God's earth who'd warrant that sacrifice. Your wife.*"

The captain's face was a conglomeration of anger, shock and surprise. His mouth worked, like a fish impaled out of water. But it was Smith, not Lindsay, who challenged McDermott.

"For Christ's sake, Max, are you saying they were working together?"

"No. Jim, when you went to Rebel's that morning, you intended to kill her. Or you never would have thought up such an elaborate scheme. But when you got there, you found her already dead. You were off one hell of a hook. Mission accomplished, and you were innocent. Except that somewhere along the line you found out who the real killer was. And that's when you decided you had to keep your own wife from the chair. Am I wrong, Jim?"

Lindsay's mouth twisted again, as if the gesture could free the words locked inside. "Where's Norma?" he asked finally.

There were undisguised pity and compassion in McDermott's voice. "She came apart, Jim. Her mind's gone; she's back in her childhood, thinking that doll Debbie called Rebel is hers. We took her to a hospital and your doctor's with her. There's no need to protect her anymore."

Lindsay put his head down between his strong hands. When he looked up, his eyes were filled with tears that refused to fall. "Will she be all right?"

"I'm no psychiatrist. I don't know if she'll ever be well

212

enough to stand trial. Before that question's answered, you've got those kids to think about. You're all they have, for God knows how long. They need you."

The pilot nodded without speaking.

"Ready to talk—for the record?" Smith asked.

Lindsay nodded again. The lieutenant summoned a stenographer and told Lindsay, simply, "Go ahead."

"Max figured it out," the captain began. "I planned Rebel's murder just as I outlined it in my confession. When I got to her house, about four A.M., the door was locked but I had my own key. I let myself in and found her body. I went right back to the airport, and I guess I must have left her door ajar, I don't really remember. I was in a daze. At that point, I didn't dream Norma was the murderer. I thought it could have been any one of the guys Rebel had been playing around with. All I felt was relief. I went through that act of sorrow just to protect myself from any suspicion. It shook me when Smith came up with that timetable possibility, so even though I knew I wasn't guilty, I kept up the act as long as I could. If you had ever been able to prove I flew back to Washington that morning, you could have hung a murder rap on me even though I didn't kill Rebel. With the circumstantial evidence you would have had, I was dead.

"It was two or three days after the murder when I found out the truth. Norma had been acting funny. She cried all the time, even in front of the kids. One night, after the children were asleep, I asked her what was wrong. I thought it was a natural reaction to Rebel's murder, on top of our admitted affair and all that. I even suspected she figured I was the killer. That's when she told me what she had done. She must have gone out of her mind after Rebel slapped her. She did drive around for a long time, like she told you. But after she got the gas she went back to Rebel's full of blind hate and totally desperate. Rebel was even drunker than before and it was easy for Norma to strangle her. Remember, my wife was a nurse and knew exactly where to apply the pressure.

"I asked her why she had done it. She said she didn't really know. That it was a combination of jealousy and desire to protect Kevin and Debbie—and me. She said something snapped when Rebel hit her. She didn't remember much until she got to the gas station, and by that time all she could think of was that Rebel had to die, and Rebel's baby, too."

Smith asked, "Did she know you already had planned to kill the girl?"

"Not right away. I didn't have the guts to tell her that. Not until the night you questioned her right here and you damned near broke her wide open. She almost confessed to you then. Later that night, she told me she couldn't stand the guilt anymore, that she was going to call you and admit the murder. That's when I confessed—to her—my own murder plan. At first, I tried to talk her out of confessing. I told her the police would never solve the murder. She said she was going to call you anyway, Lieutenant. I had only one choice. I convinced her I had to take the blame. God knows how I did it. I must have talked and pleaded and begged for hours. I said I deserved to be punished as much as she because I had actually planned to murder. I said I was even guiltier if we added the sin of adultery. For without adultery, there would have been no murder. I had to remind her that if only one of us survived this tragedy, better it be she because she could raise the kids easier than I, an airline pilot away from home so much. I kept hammering away on the children as the ones we had to think about. Finally, she caved in. It helped that Norma's deeply religious. She said God would have to punish both of us for what she had done and what I had intended to do."

There was silence until McDermott cleared his throat nervously and asked, in his old rasping tone, "The dive, Jim

214

—was that necessary? Why didn't you just confess and be done with it? Your mind didn't go blank like you claimed. You staged the suicide attempt deliberately."

"Yes, it was deliberate. Premeditated, just like the murder. I screwed up on a few trips, knowing I'd be reported to Blake, and that Blake would order a checkride. And I was pretty sure he'd pick you as the check captain. In fact, when he told me I had to have a check, I was the one who suggested you. I didn't want to pull off the attempt with a plane full of passengers, and I figured a checkride with you in that right seat was a perfect spot without endangering a lot of innocent lives. I wanted to make you believe I was trying to kill myself because it would add credence to the confession and take Norma completely out of the picture and away from all suspicion. If you had waited another five seconds before slugging me, I was going to chop power and pull the speed brake myself. But I'm curious about one thing, Max. When did you guess the truth?"

"I suppose it hit me when I saw that ALPA plaque on your den wall, right after they took Norma away. That's when I realized for sure that the suicide stunt was a fake, and that there had to be a motive behind it. All good pilots are bird-lovers. Anyone dedicated to flying like you are— enough to win the highest award your fellow pilots can give you—could never have flown a plane into the ground deliberately. I had already told Smith the dive was the part of the puzzle that never fitted. From then on, it was a question of figuring out the motive for the phony suicide attempt. When Norma came apart, the piece that hadn't fitted suddenly dropped into place."

"What will happen to my wife?" Lindsay asked. "And me?"

Smith cleared his throat. "I don't honestly know, Captain, I rather imagine she'll be committed to a mental institution. If she recovers, she may have to stand trial. As for you, damned if I know. I'll call your lawyer and see what can be worked out. It's the screwiest situation I've ever run into. You've admitted planning a murder which someone else committed. I don't know if there's anything on the books which covers it. I suspect you'll go free, because only the good Lord himself knows whether you would have gone through with the murder if you had found the girl alive. Frankly, I hope so, for your kids' sake. Like I said, it's all screwy."

"Yes," Lindsay said. "I'm the one who's really guilty and my wife is in purgatory. Except that her purgatory is my own punishment."

They took the pilot back to his cell. Smith sat behind his battered desk, fingers drumming on the glass top.

"Thanks," he said to McDermott. "I never would have cracked it without your guessing the truth. Feel better?"

"Not much. Lindsay was right. They're both guilty. The ones who'll suffer are the kids. They're losers, too."

"You forgot one loser," Smith said. "A girl named Rebel Martin."

"Yeah, the biggest loser of all, inasmuch as she's dead. But so's Lindsay, Smitty. His career is finished. After all this, Coastal wouldn't let him ferry an empty plane between here and Baltimore. I think I'll ask Blake if we can't find him some kind of good ground job."

The lieutenant lit a dirigible-sized cigar. "You were pretty damned smart, hitching your solution to that fake suicide dive. Everything pointed to Lindsay, including one little item that escaped both of us."

"What was that?"

"Doctor Decker told us Rebel's reaction to the pregnancy news. She said she was happy but the daddy wouldn't be. We pretty much assumed Lindsay fathered her kid and that should have been the first tip-off that Lindsay didn't really love her. I didn't think of it until after he confessed."

"There were," Max said, "a hell of a lot of things we didn't think about. Also some we'd better start thinking about.

216

Such as Jim's kids. Smitty, how about a ride back to my place? I'll pick up my car and see how Mike's doing."

"Sure." Smith rose. "I'll have one of my boys take you. Thanks again, Max. I still think you'd make a hell of a cop."

McDermott grinned. Their two big hands clasped.

Outside, Max waited for a patrol car to arrive from the police garage. The sound of jet engines screamed overhead and he looked up at a Coastal 727 heading for National on final approach.

Suddenly, he felt old and tired and sad.